Please return/renew this item by the last date shown on this label, or on your self-service receipt.

To renew this item, visit **www.librarieswest.org.uk** or contact your library

Your borrower number and PIN are required.

Libraries**West**

the orphans

ANNEMARIE NEARY

✺ WINDMILL BOOKS

1 3 5 7 9 10 8 6 4 2

Windmill Books
20 Vauxhall Bridge Road
London SW1V 2SA

Windmill Books is part of the Penguin Random House group of companies
whose addresses can be found at global.penguinrandomhouse.com.

First published by Hutchinson in 2017
First published in paperback by Windmill Books in 2018

www.penguin.co.uk

A CIP catalogue record for this book is available from the British Library.

ISBN 9780099592594

Typeset in 11.1/15.55 pt ITC Galliard Std by Jouve (UK), Milton Keynes
Printed and bound in Great Britain by Clays Ltd, St Ives Plc

MIX
Paper from
responsible sources
FSC® C018179

Penguin Random House is committed to a
sustainable future for our business, our readers
and our planet. This book is made from Forest
Stewardship Council® certified paper.

For Patrick

PROLOGUE

North Goa, 1992

In a hot, cramped room with a ceiling fan, a small boy is bouncing on his parents' bed. It is barely light, and the boy is still half dreaming, fighting lions by the sea. The room smells of feet, and the walls are the colour of dhal, but Sparrow tastes a tang of salty blue.

'Beeeeeeeach!' he squeals, but nobody wakes.

The ceiling fan is making the mozzie net swell, like a giant wave come to get him. He lets it sweep him away and onto his back beside his squashed-together parents. When he burrows into Mama, her arm pulls him towards her and her plait trails against his face. Her hair smells of fruit, and of the flowers that make his sister sneeze. He thinks of the funny word for sneezing, 'Hey-feee-vehhhr', and of the swaying purple flowers in their once-upon-a-garden. Sparrow misses that garden, the paddling pool and swing. But if he cries and says he wants to go there, his mother shakes her head. Gone, gone, gone. She makes a shape she calls their Old Life, and then she rips it up.

In the next room, Jess is awake too. She watches her little brother through the open door, flipping ghost-like behind the net, then landing flat on his back.

'Gone, gone, gone,' he is saying, and she knows that he is thinking about home, just like she is. She misses school, and being good at things. She misses friends who come for tea and then go home again. Not like here, in the Yellow House, where all the kids live in the same place and everything is shared, even Mama. Sometimes Mama goes away with other men, and often Dejan comes to visit, with his big moustache. Pa is always there, though his eyes are often vague, as if he is finding his way through winter fog.

Jess twists her arm round to inspect the inside part, still soft and white and babyish like it was at home. It's the only bit of her that hasn't changed. The rest is thinner, browner, blonder. Not like Sparrow, still pink and white. Jess is the one who remembers to cover him up so he doesn't burn. She is the one who carries his sunhat in her bag.

Mama is awake now, and standing naked by the bed. She has pinned her plait up on the back of her head and, as she washes in water from the bowl, a streak of sunlight turns her skin to golden glass. Something glitters on her wrist. Dejan with the moustache has given her mother a new bracelet. Mama hasn't said so, but Jess knows.

Sparrow and Jess play all morning in the wild garden where the grass is scuffed to dust. Eddie says there are snakes hiding underneath the spiky, orange flowers, but Jess has never seen them. By the time Mama and Pa are ready, Sparrow is tired and whining. To get to the beach, they walk down a narrow alleyway that is crammed with bright jags of colour, strong as tastes. Jess carries the picnic, and Mama carries Sparrow. He is happy now and singing to himself, a makey-uppy song. He takes Mama's face in his hands and covers it with hundreds of tiny kisses, while she smooths down his curls and murmurs that he is her perfect angel.

Jess knows that Sparrow and Mama are enough for each other, that they don't need her or even Pa. The terrible truth of that makes her sad, but now that she is grown-up inside, it doesn't make her angry. She turns around to find Pa, to make sure that he keeps up. He looks cold today, even though the sun has already burned the bony tips of Jess's shoulders. She reaches for his hand, and from very far away he sends a smile.

When they get to the beach, Pa leads them past the shacks and the turtles and the coconut lady and the men selling mangos and the girls who braid hair and weave in strands of cotton. Here, the only sounds are the sea and the squawk of some invisible bird and the scissor song of insects clamouring in the trees. She is glad not to have to play with the children from the Yellow House. She is tired of games she always seems to lose. Pa paces back and forth while Mama spreads the bright orange throw she bartered for at the market. Sparrow clings to her like a little monkey but she gently unpeels his fingers and kisses him on the head.

'Dig us back to England, Sparrow,' she says. 'Make me a tunnel, and let's go.' And she mimes shouldering her way into a narrow space. 'Keep an eye on him for me, Jess.'

Down at the water's edge, Sparrow starts to shovel at the wet sand.

'Je-ess? How long will it take to get back to London? Will it take five minutes or five hours?'

She says it might take five weeks or two months or maybe even a year, now that they don't have the camper van any more.

Sparrow stomps to the water's edge.

'I can dig Mama a tunnel so we can get there in five tiny minutes,' he says.

Jess thinks you would have to dig through Africa and France and Italy and Greece to get to England. And definitely Turkey, where they sold the van and started taking buses instead. Here, it is so hard to remember things. For two whole days, she has been trying to recite the stations on the Northern Line, but she keeps getting stuck at Balham.

Sparrow is digging, then swishing water at the hole to help it sink and become a tunnel.

'I can't concentrate if you keep splashing me the whole time,' Jess says.

He can't believe she's forgotten about the tunnel already.

'You're not helping by flooding it like that,' she says. And then she gets bossy and tells him to shush, that she needs to be able to count.

He holds up his fingers and tells her she can count those, but she calls him a silly billy, and says he hasn't got nearly enough fingers. She tells him to fetch shells and pebbles or whatever he can find.

'Is it a mission?' he asks.

'If you like,' she says.

He goes to the end of the beach, just beneath the cliff, and searches for the roundest stones, the frilliest shells. He fills his bucket, then drags it back and empties them out beside her.

'Treasure,' she says, and smiles.

That makes him feel proud and important, so he collects buckets more. On the last trip, he cuts his toe against something sharp hidden in the sand, a scrap of glass perhaps. The blood rushes out and, as he walks, the sea washes it away again. He thinks 'ow wow' because that's how his own blood makes him feel, but it isn't 'ow wow', not really.

On the way back to Jess, his hand goes to sleep. He puts the bucket down so he can twiddle his fingers. He thinks he can hear something in the trees. Maybe it's a lion, because it is definitely hot enough for lions. But he left his sword behind in the dream, and so he hurries on.

Jess isn't counting any more, and she isn't helping with the tunnel either. Her face makes him scared because it looks as if it's dripping off the end of her chin. When he gets up close he can see that Jess is crying, though Jess never cries. She is pointing over towards the place where they were sitting, Mama and Pa, but there's no one there. He runs right up the beach to find them, and the drier, silkier sand burns his feet. But the basket has gone, and the big orange blanket, and the food and the water. 'Mama,' he screams. 'Ma-ma-ma.'

But all there is where his parents used to be is a single mango. He puts it to his nose and sniffs. He bites hard and spits the skin away, and suddenly his face is full of sweetness. The fibres slip between his teeth and the juice drips onto his chest. Jess is running towards him now, and he tries to gobble all the mango up before she gets to him. Her hug slams into him and the mango rolls in the sand and his face mixed with hers tastes more salty than sweet.

Jess holds his hand tight and for a moment she feels nearly as good as Mama, but not really. Neither of them says anything for a long time.

'They'll come back, Ro,' she says finally.

And he thinks about the Owl Mother in the story, who always does come back. He glances over at Mama's tunnel, but it is filled with sea. They turn their backs on it, and sit facing up the beach instead, so they can catch the happy moment.

But nobody comes back.

And one sleep goes by and then two and then twenty-two then forty then ninety-five, right until the end of numbers.

And nobody came back.

1

Ireland, present day

Ro has followed his mother all his life, but the sightings have never taken him to Curramona before, not to the spot she called the home place. Ireland is wet and green, just as he remembers it. He's calmer than he's been in months, hurtling through high-hedged, dripping fields, travelling blind by a steamed-up window with no need to worry out the route himself. On these narrow roads, the coach is like a charging bull, the last fuchsias clipping its sides.

After a stretch of nothing at all, the sightings began again last summer. A family friend on holiday in northern France swore blind she'd seen his mother in the fruit and veg aisle of a supermarket in Lille. She'd tackled the woman, who pretended not to understand English, even followed her out into the car park. But it was too late. Sophie Considine was gone.

The prospect that he might find his mother in a Carrefour in Lille was so intoxicating that he'd spent three weeks touting his age-progressed photos around prefectures and gendarmeries and a succession of bar owners. Sophie with glasses and without, weight on and off, raddled and healthy, blonde and curly, dark and straight. All the bar owners, to a man aged fifty plus, recognised one version of her – a woman with a tight black pageboy cut and a determined, chiselled face. His hopes were raised until he realised that the woman they thought they'd seen before was not his mother after all, but a singer from their long-ago youth called Mireille Mathieu.

After France, he was exhausted, the hope sucked out of him. A month later, though, he was off again, to Durham this time, travelling back and forth on local buses along a daisy chain of villages. The woman did bear a passing resemblance to his mother, but she was at least ten years too young.

On the first Sunday of the season, a new vendor had showed up at the country market in Curramona with a chalkboard sign, *Sophie's Kitchen*. She was selling pots of home-made spreads – hummus, red pesto, baba ganoush – from the boot of an estate car that some said was navy blue, others black. Nobody noticed anything useful – the car reg, for example, or even the make. One customer had asked the woman, who had a greyish-blondish plait and was thought to be in her early sixties, if she was staying locally. She parried the question, but she never reappeared. That was it. She was there and then she wasn't.

At Curramona, they still remember Sophie Considine.

His mother was brave or negligent, depending on who's talking. She was talented, or a waste of space. The most you can say for sure is that she made an impression. This new sighting was news, and Ro trawled through all the speculation on online missing-persons forums. The more he read, the stronger the fizz of excitement, like sherbet on his tongue. And then he came across a name that brought him back to the days before the vanishing. Mags Madden.

As kids, Jess and he had spent a month or so each summer in the field behind Mags Madden's shop in a small country place called Drigheen, just outside the town of Curramona. There were albums full of pictures of that caravan and of the lake where they used to swim. If memories have flavours, Mags reminds him of vanilla, for the ice cream she doled out sparingly from her padlocked freezer. Vanilla, and sour grapes.

The comments on the missing-persons forum expressed a range of views on the sighting. Some people wondered if Sophie might have made the decision to reappear and then bottled it. Most seemed to think it was just a coincidence, that Sophie was long dead. But Ro was struck by what Mags Madden had written.

'*I know that one like my own sister. Take it from me, Sophie's in the Smoke if she's anywhere. She's not in some dump like this.*'

That present tense had been the lure. And now here he is.

He had expected the home place to come back to him like a nursery rhyme. But when he reaches the town, a single broad street with a Londis and a scattering of pubs, he scarcely recognises it at all. Even though he knows this is the terminus, he sits on as the others alight, in the hope that the driver might be stuttering on home a mile or two further into the bog. He imagines a bungalow with pebble dash and greying nets, a wife flipping burgers on a pan. Maybe even a bed for the night, if he's lucky. But when the other passengers have alighted, the driver climbs back up into the coach and stands there like a disobliging genie until Ro gets to his feet and pulls his backpack down from the overhead rack.

He starts walking east, though whether the Madden place is that direction or not, he couldn't say, it's been so long. It's dark already and drizzling as he makes his way towards the comforting plastic glow of a petrol station concourse. Beyond that, there isn't even a footpath and he is soon wet to the knees from the long grass on the verge. A truck skites him as it passes, but on he walks into the black, past fields of snorting beasts, to the slow gurgle of rainwater in the ditch. He remembers a crossroads, a huge tree, but as far as he can tell the road ahead is flat, the landscape unrelieved by trees of any kind. From the greenish glow-in-the-dark hands on his watch, it's already ten o'clock, and so he heads back to the town to get his bearings.

He passes a little square just off the main street. Its rickety-rackety houses are crowded in around a park where great clumps of giant rhubarb lord it over the dried-out annuals. He wonders if that's where the market was held. *Her* market. He closes his eyes, but he catches nothing. And how would he know what to sense anyway, after all this time? What version of her would he hope to find?

He comes across a chipper that reminds him of a thousand others – sub-Heinz beans and Kylie on the speakers. The woman behind the counter shovels his chips onto a hospital-green plate. She dredges them with salt and soaks on operatic quantities of vinegar. When she hands him his tea, it slurps onto the saucer, flooding the complimentary biscuit. And, even though he doesn't care much for biscuits, he finds that disappointing.

'Have you heard of a shop called Madden's?' he asks. 'It's in a townland called Drigheen. Not far from here.'

He knows you don't pronounce the 'g', not here. It marks you out if you do. But he can't bring himself to drop it either.

'Sorry,' she says, though she's clearly not.

He takes his seat and spears a couple of chips. Despite the yellow walls, the swallows scissoring across the wipe-clean tablecloths, this is a drab hole. Somebody has attempted a mural on the opposite wall – clownish figures in motley and masks beneath a dark red Vesuvius. The tinny radio announces that Murray is through to the next round at Wimbledon, that there has been a debate somewhere on climate change. But you can't take Curramona out of the chipper; the traffic lights are out in Synott Street, and there's a diversion on the bypass. He can't imagine the kind of life where such things matter.

Over to his right, a baby perched in a high chair is playing with a knife. The child's mother has an old face on a young body, her thin brown legs displayed in cut-off jeans.

As mothers go, she is clueless. Each time the kid drops the knife onto the tiled floor, she lifts it up and places it back in his fat little fist, so it's only a matter of time before that kid gets it in the eye. He reminds himself that he's keeping a low profile here. But he can't help thinking, what's wrong with a spoon? He can see his own history in the kid who isn't strapped into his seat, the mother who doesn't see the knife coming. And he wants to go and shake her by the neck. Wake up, wake up, wake up.

Back in 1992, the disappearance of both his parents had dominated the news for months on end. His family acquired block capitals – Mama became TRAGIC SOPHIE, while he and Jess were THE ORPHANS ON THE BEACH. The papers made it into a morality play, but it was also that irresistible weekend staple, a mystery. Auntie Rae kept the cuttings in her scrapbooks, his legacy she liked to say. Even as a kid, he'd noticed how seldom Pa was mentioned; all the speculation was about Mama, while Pa remained an insubstantial figure. In retrospect, of course, the inference was clear – a drug addict with more money than morals, Pa was as likely to be the perpetrator as a victim. So, a couple of years later, when Pa's remains were discovered in undergrowth just metres from the beach, things began to look more complicated, and Auntie Rae put the scrapbooks in the attic.

In the end, Ro takes a taxi. The driver bores on about how there hasn't been a shop there for years. Health inspection. Mouse droppings. Blahblahblah. When they reach the house, it looks different, smaller. Even in the dark it seems desolate, its windows half curtained in grimy nets. The name remains above the door, though. Six letters, M A D D E N, spelled out in little plastic blocks – upper case, sans serif. If he strains hard enough, he can place Mags Madden behind the counter of the shop, dinging at the cash register, giving off. He can picture the puce lipstick sunk into the cracks in her upper lip, the downward drip of her eyes and, ear to ear, the drapery of skin. Auntie Rae took them over for a last visit when he was no more than eight or so, but Mags wasn't exactly welcoming and he hasn't been back since.

'I don't know who you'd be looking for here,' the driver says. 'I'd say it's just been left, like.'

But Ro says it's OK. In fact, he says it's grand, and he's pleased with that. The front door has been replaced in white moulded plastic with an eyebrow fanlight. He squints through the peephole, but there's nothing. He walks around the side and peers through the back windows, but there's nothing there either. Empty, like France. Empty, like Durham.

As he rounds the corner of the building, a security light flashes on and he notices a metal plate still screwed into the wall – *Player's Please*. Rushing back, a memory of this place when it was still a shop that smelled of tea and yellow-crumbed ham. That big chest freezer with H B on the side, a treasure trove of ice cream. And just as cold, Mags Madden, who had been his mother's friend once.

At the centre of his memory of this place is a caravan in a thick green field and a scrum of Irish cousins with hedge hair. And, sure enough, there is still a caravan out back, shucked up on breeze blocks. He feels in his pocket for the mini Maglite and whips the beam around him like a blade. It's no longer possible to say what colour the caravan once was, but it's green now, merged with the fields that stretch off towards the mountains. Nature has crept through its skin, spawning and withering, season on season, so that now it resembles a giant carbuncle, sappy and swollen to bursting.

Behind him, the house is no longer dark; there is a light on upstairs, but no movement, no shadow. Downstairs left, another light snaps on, but he knows how easy it is to simulate a presence with timers and the like. Out here, in the sticks, you might be wise to take precautions. And so he doesn't let the lights bother him. Even if there are people in there, they won't notice the small beam of his torch flickering like a will-o'-the-wisp. He looks for traces of a car, a dark estate, for pallets or boxes or jars, some sign of Sophie's Kitchen. And then he checks out the caravan. Even partially stripped out, it looks tiny. It's hard to imagine how they fitted in, the children they were then, the mother. His father never used to come to Curramona. He would take himself up to Yorkshire to go shooting with his brothers, which suited Sophie, Rae used to say, because she couldn't stand the smell of blood off him. That sounds like something Sophie might have said, all right, but you never know.

Suddenly, he is faced with the futility of his existence, and all the barren years of search and disappointment. Who would miss him if he disappeared? He, who has left hardly a trace on the world. Not like Jess, whose days are wound tight into the lives of other people: her kid, her pompous husband, that leech Eddie Jacques.

He is just concluding that there's nothing here for him when the security light is activated. Footsteps on the concrete path around the house, a key scribbling at a lock. For one wild moment, he imagines that he is about to encounter his mother as she is immortalised in family videos – still blonde and young and sceptical, still cradling her guitar. As for the gesture she makes to the camera – peace or victory? He's never been quite sure.

He steps down out of the caravan and there, about to enter the house, is a woman in a yellow top and a pair of black jeans who could never, not in a hundred years, be his mother. This woman is old. She is skin and bone, drunk and teetering, and the moment of elation is gone.

She squints at him, as if struggling for perspective. And then she goes on the attack.

'Who the fuck are you?' she says. She nudges the door open with her hip, then glances back at him. 'What happened to your tongue?'

'I'm Ro,' he says. 'Sparrow. They christened me William, but everyone used to call me Sparrow.'

And even he is thinking – way too complicated, way too many names.

'I was Sophie's boy. Remember?'

She doesn't say she does and she doesn't say she doesn't. When he folds himself in through the door behind her, he allows her a moment to think about the fact that she's let him into her house, a moment to reflect. And then he has a question of his own.

'Anyone else here, Mags? Any company?'

She laughs at that – a great wheezy laugh.

'Not unless you count the altar boys I keep up in the attic next to the leprechaun.'

He'd expected to recognise the kitchen, but he doesn't. It has an overhead light in a basketwork shade, a white table and four matching high-backed chairs. The chairs look like a recent acquisition, a job lot from a bargain centre maybe, but even the ancient Formica cupboards, edged with stainless steel, ring no bells. He glances back at the window, the little bunched curtains printed with sprigs of tiny flowers. He's sure he remembers those curtains, and his heart shrinks.

Mags Madden winces up at the overhead light. She scrapes back her chair and makes for the switch, and there is a moment of darkness before the neon strips above the counter pop into life. That seems to suit her better. She reaches into a cupboard for an unmarked bottle, splashes some clear liquid at a glass.

'Have you got any of that to spare?' he asks, shrugging at the bottle, not that he wants any. He watches himself rise in her estimation, and already he hates her for it.

'You'd like a taste?'

And there is something in that word and the flattish way she pronounces it – a taste, a sip, a little something – that conjures up the last slick of batter in the bowl, a rap on the knuckles with a wooden spoon.

She opens her eyes comically wide, like they might eat him.

'I remember you right enough. Now that I think of it. Is your sister with you?' She hands him a glass, and nods at him to help himself. 'I suppose she's more sense.'

'I came as soon as I could,' he says. 'When I got word.'

'When you got word.' She repeats his phrase without applying a question mark, and in her mouth it sounds ridiculous, pompous even. Now that Mags Madden is a presence and not just a name, he is remembering her true flavour. Mags was always mean as grapefruit, her freezer crammed with jewel-coloured ice pops that no one was allowed to touch.

'Don't tell me this is the first word you've had?' she says.

He has a sudden urge to justify himself, so he starts to tell her about the run of bad luck he's had this past while – France and Durham and all the woeful litany of sightings that, no matter how unlikely, couldn't be ignored.

But she cuts him short.

'I could have saved you the bother. If you'd only asked.'

'She's alive?'

'I'd say she is, yeah. She *was* alive, that's for sure. She didn't die on that beach anyway. Is she *still* alive?' and her hands spread.

He thinks his ears have failed him, because all he can hear is the hum that is always there at the base of things, like the motor of the world churning away whether you like it or not. At times like this, your senses fail you but your blood beats on.

'A word of advice about your mother, Sparrow.'

He wishes she wouldn't call him that. He is sorry he mentioned it now, when he dropped it years ago.

'Your mother's the kind who stays somewhere for a

while, then moves on. She's the type who'd go to ground if she needed to, then surface when the notion took her.'

She doesn't care, that's what he notices first. She doesn't give a damn about his feelings, and she couldn't care less about Sophie.

'What are you saying to me?'

'What am I saying to you?' And she is imitating him again, affecting a kind of baby talk.

'I mean, she was your friend, right?'

She screws up her face at that, and her hand makes a rocky road. 'We didn't always click,' she says.

When he takes her by the arm, she feels frail, revoltingly so. She smells sweet as bubblegum and sharp as urine.

'You've come to the wrong place, Sparrow,' she says, 'and way too late.' When she throws her head back, she's like some TV-drama drunk. 'Your mum won't be calling on me, kiddo. I'd give her too many home truths. Sophie never liked to be told anything. That was her problem.'

'When was she last here?'

She juts out her chin at that. 'How would I know?'

'Maybe you would, though.'

'If you're after the woman at the market, you're wasting your time. There's no way Sophie's spending her days making hummus. That wasn't part of the plan.'

'There was a plan?'

He gets the feeling that she's winging it now. And then he realises that, even through the fug of booze, she is relishing this. It dawns on him then that the only thing he knows for sure about Mags Madden is that she hates his mother. For whatever reason, Mags would sooner see his mother dead than have her reappear and find her son still loves her. That shocks him, and intrigues him too. But mostly it angers him.

'Ah, don't mind me, love.' She plants her hand on his arm and gives it a squeeze. 'Give your Auntie Mags a cuddle.' She puts her head on his chest, her arms around his waist. 'I know all about Sophie,' she murmurs. 'And I hate to tell you, Sparrow, she was no fucking good.'

All he can hear is *was*. Ro isn't interested in was.

'None of us knew the whole Sophie. None of us.'

He pushes her away. 'You don't know the first thing about her.'

'You don't know anything about my mammy?' She puts on that simpering idiot voice again, but, though her lips move and her eyebrows arrow, her volume is fading. The hum is in his ears again, messing with his blood.

And then she stops. He can't interpret her expression. It might be pity or it might be fear. For a moment, she seems almost sober.

'You don't believe me, Sparrow? Come and see.'

She stretches her hand out to him as if he's still Sparrow Considine, motherless boy. When he doesn't take it, she makes for the door ahead of him, ricocheting between the table and the counter, then slumping against the trembling fridge. While he waits for her to move, he concentrates hard on those little bunched curtains with their sprigs of blue flowers. Forget-me-nots. Of course. What else would they be?

His mother's voice is in his head, and Mags Madden is blundering out across the long grass with a torch in her hand, slashing at the night like a Dementor. As he watches her struggle through thick clumps of field grass and bracken, he is already deciding not to believe a word she says. When he joins her at the caravan, she turns and reaches out to him in a non-committal kind of way. *Have a little taste.*

She stumbles, and when instinctively he stops her fall, it's remarkable just how light she is. A dried-out old husk of nothing. She scrabbles away from him into the caravan, and when she drops the torch it dies and he is dowsed in darkness. The world doesn't get much darker than a night at the home place. Her voice hovers somewhere over to his right, and he knows that, whatever else he does, he mustn't let it get inside him.

'You were a lovely little boy, Sparrow. You didn't deserve what you got. And poor old Will, sure he wasn't half the villain she made him out to be. Oh, there were drugs, all right, and other women. I had a moment there, myself. But you think she didn't have other men? You think she didn't take whatever pleased her?' Her voice is hard now, and she's no longer able to hide the spite in it.

But Ro is focusing on that voice in his head, his mother's voice, all silk and soft flesh.

And he is on that beach, too, and straining to look behind the light to see what might be happening in those trees.

'She used people, you know? Used him, tried to use me. She was a heap of shit.'

'Don't say that.'

'Here. Let me show you something.'

He doesn't want to see, and yet he wants to know. It's hard to drag himself away from that bright beach from long ago, the moment before disaster. But Mags Madden won't let him stay there. He should leave now, he knows that. He should leave before her poison gets to him. But he needs to find out if he's ever come close.

'Is she in France, or Durham, or—'

'I doubt it.'

'I thought I saw her once in a McDonald's in Newcastle.'

'A McDonald's? Jesus, you don't know much about Sophie, do you?'

It infuriates him that she could tell him anything at all about his mother and he wouldn't have a clue whether it was true or not. He barely knew his mother, after all. A kid like that, what could he know?

Maybe Mags senses that she's losing him, because her voice is hardening now.

'She'll be with Jess,' she says quietly. 'That's where she'll be. With perfect little Jess. Just you see – she'll have tagged herself on to Jess's life, one way or another. Taking the pleasure of it, without any responsibility. That was her, all over. That was your mother.'

He is desperate to ask her why she thinks his mother wouldn't want to be with him. But she gets there before he does.

'I don't think she'd have wanted the trouble of the likes of you. She'd not have had the time to mop you up. Normally, I wouldn't say that, but . . .' And the way she is speaking now, the consonants sound drenched in whatever it is she's been drinking so that the sense of it is fading, melting.

He can hear the scrape of cardboard pulled along a gritty surface. 'Since you've come a distance, Sparrow, it's only fair you go away with—'

But it's too late. Something has gone off in his head, and he knows for certain now that all she has to offer him is humiliation. He needs to get back to that town where a mother sits eating chips while her kid prods at his own cheek with a knife.

'You've been chasing the wrong rainbow, kiddo. No point looking for Sophie Considine. She's long gone. Little Mary Callan whose mother couldn't keep her, the girl the Considines took in.' She touches his arm. 'That's who your ma was. God only knows what she's calling herself now, with the notions she had. Come here,' she says, and before he knows what's happening she has clamped her hand to his crotch.

'Get off me!' He kicks out at her, and in that moment there is hate enough in him to want to catch her chin or nose or the back of her befuddled head. His kick connects to something with give in it, and he hears it yelp and sigh. He kicks again and again and again before stumbling his way out of there, out into the wet grass, knee-deep in root-twisted earth packed tight with bracken.

And there is still no light. Nothing but the faint glimmer of stars hazed with cloud. My God, where is the moon when you need it? He howls at the dark to rip the moon from it, but there is nothing. And so he stumbles on in darkness for an hour or more until he gets to the town, where he sits at the Civil War memorial and waits for the first bus out. He doesn't feel much, really. Just cold, and something squirrelling away inside him.

Then the night slides into a new phase. It reaches the point when the birds shut up and the engines take over and the struggling day emerges. He takes the first bus that arrives, which, as it happens, is heading for Dublin. He slings his backpack up into the rack and takes a pair of seats for himself. And as the bus pulls away he feels OK, fine, though there's still a tug tug tug of something at him, like a small child at his mother's sleeve. Half an hour into the journey, he realises what's bugging him. She might have had the answer. He might have heard it had he stayed.

2

London, present day

At the firm's Summer Party, waiters bearing shiny palettes of pre-poured drinks flank the Physic Garden lawn. The marquee has been planted well away from the specialist displays; here the borders are stuffed with summer mainstays – foxgloves and lupins, temples of astilbe, clusters of agapanthus bursting blue. Were it not for the dirty tide of traffic, the planes roaring towards Heathrow, they might be deep in the Oxfordshire countryside where Jess's in-laws live. Over to the left, where the gravel paths converge, concentric circles of potted offerings surround the statue of the garden's bewigged founder, tributes from hopeful amateurs, perhaps. Jess has a garden of her own now, but she is no enthusiast. She favours gravel over lawn, obedient specimens in zinc planters over the unpredictable sprawl of the herbaceous border.

Inside the marquee, a string quartet is playing

blanched-out jazz standards. Most of the female lawyers, bare-legged and wearing florals, have regressed to girlhood. Most of the men have removed their suit jackets and ties. Jess left the office with Sarah and Max at six, and they have been here ever since – gossiping, laughing, drinking. It is almost ten, and she has eaten nothing but tiny bundles of asparagus and balls of salmon and black rice. Her stomach is raw, and she is beginning to dream of fish and chips from that place near the station. This is the longest she has ever left Ruby – over fourteen hours, and counting.

'You're not fading on me now, Jess,' says Sarah, taking her cloudy glass away from her. 'You need another Bellini.'

'Fine for you to say, on soft drinks all night.'

Sarah sidles through the logjam at the bar with her neat bump. Elbows out, drinks held high, she bends to a double-cheeked kiss from Delia, who is mentor to them both, pristine in taupe Armani. Jess shunts their laptop bags under the table. As she stands back up again, she becomes aware of someone behind her, too close.

'What are you worried about?' he says. 'It's a room full of lawyers.'

She feels for the table as she steps back from him.

'Yes, well, you never know.'

Miles arrived at the firm while she was on maternity leave, a new partner poached from Carrier's, along with half the M&A team.

'Good to let the hair down now and then.' He slicks a hand across his bald patch.

She laughs, but perhaps the gesture was unconscious

because he doesn't respond. She glances over to see if Sarah is still with Delia.

'Bet you could do with a bit of down time,' he says.

'Couldn't we all?'

'New mother. Hard to keep the pace.'

'Excuse me?'

'No room for passengers on a team like this one.'

He isn't smiling any more, and she feels a jab of alarm.

'You're joking, right?'

Her work record is impeccable, she's on the cusp of partnership. She keeps on smiling, though. Because? Well, because she doesn't know how else to react.

'Husband pulling his weight?'

Max is waving at her now, pulling faces behind Miles's back, and she prepares to move away before she loses her temper.

'Oh, you know what US clients are like. They think he's a twenty-four-hour drive-through.'

'So, no.'

'I didn't say that,' she laughs. 'Did I say that? Surely not.'

She had forgotten this side of work, how tiresome it can be, dealing with people like Miles. He takes a step towards her, and there's a sheen of moisture on his upper lip.

'Are we going to dance?'

She glances at the empty dance floor. 'I doubt it, Miles, but thanks.'

'I think you're wrong there. I think it's only a matter of time.'

Sarah has returned. She stands there a moment, looking from one to the other, then hands Jess the Bellini.

'Waylaid. Sorry. You must be dying for this.'

'Catch you when the music changes,' Miles says, and walks away.

'What was that about?' Sarah says.

'I honestly have no idea.'

She pulls a face. 'He's an idiot. Come on, let's find Max.'

Max gives her a puppyish hug, and almost knocks the drink from her hand. He is talking holiday destinations with some of the trainees.

'Already had mine, sadly. Just back from Italy,' Sarah says.

Max says he's going to Slovenia. 'We're staying at a place called Hisa—'

Jess's phone purrs in the little bag she wears slung across her like a sash. She glances at it and sees it's Hana. And then she notices the three missed calls, all from Hana too.

'Hang on a sec,' she tells them. 'Ask me about it when I get back. It's just outside Kobarid, but I've got to take this.'

She steps away from them to make the call, which Hana answers on the second ring.

'OK, Hana. OK. Just slow down a bit. Hang on, I can't hear a word with this racket. Let me call you back.'

She walks out the other end of the marquee, where a huge *Gingko biloba* blots out the sky. Her heels sink into the lawn, so she moves on to the gravel path where the cellist from earlier is leaning against a tree, talking intently into her phone. To preserve the woman's privacy, Jess moves deeper into the garden, to a bench by a clump of artichokes sprouting punk shocks of purple. She presses the speed dial. Behind her, the genteel jazz has given way to a beat.

'Hey, Hana. That's much better.'

'They wanted to stay and wait, but I said no, better to come back later. No uniforms or nothing. Just a badge that could mean anything. And so—'

'Who are we talking about?'

'They say they are police. But when I ask is it about a car parked in wrong place, or a break-in in house down road, or what is it about, they just say it is not urgent matter, but they need to speak to you.'

Hana sounds insulted by that.

'Oh, it's probably just the community support people. I'm sure you know not to let anyone into the house unless Charlie or I—'

'They will come back tomorrow. Ruby is sleeping now, so you can stay out late if you want.'

She does not want. She closes her eyes a moment and inhales the complicated fragrance of a summer evening on the turn – cinder and basil and something that might be chamomile. The crunch of gravel alerts her. When she opens her eyes, Miles is standing over her. The first thing she notices is that he has nothing in his hands, no drink or phone or cigarette. The top two buttons of his white shirt are open.

'Oh, hello there.' She is startled, and doesn't try to hide it.

'You're not slipping away.' The question comes out as a statement that she chooses to translate back into a question.

'In fact, yes, I am. I've got something to deal with at home.'

'And nothing to deal with here?'

He seems angry with her. She is puzzled, and searches their earlier conversation for clues. She wonders then if something might have hit the fan in the meantime – a deadline missed, the wrong client copied in on an email?

'Is something the matter, Miles?'

He leans forward and presses her shoulder into the bench, applying his weight to it. She is so shocked that she is unable to speak. Everything is suddenly indecipherable – the galaxy of multicoloured paper globes that hang from the trees, the luxuriant vegetation, this man who has taken ill or lost his balance. But when he shoves his weight down on her other shoulder, she realises that something is going very badly wrong. She has trained herself never to take risks – there are no dark alleys in Jess's life, no unlocked doors – and yet she has been caught, pinned like a moth.

'Stop pretending you don't remember me,' he says. 'Just stop it.'

His voice has changed. She can see the underside of his chin, where he has nicked himself shaving. He is not looking at her at all, but at something above her head. She realises then that he is keeping an eye out, and the fact that he is sober enough to be cautious worries her more than anything else. She smells sweat, and something fishy, and then she remembers the rice balls and thinks she might be sick. Instinct tells her to stay silent, to let his anger blow itself out, but her mouth does the talking.

'I've no idea wh—'

'Cut the crap,' he says.

She catches a speck of spittle on her upper lip and turns her face away. The slats of the bench are pressing into her back, and she can't heave enough breath to power a scream. The pathetic squeak she does manage is soaked up by the ambient traffic and the thud of music from the marquee. But he has only two hands, and they are both necessary to hold her firm. In the split second that he reaches for something – his pocket, his fly – she kicks hard and he falls back, flailing.

She is gone before he gets to his feet. She makes for the marquee along the gravel path, then takes to the lawn instead. Her shoes are off now, tucked under her arm, and she weaves in among the display beds until she reaches the gatehouse. A nice lady in pearls who is selling memberships surveys Jess's wild hair, her bare feet, then tactfully resumes reading. Out on Swan Walk, Jess puts her shoes back on and is instantly stronger. She hastens her step, leaving behind her laptop, and the Oxfordshire garden, and the thick, squat palms that might have come from Goa. Over the wall wafts 'Viva la Vida'. She already knows she will not tell anyone this story. She needs the job too much. But the thought of Miles hauling himself out of the flower bed and charging after her like a maddened bull frightens her. It makes her think she would be wise to report a man like that.

She reaches Royal Hospital Road, where there are always taxis, and hops in one to take her south. In the comforting dark of the back seat, she is aware of her own breath, coming ragged and fast. The driver seems to notice it too. He glances up at her in the rear-view mirror. 'You all right back there?'

She closes her eyes as they cross the river. She leans back in the seat and starts to call Charlie, but her hands are shaking and he will still be with the client. And what would she say? What did happen, exactly, in that garden?

As the taxi sweeps through the summer evening, people are still standing outside bars, light-hearted and loose-limbed. And all the while Jess is picking through memories – awkward encounters, rows, drunken parties, people she might have slighted without even realising. She relishes a professional argument, but backs off at the first sign of a personal clash. She is careful of people's feelings, is never rude. She can't imagine what she could have done to provoke such anger. There was once an incident of road rage, memorable only for the fact that it was so unusual, but the driver who threatened her was older, she is sure. But by the time the taxi reaches the Common she has remembered something. It must be eight, ten years now, soon after she left uni. A group of them had travelled over to Switzerland for a long weekend – a friend's birthday. Faithie, that's it. There was a flight to Geneva, a train ride along the lake past Montreux, and then a bus up to Villars, where Faithie's parents had a chalet. They were all lawyers, and the same vintage, give or take. But there was this other guy, a little older than the rest of them, who was someone's flatmate's brother and who'd come along at the last minute. She remembers a mix-up in the queue that left her sharing a six-person chairlift with him, just the two of them on one of those long, long climbs to the top of the mountain.

No matter how hard she tries she can't remember his face, though he did have a similar physique to Miles Rennie – stocky, with a rugby-player heft to him. Could it have been Miles? She supposes it could. They had talked a little – ski runs, other resorts, whatever – and they were about halfway up when he made some kind of move. It was nothing, really. He might have placed a hand on her Michelin Man padded leg, but she doesn't think he tried anything too overt. As far as she remembers he didn't even try to kiss her, though he did say something crass about the two of them going off-piste. It was embarrassing rather than frightening. She just wanted to get away. And she did cloak it with a sort of excuse, something weak about meeting someone halfway down. She remembers gripping tightly to her poles, and shunting herself forward onto the edge of the seat as the top of the mountain approached. Raising the bar and then just skiing away.

It hadn't really bothered her, and she didn't acknowledge the incident to him or to anyone else. She just stayed out of his way for the rest of the weekend. It was easy, in a big group like that, to lose him at the opposite end of the long rough tables in the mountain restaurants where they ate endless servings of raclette. And that was that. She is amazed that anyone could consider the slight worth nurturing. And so perhaps she is wrong.

As the taxi pulls into Riverton Street in front of this house she loves, that they can't really afford, she feels calmer. Perhaps she will try to forget the incident in the Physic Garden ever happened. As soon as she gets in the door, she can hear the snuffle of Ruby's breath on the baby monitor. Charlie isn't home yet and as she rushes up the stairs there is a blur of television voices from Hana's room. She eases open Ruby's door and home drapes itself back around her. It's all she can do not to lift the child out of her cot. She stands there and listens to Ruby's soft breath. She lets it comfort her, and then she gently shuts the door.

Ro's bus didn't go to Dublin after all. Instead, it left him stranded in the middle of the bog, some place he'd never heard of where he waited for hours for another one to twist its way around two counties before dropping him off at the Busáras. Now that he's finally at the ferry port, he can feel Mags Madden all around him – a wispy presence, rustling like a sack of old leaves. To drown her out, he clamps his headphones to his ears and lets Jon Hopkins surge right through him, pumping at his heart, taking a wrecking ball to his head.

The last ferry out of Dublin is full of the kind of people who are normally invisible. Here, isolated from those who run in packs, they are forlorn and obvious. Ro has been on a lot of boats and he has seen a lot of people like the fat man at the next table who is boring on about his time on the rigs to a couple playing Candy Crush. Caspian Sea. Ten years. If he went back he'd be a supervisor, but they can stuff their job.

He feels sorry for the woman opposite, whose head is already a skull, and yet part of him hates her too, like he hates all this tribe of losers, for being in the same boat as him. Now that he's removed the headphones, the hum is in his ears again. Although it is possible that the real Mags is recovering from her hangover in her Formica kitchen, frying rashers against the late-night munchies, it doesn't sound like it because the Mags in his head is papery and rustling, dead as autumn.

Once the ferry trembles into life, Ireland passes behind him quickly enough – the fat, round storage tanks, the rat-tail rain. He remembers what it felt like in that caravan – to place one kick, and then another, and another, and then to walk away.

As he queues for coffee at Blazes Boylan's Bar he wonders at being able to hide what's in his head – the flashing metal and the battering drums, the Mags Madden shuffle. But this tribe of losers notice nothing, because everything they see is grey. Not like Jess, for whom everything is etched in black and white. The thought of Jess agitates him. Jess, and her inside track.

He isn't taken with the doughnuts or the crackle-glazed croissants, so he moves on to the Nora Barnacle Food Emporium instead. As he stands in line, he looks out at the approaching dark. There is no horizon, only mist and waves. Rain streams down the sealed, metal-framed windows that are streaked with the rusty tracks of other journeys, and it occurs to him that his mother might have taken this same ferry herself, sat in the same seat, even. Somewhere between Ireland and Wales, he wakes to find the waves have thickened. Sealed off behind those windows those silent waves are menacing. He plugs himself back in to Jon, and it's like a fuzz in the blood, driving him on and on, to London and Jess and answers.

When the ferry docks at Holyhead, he discovers that there isn't a train for hours. He takes a bluey to keep him going and goes in search of alternatives. The car-hire place is still open, though the guy there could be moonlighting for all he knows. The only vehicle available is a two-door Bug with a 1.3-litre engine. Apart from the Merc, that is. Once seen, he's sold, but an epic grovel is required before Mr Moonlight will deliver the keys to the Merc in return for a wodge of cash.

It's a long time since he has driven, and this night driving is like a hallucination. Halfway across Anglesey, there are roadworks, great red Xs overhead that might be a comment on his life. No entry, no entry, no entry. He meets a line of lorries travelling in the opposite direction, cabs with flatbeds strung out behind them. To escape from what looks like a bad omen, he floors the accelerator. Sometimes, he loses the run of the road, no longer sure where the centre is, and it's exhilarating, this tangle of light – blue ahead, and flashes of red that might be a perimeter, lines of white that might mark an airfield. And still the car surges on. He is tired of choosing, of being let down. Frustrated by all the roads he didn't take, the leads he didn't reach in time. Some will-o'-the-wisp is as likely as his rational mind to lead him to his mother.

There are eight pre-sets on the car radio. He tries them all before settling on a chat show with the usual late-night lunatics, the mystery voices and the kiss 'n' tells. Story after story, lie upon lie. As for their own history, Jess has always claimed to believe the simplest theory, that their parents were attacked on that beach and dragged into the trees, that they were robbed and their bodies hidden, and that it is mere chance that their father's body has been found and not their mother's. But his heart is popping now at the thought of those years spent trailing off after Sophie Considine who probably was no longer Sophie Considine at all. Even now, he can hear Mags Madden, whispering in his ear. 'She won't be far from Jess.'

Somewhere south of Birmingham, between trance and sleep, he jolts awake to find himself veering off the road. Wresting back control, he pulls onto the hard shoulder while his heart batters and his mind swerves. He puts his head down on the wheel for a power nap until, woken by the shuddering of a Sainsbury's juggernaut, he decides to come off the motorway instead. At the next services, the stench of old sausage greets him at the door. The bluey has worn off now, and he is yearning for a bed. Ten minutes later he is in the Travelodge, and sinking into beige and white and glorious sleep.

3

The morning after the Summer Party, Jess goes to the office just as she always does. But, bubbling there beneath the skin of things, there is a sense of dread. She knows how this goes – the day will stagger on, and then whatever peril she has half perceived will hurry in and swamp her. She has trained herself to pick up the warning signs – a feeling of unease, a weight in the air. When she passes the knot of PAs beside the stairwell, two unfamiliar faces – temps, she supposes – look up at her, as if they sense it too, this clinging apprehension. She skips the weekly know-how meeting and leaves the office at lunchtime to try to clear her head. On her short cut to the market, she almost collides with a man peering up at the clouded peak of the latest trophy high-rise. There is no one else around and, when he whips round to face her, she is terrified that this is it, this is the moment. But then he steps aside, and it was nothing after all.

No sooner is she back in the office than Miles is at her

door, and she knows for certain then that this squat, balding man in the purple tie is the source of her unease. She offers him a seat, but he remains standing. Leaning there against the door frame, he looks hung-over, shifty. She waits for the apology, but it doesn't come, and then she is angry with herself for allowing him to make her feel so vulnerable.

'You look tired, Miles,' she says. 'Late night?'

She focuses on a large, angry spot on the side of his nose, horribly compelling in a man of his age. The focus helps her hold back her fear, because she is shocked to find that she is still afraid and therefore that whatever happened was real enough. And then she steels herself to confront him.

'You seemed upset last night.'

He does a double-take, as if he can't believe she's had the nerve to raise the matter.

'Corporate jollity, it does my head in.'

'That explains it then,' she murmurs blandly. 'Have you seen Faithie recently then?' she says.

He looks her straight in the eye.

'I have no idea who you're talking about.'

'I remember now,' she says. 'Villars, right?'

And now that it's clear that last night never happened, that she imagined it all, she wonders why he is here at all. She isn't left wondering for long. He starts with generalities – never good when a client is unhappy, any lapse in professionalism, lack of attention – so that by the time he has reached the nub of the issue, Jess is relieved to be able to work out the general thrust of his attack, this being the best means etc.

'The subclause, the one we had to wrench like sticky toffee from Trentino's hot little hand?'

Now she's with him.

'What about it?'

'How could it not have found its way into the execution copies?'

That is Sarah's file. Jess did some work on it when Sarah was on sick leave, but only at the early stages. She didn't even work on the S&P. The obvious course is simply to say it's nothing to do with her, but somehow she isn't able to do that, it seems so petty. Somehow she doesn't seem to be able to say anything at all, so intent is she on holding his gaze.

'You'd better fix it,' he says.

'My pleasure.'

'Your what?' He has resorted to sneer mode.

'Don't fret. I'll sort it with the other side.'

As he turns to go, she wonders if Sarah has rebuffed him too. It seems to make him want to put the boot in.

'Before you go,' she says. 'If you ever so much as touch me again.'

His mouth sinks into a grimace.

'Touch *you*? I'd rather suck a dick.'

When he's gone, she looks at the phone. She looks at it for at least a minute and considers whether or not to call someone, whether that someone should be Sarah or her mentor Delia or HR. Whether she should tell Charlie. But in the end, she doesn't call anyone. It makes her feel superior to Miles Rennie not to lift that phone. She has risen above. She supposes she is almost sorry for him, though she is sorrier still for his wife, because apparently there is one of those.

One of the other partners drops by a little later. 'Not to worry, Jess,' he says. 'That Trentino contract? At least we caught it.' He flicks the air to say it was nothing, all's well, and not to give it another thought. But Jess has seen him do that before when it did matter and the comeback was already on its way. She brushes the thought away.

To make up for not having seen Ruby the night before, she slips away early. By six thirty, she is walking home across the Common, the light driving slantways across the grass that is already beginning to yellow, past the stately summer trees. Players circle the torn green carpet of the cricket crease, and there's music in the puck and cheer of their game. She passes the hordes of fitness fanatics gathered at the low-slung bar that marks the Common's perimeter as they stretch and flex in strictly marshalled groups. As she weaves through the groups of friends sipping Prosecco on picnic rugs, she gives a moment's thought to all the other lives she might have chosen, and then she quickens her pace towards her own. Passing the bandstand and the wildflower meadow, through the waft of onion from the twenty-four-hour burger stall, she reaches the cut-through, where cops idle in their squad cars, playing games on their phones. A right turn, another stretch of grass, and the Common shrinks, giving way to a tight matrix of tarmac and red brick.

They bought the house on Riverton Street the year they got married. Nobody else had a place like this – a three-storey house with a filigree balcony, a veranda, a gate that leads directly onto the Common. Most of their friends were struggling to afford a one-bed flat five stops away on the Tube. But this solid permanence meant so much to Jess that she would gladly have alienated the whole world if she could have a house like the one she spent her schooldays in with Auntie Rae, somewhere she would create her own stability, no matter how much they had to scrimp and borrow.

Riverton Street is a place of order and plenty, of plantation shutters and lavender bushes. The waist-high walls that separate the front gardens from the street are topped by occasional hedges – wafts of bamboo or close-cut privet. There are foreshores of gravel, with hip-high pots in zinc or terracotta, and woodwork is painted sludge green, pewter, putty. No clear colours, no shouting. Living on Riverton Street, it would be easy to imagine that all the suffering in the world – the cruelty and starvation, the endless hate and fear – merely exists in the collective imagination, on a screen, on Mars.

Nowadays, Jess tries not to think about what happened on the beach. She has safeguarded herself with walls, inoculations, insurance policies, invested in a decent alarm system. She has acquired a profession, a marriage, a single, much-loved child. She has made a fortress of her beloved house and, although their equity is just a thin screed on an edifice of mortgages and investments, they just about manage to cling on to it. But Jess knows how quickly things can change. She has no blithe confidence in the world, and she no longer really has a brother.

Just as she reaches the end of the street, a message pings in. Hana, asking how much longer she's going to be. She imagines Hana sitting on the closed loo seat, jabbing at her phone, while Ruby splashes at the bathwater, then covers her face in the foam. She sees the two men sitting in a blue car a few doors down, too, but she's so anxious to get home now that she doesn't pay them any heed.

She is just about to put the key in the door when it opens for her. And there is Hana, startlingly blonde, with her frosted lipstick and the two furrows of permanent displeasure on her brow. Ruby is in Hana's arms, her pearly teeth bared as she strains for Jess.

'Silly billy,' Hana says. 'Let Mama get her jacket off first.' She moves Ruby out of reach and although the only thing Jess wants is to cuddle her child she does what she is told, takes her jacket off, her bag. But then the doorbell rings and, as Jess moves to answer the door, Hana swings Ruby round to face the garden. 'Come on Rooby Roo, let's do swing.'

Ruby's arms are flapping wildly now, her face contorted with disappointment. Jess has opened the door and is about to greet the men on the doorstep when Ruby grasps her sleeve with her strong little fingers. Torn between her wriggling child and the open door, Jess stands there blankly for a moment. And then Hana expertly unfastens Ruby's grip and carries her away towards the garden.

The two men on the doorstep are watching her closely. They flip their cards at her and move to enter.

Embarrassed by this glimpse they've had of her home life, Jess stands her ground.

'Mind if I have a closer look?' She gives them her professional smile.

They don't smile back, but they hold their badges up anyway. Point made, she gives each ID a cursory glance – Reynolds and Crowe – then stands aside to let them in. This is not the uniformed bobby who came to advise them on home security. This is something else. She watches the backs of their heads as they take in the TV room with Charlie's mega screen, the gleaming expanse of the drawing room, the succession of ink-blot lithographs that line the staircase until they disappear out of view.

The first officer, Reynolds, is ostentatiously dressed down in scuffed trainers and a pair of sweatpants that still bear the shape of his knees. He is young, perhaps no more than thirty. Crowe looks like he ought to be in retirement. He is going for the golfer look in a diamond-patterned sweater and cords, and is carrying a black daypack, a little incongruously, she thinks, which he eases off his shoulder and rests on one of the stools at the breakfast bar that no one ever uses. She scans her visible life through their eyes. The carousel of exotically named coffee capsules, the huge glass dome on the cake stand, the precisely judged colours. She wonders what ruin they are about to bring on her. Meanwhile, in the garden, Ruby is screaming.

Absent-mindedly, she reaches for the coffee machine, but the golfer says she really doesn't need to bother about that.

'We're all caffeined out,' says the man in sweatpants. 'Mind if we sit?'

'Oh sorry,' she says. It slips out, this word she's almost been trained out of using. 'Yes, of course.'

They sit together at the breakfast bar, which is too uncomfortable to be the informal spot the kitchen designer assured her it would be. The sweatpant man has trouble balancing on the stool so he props himself against it instead, one buttock anchoring him in place. The golfer seems to be the boss, if that's the word. He looks at the black backpack as if it might explode right there in front of them. Once they are, all three of them, gazing at the bag, he reaches into his inside pocket. He unfolds a piece of paper and pushes it across the table to her. Before she has a chance to read it, he pounces on it with his index finger and draws it back. 'I should really give you a bit of context first. This is an email from the Irish authorities.'

Nobody elaborates and she doesn't say anything either, and when the silence has stretched a little thin for comfort, the golfer continues.

'I'm afraid this might upset you, Mrs Clark, but your mother's passport has been found.'

They are both looking at her now, as if there is a line she is meant to contribute here. But she doesn't know that line, and nobody says anything to prompt her. Hana sticks her head through the door and then moves away again. In the hallway, Ruby seems to have calmed down. Her scooter will be getting cold outside, she says. Can Hana put it to bed too?

The other man is getting impatient with the golfer.

He butts in and, from the release he seems to gain from talking, she can tell right away that she will get more sense out of him.

'What you have to understand,' he says, 'is that we know very little at this point. The passport was discovered—'

'But I thought the passports were found right away, back at the hotel.'

It's one of the few things she does remember from the day itself. She recalls clutching on to the little blue books because they contained the photos of her parents, and not being allowed to keep them, and the rage she felt at that.

They glance at one another and she realises then that there is something she has failed to grasp.

'Ah,' the golfer says. 'I should have explained. This is a different passport. An Irish one she applied for in her maiden name, a matter of months before she left.'

'Her birth name,' the other man offers.

'OK then, her birth name, whatever difference that makes.' The golfer smiles curtly at Jess, then moves on. 'What I need to tell you, though, is that the passport was used after she disappeared.'

And then she feels something. She isn't sure what the emotion is, but it's complicated and unpredictable.

'The focus of our investigations will be whether it was used to gain entry to the United Kingdom after your mother disappeared. And if so, when.'

'And by whom,' the tracksuit guy adds. In case she hadn't had that thought already.

He flicks a few images further along on his phone and turns the screen towards her.

'Looks good as new, don't it? Only used the once, far as we know. Delhi to Paris. After that, who knows how it got to Ireland? It might have been used again, and it might not. Either way, it was kept inside a leather bag, inside a plastic bag, inside a cardboard box. The Irish found it in a caravan in the middle of nowhere. A place, I believe, you know well. Curramona.' He scrolls again through the images on his phone until he finds the one he wants. He comes alongside and puts it in front of her, a little too close, so that she has to move her head back to see it properly.

'It was located in a townland called Drigheen, on a plot of land behind a former shop, latterly the residence of Margaret Madden, a woman in her sixties who lived alone.' He looks at her as if he's expecting her to corroborate that.

While she does remember the place – the shop and the caravan, and summer days spent longing for the rain to stop so they could get to the lake where they weren't meant to swim – Mags Madden is not someone she ever thought she would hear of again. Auntie Rae fell out with Mags years ago and, though maybe she should have got back in touch herself, somehow there never seemed to be the time.

'The passport was found next to the deceased woman's body.'

'Mags is dead?'

She doesn't feel any particular grief for Mags Madden. But the very fact that these men have come here makes her feel as if she should.

'I'm afraid so,' says the golfer. 'And in suspicious circumstances, too. There's been a spate of rural crime in that area recently. They think this might have been a robbery that went wrong. On the other hand, the shop has been closed for years, and there's not likely to have been a lot of cash around the place. No jewellery seems to have been taken, nothing like that. And the woman had drunk a lot – I mean, well over three times the legal limit. She was frail, so it's possible she tripped and bashed her head. For some reason, the cardboard box in which the passport was found was in the middle of the floor. Not sure what that says. The post-mortem will reveal a bit more.'

There is only one question worth asking. But she is afraid to hear the answer, and so she doesn't let it pass her lips. Does this make it more or less likely that my mother is still alive?

But that one question breeds others until her head is crammed with them. She calls up that stock picture of her mother she has curated for herself. The one she keeps at the very back of her mind to use when she needs it. Blonde, demure, that long plait slung over one shoulder. Half smiling, half disdainful. Those beautiful eyes she once heard Rae describe as cold. But one sister's account of another, how reliable is that? Rachel and Sophie. Dark and Blonde. Home and Away. Good and Bad. Those lazy binaries, they're attractive, but they only tell one side of the story.

And perhaps she doesn't want to know any more. Perhaps it would be better if her mother simply stayed where she was. As good as dead, as dead as Dad. She barely glimpsed the image of the passport photo page, and now that the officer's phone is resting face down on the counter she feels bereft.

'Could I see it again?' she asks. 'The photo of my mother?'

The men seem uncomfortable now. Their message delivered, perhaps they just want to get away. They look at one another as if the request is somehow improper, but the man with the phone scrolls back through the images until he reaches the ID page. He focuses on the passport photo, enlarging it, then turns it towards her. She takes the phone from him and gazes at the screen. She would barely have recognised her own mother. Her hair seems darker, though it's hard to tell, and she is wearing glasses. Glasses? When did her mother ever wear glasses? She starts to tell them that it isn't who they think it is. But when she looks a little closer, she realises that, while this is an entirely different look, it is still her mother. She doesn't let herself explore the implications of that. Not yet.

The tracksuit man is saying something now. Jess thinks he might be asking her if she's OK. But she is ankle-deep in warm seawater, her feet sinking in the gently scouring sand of that Goa beach. Around her calves she can feel the flick of tiny fish. And she is still blissfully unaware of what is about to happen. She is surrounded by her last ever moment of untainted joy. Her eyes prick to think of that. Sparrow is there too, standing at the water's edge, howling. He has sliced his foot open, a sharp stone perhaps. It's not a deep cut – no sooner does the blood well to the surface than the sea takes it – but he wants his

Mama. Baby shark, he is saying. Hungry shark. Only moments earlier, Jess's eye had caught the blaze of orange on the sand, that big orange square of cotton Mama used as a picnic rug. It was as if the sun had burnt itself onto the sand. But there is no orange now. There is no Mama now either, and no Pa. Jess feels a hand on her shoulder. And as she turns and looks into the golfer's face, she is momentarily confused by his solidity in the here and now until she catches a buttermilk-sourness off his breath.

'You OK there? You see, this is what you need to understand,' he says. 'Your mother applied for that passport in an entirely different name, one we don't think she used at any other time.'

She wishes they would go now and let her think. The golfer asks for a mobile number, says he'll be in touch as soon as he has anything else.

'Oh,' he says. 'Just one more thing. Your brother – any idea where he might be?' He glances down at a piece of paper. 'Sparrow Considine? Gets about a bit.'

'Not really,' she says, immediately on the defensive as she always is about Ro.

Her throat tightens. Guilt, of course, because she came off luckier. Fear, too, in case they're about to tell her something about Ro that she doesn't want to hear. Sadness, for the lost boy he still is.

'Thought he was a bit of a nomad, no?'

'So what if he is?'

'Anyway, when you see him, get in touch, yeah?'

They look strangely at her as they leave, as if she hasn't quite displayed the correct emotions. She wonders what they expected. Elation? Gratitude? Should have sent someone with a speck of empathy about them. Should have sent a woman. Although she stopped feeding Ruby a year ago, her nipples prickle and she is glad that, in her case at least, the instincts do their job.

Upstairs, in the bathroom they decorated with waves and whales and dolphins, Hana is pacing the room like she's in a cage, while Ruby seems to have forgotten all about earlier. She gives a 'yay' as Jess appears, and tries to haul herself up by the side of the bath. Jess is so transfixed by Ruby that she hardly notices Hana leave. Hana has a room here, but you'd never think it. Each evening, she departs as soon as Jess gets home. Jess assumes there's a boyfriend, but the one time Jess asked, Hana screwed up her nose and said she didn't like the word. She can't imagine sharing any of this with Hana, who declared soon after she moved in that people lose what they deserve to lose. Jess found the idea of that astonishing, brutal even. But maybe it was no stranger than the belief she clung to for a long time that her own loss had a prophy-lactic effect, that it would protect her like a magic charm.

'The worst has already happened,' she told her friend Carrie, as she threw back her head and let the stars shatter her face. 'And that makes me freeeeee.'

They were drunk on a rooftop bar, with their hair streaming around them, full of power and possibility.

'Don't kid yourself,' Carrie said. 'That's not how it works. One disaster doesn't stop the others from lining up to take its place.'

Even so, Jess spent her college years convinced that

she'd had all her bad luck in one clump. She raced down black runs, went home with risky men, drove fast.

But now she is fearful. She is afraid of having to face a truth she has trained herself to live without. She is afraid of pain and loss. Already, she is sure that the incident with Miles Rennie will have a sequel. And now there is this. She is not sure yet what to make of this.

She reads Ruby two rounds of *Owl Babies*, and as usual the mother owl comes home. Each time, Ruby squeals with delight, clapping her fat little hands. Except that tonight it is the wrong book for Jess, who can hardly keep the tears from her own eyes as she waits for Ruby's to take on their clouded look, pre-sleep. Jess slaps all the shutters closed and waits there in the semi-dark for her to drift away. And as she watches Ruby nuzzle her way towards sleep, her heart clenches for her own lost mother. By now, the news is hurtling around inside her head. She tries Charlie's phone, but it goes to voicemail. She didn't think he had another client dinner, but she is never sure. She is bursting to talk to someone. She could ring Martha, but Martha has three toddlers to contend with. She could ring Sarah or Max, but she doesn't want to bring this into the office, at least not yet. Contemplating the gleaming floor, the airy space of the room, she thinks of all those people who just disappear. The faces at the station, the people who stare out of 'Missing' posters. Do police routinely turn up to discuss someone who disappeared years before? She doesn't think so.

She splits the last bagel and pops it in the toaster. It burns, even though she thought she'd checked the setting. Once she has scraped off the black and smeared the scarred surface with butter, she no longer feels like eating. She busies herself with the iron instead, swiping a damp piece of kitchen roll over the rusty residue that has attached itself to its leading edges, until she realises she has no idea where Hana keeps the ironing board.

And while all this is going on, or not going on, she is developing a theory. Immediately after Goa, press interest in the case gave the police a child-protection role – not too much hassle, no more attention than they could bear. They were assigned two young officers who tried to inter-est Ro in football. Jess told them it wasn't his thing, but they wouldn't listen. It was her thing, though – skills, stats, whatever. They told her she was marvellous to know so much, and about Stoke City, too. While she detected the condescension even then, she was grateful for the praise. And then someone else took over, a girl with lovely nails who staked her professional pride on making Spar-row better. There was no more football after that.

She realises then. The older policeman, the golfer, must be one of those officers from the old days. It softens her heart to think he cared enough to come along and break the news to her himself. She wishes she'd been kin-der, less snippy. The fact that someone else still cares, it matters. She still cares too. She's just not sure she can afford to.

And then there is Ro.

Sitting there in the shuttered room, on the polished floor that is still warm from the day's sun, she listens to the baby monitor and the rise and fall of Ruby's breath, the snuffle as she turns and the cot rattles and the little mobile above her head gives out the first two notes of its tune.

There is no place here for Ro.

The gate creaks open, then clacks shut. There are footsteps along the path, a shuffle at the letter box, a drop. When she goes to check, it's just another flyer. *Robert has sold another home on your road.* And that's how it is when the world shifts. Sometime in the velvet dark, she senses Charlie arrive, but it's much too great a distance for her to clamber to the surface, and she can't muster the energy to speak. As he undresses in the en suite, she catches a sliver of light, the whine of his toothbrush. In bed, he curls right up behind her and that reassures her, though she's not sure why. He smells meaty, and she can feel the rasp of his stubble on her shoulder, his cock at the base of her spine. He folds his arms around her waist, and then they are both asleep.

4

At the Travelodge, Ro has taken another Ambien, and is just descending into a bout of Mags-defeating sleep when, in London, Jess is getting out of bed. She is standing at the double basin in the en suite, sawing at her teeth while Charlie takes a shower. Each moment that passes somehow makes the subject of the passport more difficult to raise. Reaching for a towel, he bends to kiss her. His breath tastes sour from the night before, and she turns her head away.

'Sorry I was so late,' he says. 'Bloody client couldn't get enough of me.'

She hasn't the will to question him. As she watches him dress, sliding on smooth cotton, rolling back the cuffs and threading through the gold links she bought him out of last year's bonus, she has a flash of him in an entirely different life, where the cotton is polyester and the shoes aren't clean and the bathroom is shared with people he isn't sleeping with. She tries to dress him in that other life, but her imagination fails her.

Breakfast is hurried, as it always is midweek. A thick yoghurt with a splodge of honey, a thimbleful of coffee. Ruby asks for 'holiday', as she has done every day since May, when they went to France, just the three of them, and walked with her on their backs for hours, taking turn and turn about. Being carried through the green by people who love her. This is holiday. But Jess needs to sit in a room and hold her head between her hands. She needs to decide whether to contact Ro, and how to do that even if she wants to. The very thought of what will come from Ro learning of the passport is exhausting. It frightens her too.

Charlie slides his cup out from under the coffee machine. He looks at her, then knocks the coffee back. 'What is it, hun?' he says.

She manages to speak calmly – the two men, the passport. She doesn't say she thinks she recognised one of them because Charlie would pooh-pooh that. And she doesn't mention Ro.

'So, what are they saying?'

'I suppose they're not really saying anything. Not yet anyway. They just thought I should know, that's all.'

'Not very helpful, is it? We don't have any answers but just in case you were managing to get on with your life, we thought we'd—'

'Please don't, Charlie.'

'I'm not criticising you, Jess.' He reaches out for her, but stays just out of range. 'It's just this mania for excavating everything when we all know there will never be any real answers. It pisses me off. So, there was a second passport. So what?'

She feels frozen, as though the emotion inside her has shut itself off for fear of being called out, named and shamed. She puts out her hand to lift the cup in front of her, but it doesn't seem to want to obey. Perhaps something shows in her face though, because he launches himself towards her and she finds herself buried in his jacket, which smells of old rain.

'Oh my love, I'm sorry. I didn't mean to upset you.'

She doesn't cry, she merely notes that he doesn't seem to grasp the significance of this at all. And then she begins to tell herself that his reaction is the right one – it means nothing. In the gleaming temple of efficiency that is her kitchen, it is difficult to conjure up a Goa beach, the confusion of being abandoned. It still seems impossible, the comprehensive loss of both parents. Not a scrap of evidence. Just the disbelief, the sudden void, the constant chatter of voices she didn't understand, the fear that nothing would ever be safe again.

Charlie draws back from her and smooths down her hair. He kisses her cheek, a chirpy kind of kiss that is just not the right one to serve the moment. She remembers the sadness in the golfer policeman's eyes, and she knows he thought the passport mattered. She thinks it matters too. She wants to scream it out loud so that everyone can hear – she's come back, she's come back – but not here, not now.

'I'm sorry, Jess. It's not nothing. I know that. It's just— We can't keep doing this, can we? Theories, more theories.' He bends down and kisses her head. 'Let's plan something nice for the weekend.'

'Well I guess we have your birthday on Sunday, so that's something.'

He misses the sarcasm in her voice. His face lights up. And she realises he'd forgotten it was his birthday, which must be a first. Charlie is like a kid when it comes to his birthday. Parties need to take place on the actual day. There must be candles. It's one of the things she loves about him, this candour when it comes to his own pleasures. Somehow, it seems to make him generous, mindful of celebrations even when he's not the centre of attention himself. He goes to Ruby, and nuzzles her face. 'We haven't had much time recently, have we, sweet pea? So, yep, a party will be nice.'

And for a moment she wishes she never had to leave this room. This is the kind of life she has striven to achieve, and it is doing its work now. It is making her feel safe. The smell of bitter coffee, the warmed sweet milk, the daughter rattling at the tray of her high chair with a plastic spoon.

Moments after Charlie shuts the front door behind him, Hana comes downstairs and the choreography they have devised begins, Hana distracting Ruby with her blue teddy to give Jess time to disappear without a fuss.

She stands all the way to Liverpool Street. In the crush of strivers fighting for the escalator, she grieves for all those days when she needed a mother. She runs a finger under her eyes to preserve her mascara, but the sadness is like a wave and it drowns her. She sits in a booth at the back of the Prêt on the corner and forces down a harsh espresso against the heave of tears. Now and then, someone glances at her. A girl in a pink mac looks her straight in the eye, then swirls the straw round in her smoothie and turns away. And maybe she looks like a mad person because no one asks if they can help, which they can't anyway.

For a long time, she had been unable to remember anything about the day her parents vanished. It had been bleached out by light – the sun in her eyes on the beach, the blaze of naked bulbs in the police station afterwards. They said she must try harder to remember, but the glare obliterated everything. Once the questions stopped, and she was able to make a space for herself that didn't involve a beach and a vanishing, hazy shapes began to form behind that memory of light until one day the outline of a tree emerged. It was the kind of tree they use in ads for things that smell of coconut. But Jess smelt mango, and she knew for certain then that somewhere beyond the light was the beach. It would begin to materialise just as her head hit the pillow. Each night, it seemed, she could see a little more. Soon she perceived a stretch of sand, a red bucket. That single dreadlocked tree became a row of perfect palms straining out towards the sea. She sensed movement in there, people. But no matter how hard she tried they stayed hidden. She swirls the dregs of coffee around the little paper cup and knocks it back.

When she enters the revolving doors of the offices, she glances up at the extravagant glass installation suspended from the top floor of the building. It seems even more inappropriate than ever today. Rope after rope of multi-coloured baubles and tentacles and strange whimsical flourishes sweep through the central atrium from somewhere out of view all the way down to the entrance hall. The rest of the building is prim, dove grey and walnut, but this is a carnival of every wild imagining a lawyer needs to curb. It reminds her that she is beginning to hope, and she mustn't do that.

She swipes an *FT* from the rack by the lift and scans the front page – another orange jumpsuit against another blue sky. The shocking cruelties are all still out there. And yet, today is not the same as yesterday, because her mother might not be dead. Then again, if Sophie is alive, she must have opted out of contact for all these years. Something hardens in Jess with that thought. Her mother is dead.

She takes a detour to the Ladies, locks herself into the first stall, and throws up the coffee in bitter little retches. Outside the cubicle, someone has come in to wash her hands. There is the clink of make-up, the muttered solo chat of someone who doesn't realise they're being overheard.

'It's not rocket science, for fuck's sake. Jesus.'

Jess sits on in silence. She puts her head between her legs and waits for whoever it is to leave. When the door of the Ladies closes with a rubbery little kiss, she unlocks the door and starts to run through the immediate list of tasks. Review the distribution agreement before the ten o'clock meeting, deal with a pile of routine assignments and novations, correspondence with the department, check through the new production-sharing contract for Namibia. Normally, she doesn't find these things daunting. She likes to put a form on things, to fence emotion behind verbal formulas. Her work is as important to her as her gleaming kitchen, her gravelled garden. She purchases a toothbrush, ready-pasted, from the dispenser that deals with every unexpected eventuality from a sexual opportunity to a ripped-off button. She fixes her make-up and goes.

The corridor is lined with all the new art that the young Spanish partner has bought on the firm's behalf. His taste is provocative and nobody could believe he got the naked buttocks with the purple butt plug past the Acquisition Committee. By the time she reaches the central pod of PAs, she has pulled herself sufficiently together to be able to talk holidays, and whether you can ever really trust the reviews on TripAdvisor. But then it's back to the swivel chair and the pile of documents that she must trawl through patiently enough to find the trap. There will always be a trap.

As far as she knows, Ro has never had a phone. Under his name she has stored six or seven numbers. There is Ro – Clare, Ro – Juliet, Ro – Saski, Ro – Pia, Ro – Fay. None of these relationships has lasted. None of these numbers is worth ringing. She's done it before. It's an embarrassment, that's all. She tries to imagine how Ro lives, where he goes, what he does. She supposes the trust gives him enough to keep him above the poverty line, that whatever he has he still spends on travel, on the quest, but she doesn't know.

She pushes back her chair and the half-finished mug of coffee she left down there earlier is spilled. She watches the brownish liquid bead onto the carpet tile, then soak into a heart-shaped stain. There was a stage when Ro would have seen that as a sign. Clouds, birds, an archipelago of freckles on a new face – everything was scanned for what it might have to say about the only thing that mattered.

The latest draft of the distribution agreement is printing off next to her. The smell of baked paper is overwhelming, and she wishes she could open the window. Better to let the summer in than to freeze-dry it, that's what she told HR when D3 petitioned them for the keys to the windows.

'You've a way with words,' the woman said, as if that were suspect in a lawyer.

But in an office full of harassed perfectionists, the windows remained sealed.

The agreement is routine – she can already guess which will be the contested sections – it's the clients who will be time-consuming. There will be egos to salve, losses to gloss over and pointless gains to be dressed up as stunning victories. Meanwhile, accumulating in a corner of her mind, the list of things still to be arranged for Charlie's birthday party in a couple of days' time. In another corner, Ro.

She sits side-on to the glass panel that looks onto the

little cluster of PAs and beyond them to that carnival of coloured glass plunging through seven storeys of prime real estate, past Probate and Chancery and Estates and Private Client, through Commercial A and Commercial B.

A call comes in on the extension, which is unusual. Most clients call her direct line. The woman at the other end sounds confident, friendly even. She introduces herself briskly and, leaving no gap, she cuts to the chase.

'I'm ringing to let you know that we'll be running a story in the *Daily Post*.'

Jess has never even read the *Daily Post*.

'We want to get to the bottom of the story of your mother's disappearance, just as much as you do. The passport, it's significant, I think.'

Having only just heard about the passport herself, Jess is shocked that anyone else has heard. Immediately, she thinks about the policemen. Which number did she give them? She can't remember.

'I was hoping for a quote, you know? About the whole experience?'

Whatever that is. She suspects she hasn't had the whole experience yet. When Jess doesn't say anything right away, the woman just keeps on talking, as if to pause would break a spell. 'I'm sorry to have to disturb you at work. I know what it's like, juggling, with Ruby still so young. Hard work.'

She is taken aback that this stranger, who has muscled in on her day, could know about Ruby. The woman seems more powerful now, and that makes Jess keen not to offend, not to make an enemy of someone who writes for the *Daily Post*. And then there is the client, who must not be kept waiting, and his agreement, which must be perfect.

'Just a few words, Mrs Clark, that's all I need.'

She can't imagine that anyone at work reads a rag like that. What will it matter? And so, Jess tells the woman she can have her quote. She supplies a rehash of something she said to a missing-persons charity once, as far as she can remember it. Something a little grandiose about life and challenges and surmounting them. But as soon as she puts down the phone, she regrets it. She should have spoken to Ro first. And now it feels like she's unlocked all the doors.

Running out of time before the meeting, she scans the numbers she has for Ro. Ro – Fay is the most recent entry, so she tries that one first. She has never met Fay, but all Ro's women are tiny and blonde and surprisingly feisty, so maybe she doesn't need to. Fay doesn't recognise her name, but as soon as Jess starts to explain, she butts in.

'I'm not being funny . . .' she says, ' . . . but your brother's way out of order. Four in the morning, he's flinging gravel up at my neighbours' windows. Woke half the street before he clocked which house was mine. That must be six months back.'

The only other possibility is Pia. She met Pia once, and liked her. Pia supplies little green marzipan cakes to a shop in Notting Hill according to a recipe a forebear devised for some nineteenth-century Swedish princesses. They bonded over an obscure Kentucky rock band whose name Jess has since forgotten. For a while (well, for three months or so), it looked as though the relationship with Pia had legs until Ro ended up behaving just as badly as he'd done with all the others. She tries the number, but the call fails. She feels suddenly overwhelmed by all the things she can't control, the numbers that aren't the right ones, the people she can't read.

Ro has lost himself to Ambien, but he has shaken off Mags. If anyone has tried to enter his Travelodge room, he's been blissfully unaware. He slips down the stairs and out a fire exit into the car park while the girl on reception is playing with her phone. He is restless for London, hungry for answers. And he needs something else, too, something soft and sweet. Pia, that's what he needs. Because the bitterness is creeping back again, soaking in with the daylight. All those wasted days spent sitting knees-to-chin on a stinking bus on some shuddering road, in search of Sophie who was really Mary who was all the time with Jess.

He screams into reverse, then puts down his foot and goes. For most of the journey, Mags stays away. In the breathing space of the long drive back he concedes certain things, and maybe that's what shuts her up. He should not have held her head like that, or twisted her arm. He should never have kicked, then kicked and kicked and kicked. You are always the loser when you lose the rag. Who taught him that? Not his mother anyway. It must have been Auntie Rae, who had him figured out all right.

'The trouble with that fella,' he heard her tell the priest

who came to the door that first Christmas after Goa, 'is that he doesn't want to grow up. He thinks if he grows up he'll be turning his back on her for ever.'

Even now, he knows he looks immature, half built. He is a sparrow of a man, just as he was a sparrow of a boy – more frame than padding, more bone than brawn. But he is more resolute than he looks. There are powders he could take, no doubt. He could probably make some difference without ever entering a gym, but why bother when this deceptive appearance gets him everything he needs?

It is late morning by the time he has dropped off the car and taken the Tube to Brixton. Pia's flat is in a Victorian terrace not far from the market. He knows the route by heart though the shops have become funkier since he came here last. She will be happy to see him, even if she isn't. The happiness will be unspecific however, because Pia herself is never less than sweet. But though the door is still purple, the first-floor blinds have changed. The white linen has disappeared, and so has the little glass heart that used to catch the light, and when he rings the doorbell he has already guessed that Pia no longer lives there. From upstairs, a middle-aged woman glances down at him. She moves away, and he waits awhile, but she never comes to the door.

It is just another ending, and there have been many of those, but it brings Mags back. Nagging at him, whispering in his ear, all breath and spittle, and struggling to keep her balance. She is poisoning his day before he has even got it started. He uses a cashpoint near the station and finds the Merc has nearly cleaned him out. A pity about the state of his finances, he thinks, as he appraises his reflection in a nearby window. He could do with a haircut. Although there is money somewhere (at least, he thinks there is), he has lost the means to access it. Pin numbers long forgotten, cards lost. There is just one account now, with monthly subventions from the trust set up by his paternal grandparents, a sum he supplements from time to time with casual work in hipster bars that like his look. He wonders about moving back here, putting down roots one day when all his questing has been done. As he walks away, the rain begins – a proper, pelting shower – and he lifts his face to it, and lets it cleanse him free of both of them, Pia the sweet and Mags the sour.

He darts into a newsagent's, partly for shelter, partly for information. He picks up one of each of the red tops, five or six in all, and tucks them inside his jacket. He stands under the bowed blue awning while the rain drips onto the back of his neck and drenches his Converse. He is aware of the cars swishing by, until the moment when they no longer swish and the rain has stopped. When he has figured out the access to a rank of rental bikes lined up by the Tube station, he rides off into the traffic, pedalling furiously until he reaches the Common. Ahead of him, a small boy with a shiny red and black helmet, his knees like tiny pistons, is powering away from him. The boy is hunched over the handlebars, peeking up now and then at the punting, swearing footballers, at the white girls working off the baby fat under the instruction of lean black men.

He cycles the perimeter first, then edges closer in. On the outer circle, a knot of leggy guys are whacking a basketball around a fenced-off rectangle. At the half-pipe next door, grown men swoop and clatter beneath a wire slung with braces of ruined trainers. There are the usual bubble-written tags and, on the gable end of the café, a family of psychedelic owls. The grit sizzles under his wheels as he cycles across the beaten-earth path where summer has exposed the Common's archaeology – tree roots like bones and the glint of long-broken bottles. Over in the distance, a red van is parked haphazardly across the grass. Propped in front of it, a sandwich board: *Ed's Organic Ice Cream.*

He passes a woman who is holding the hand of a little boy. She is so much taller than he is that his arm is forced almost upright, at five to the hour. He recognises the uniform – the dark green trackie bottoms, the white shirts with a splash of purple on the pocket. Before Goa, he'd felt safe in that nursery. He has never felt safe since.

He overtakes the kids and passes the café on the Common where a woman with dreads who looks like Queen Nefertiti is stacking away the chairs. Years ago this was a sad, sallow place, yellow with grease and nicotine. On better days, there was chess played at tables outside by old men who had pissed their pants. On worse days, there were fights. Round the back, there was a place he used to visit when he wanted to get away from them all – Auntie Rae and Jess and the girl cousins who treated him like he was one of their Care Bears. A slice of dank space between two walls – the back wall of the café and another wall that seemed to have no purpose other than as a canvas for graffiti or something to kick a ball against. It smelled a bit in there, but it was his secret place.

Nowadays, the café is all pistachio madeleines and almond cannoli. It is redundant, sad-eyed dads in shorts, and harassed mums whose heads are dulled by Nurofen Plus and last night's bottle of supermarket white.

He stops his bike outside the café and the girl with the Nefertiti hair eyes him, then the bike. 'You looking for a docking station?'

How pretentious, he thinks. OK then, a docking station.

'Might have to go back to the Tube.'

Instead, he wheels the bike inside the café and props it up against the wall.

Nefertiti is at the levers and pistons now, making a drama out of her coffee-making. He spreads the papers out in front of him, flicks through the pages. He draws blanks with one, two and three. No mention of Mags at all. But he finds her in number four, on an inside page of the *Daily Post*. And there, on the same page, is Jess. Jess and her house. Her big new, big old, big big House. Charlie's arm is clamped around her shoulders, so tightly he could be a parliamentary candidate. How do the papers get these things? Facebook? A treacherous friend?

And then he realises that dead old Mags is not the main story at all. The main story is Sophie Considine and those two little children on that Goa beach. It seems the Orphans are still news, even now. This is a piece about the discovery in dead Mags's caravan of a passport that says what he knew all along – that his mother didn't die on that beach. He speed-reads the article, gulping down the paragraphs, then goes back to the top and reads more carefully what Jess has to say.

I found it hard, growing up, not knowing. I suppose that was the worst thing. Not knowing if she'd come back, if she'd suffered. Each Christmas until I was fifteen or so, I fantasised about her turning up at my aunt's doorstep dressed in a Christmas jumper and bearing the kind of parcel you see in Home Alone, *a big one with an oversized red bow.*

Where the hell did that come from? And where the hell is he in all of this? If it weren't for that old photo of the two of them by the water's edge, he'd have been air-brushed from history by now, purged. Jess has nothing to say about the passport, nothing about Sophie Considine. She doesn't even mention him. This is all about what it feels like to be Jess. And yet, none of this would have been discovered were it not for him. He's been grating the side of his hand on the rough wood at the edge of the table. He doesn't even notice until he's rubbed the skin raw. As he rereads the article, he puts the wound to his mouth and sucks.

When he goes to drink the coffee, it tastes harsh and bitter by comparison. He approaches Nefertiti at the counter and asks her to tip it into a large takeaway cup and top it up with foamy milk. He adds sugar, two tight twists of it, and a generous shake of chocolate powder on top. He hugs himself, just because. It's a habit he's retained. And he is definitely taking up less space these days. He splays his fingers out in front. Getting thinner, no doubt there. He looks speculatively at Nefertiti. He'd prefer a blonde tonight, but it's not a deal-breaker. Besides, it's early yet. Retrieving his bike, he catches her eye and when she smiles he decides to come back for her later.

The sun slips behind a cloud. Without it, the Common feels like what it really is, a vast field in the city. For a moment he loses all sense of connection with the place; it is rendered alien, meaningless. But the Common mattered to him once, just as he and Jess were once the best of friends. Even before the beach, he can remember dancing with Jess in the garden with the purple flowers, and singing and stomping along an imaginary yellow brick road. And all the adults laughing and Jess lifting him up and carrying him to Mama who put a party crown on his head and told him he was her little golden prince.

As he spirals out from the bandstand towards Jess's place, he passes the choppy little pond where old men in padded jackets used to race their remote-controlled boats. Over in the distance, a rash of boys in red football tops are spreading and clustering. Ref. Ref. He passes the fishing pond, where the fishermen are all camouflage and bivouacs, enacting some fantasy he can't access. There is a guy in army fatigues – *Atomic Tackle* on his back, 'Mellow Yellow' on his speakers, his three rods propped over the soupy water like tripwires. Men whose tiny cycling sweaters are stretched across their big chests are eating burgers by the sheen of the pond as a flock of Greenland geese honks overhead and a duck skids onto the water, settling on its surface.

One warm summer night during a long-ago World Cup, he got high on the muddy bank there and waded out through the green water, thick with duck shit and fronds of menacing vegetation. The hardest part was clambering up the steep bank of the island. Several times, he'd grabbed at dead branches or lost his footing on the mud and found himself thrown back again into the water. He dreamed of bringing a tent over there, just to see what it felt like to disappear, but he never did.

He is almost at Jess's house now, but if Jess knows he's here, she'll pull up the drawbridge and he'll find out nothing. He needs to watch. To wait, if needs be. He needs to be calm. He stops a moment at the back wall of her garden, where a wooden gate gives directly onto the Common, then moves on to where there is a break in the terrace and a passageway links the Common to the road in front. Most of these houses have shutters, slatted off-white or cream or chalky blue-grey. Most of them have tubs of lavender or box that sit demurely on the pale gravel. He hates the greyish foliage and old-lady scent of lavender. He wonders what would happen if you planted a row of fuck-off sunflowers in a street like this, installed some plastic planters of begonias and marigolds, let the whole thing go wild. If you put a rusty swing in the front garden or a shed from B&Q, if you failed any one of the rules of taste and order, what would they do? It's impossible to walk up to any of the windows without crunching on the gravel and attracting attention. And so, he gives up on the front of the house and returns to the closed rear gate instead.

When the rain begins again, he stands in under the trees while it splatters the bald earth track that's been beaten into the grass by runners and cyclists. He is soon bored; there's nothing to see, and a little worm of wet has worked its way under his collar. His thoughts shift to Nefertiti and the sweet smell of coffee. He's just about to go back there when someone stops at the gate. An ice-blonde girl with a buggy is punching a code into a box recessed into the wall. She angles the front wheels up onto the step, and then she's in. And once she's in, there's nothing else to amuse him until, minutes later, two burly men approach the back gate with the thud of cardboard, the clink of bottles. They bring one case of wine, then another and another and another. And then the beer, so much beer, stacks of beer. Next, it's speakers, tabletops and trestles, moulded plastic stools. A party? With all that booze piled up outside the gate, one of the men stands guard, eyeballing Ro, as the other disappears back through the gap in the terrace.

Ro sees his chance. 'Need a hand there, mate? Just waiting for my football crowd.'

The man looks him up and down. Football crowd? Like he's swallowing that.

'Nah, 'sfine. No worries.' He answers his phone, then jabs at the buttons on the gate and lets himself in.

Ro is glad that it's a keypad and not a lock. There's a tip he learned once from a guy in Hamburg – a couple of strips of Sellotape will do the trick, that's all. He's sure he could find his way in there if he wanted to.

'Happy to help, mate. Not doing anything sitting here.'

'You sure? There's a warden outside so he's had to go round the block. Cheers, 'preciate it.'

Ro stacks one carton of beer on top of another and follows the deliveryman into the back garden. It's like another world in there, a very precise one. The garden is composed of four squares edged off with knee-high box hedges. The rest is gravel, raked and golden. A couple of pale blue wooden benches curve along the side walls. There is a purple scooter, a small child who must be Ruby, the ice-blonde girl. But the only movement is from the magpies opposite. He can hear the triple rasp of their call as they dig for something on the roof.

'Where do you want them?' he asks the deliveryman. 'In the kitchen?'

'No, mate, I'm good.'

The girl with the blonde hair is looking at Ro, and the kid is looking at him, too, and he's wondering what makes him so interesting all of a sudden.

'Got a lot of booze here,' he calls over to the girl. 'Birthday coming up?'

She shakes her head. 'Not my birthday, not my nothing. Boss's birthday at the weekend. Big party.' And then she yawns.

The deliveryman is looking at him strangely. Time to go. As he walks back out through the gate onto the Common, he glances back and the guy is still standing there, watching him. No thanks, no appreciation at all.

It's easy to visualise them – Jess and little Ruby, who is less baby than she was last time, sitting with his mother on the other side of that wall. He can imagine them discussing the passport, and how it's just like Mags to hold on to something she was never meant to have in the first place. He can imagine Jess keeping their mother to herself.

He grows gloomy with the light. And then, at a first-floor window, the girl with peroxide hair appears for just a moment and sticks her phone out for a pic.

5

GOA ORPHANS. MOTHER MAY HAVE LIVED. The piece in the *Daily Post* is accompanied by a photo, *the* photo. The image itself is unexceptional – two golden children on a golden beach. But once you know that those children are about to be orphaned, its nature alters. It is no longer just a depiction. It is a reminder. Look at the beauty, it is saying, the innocence. See how unknowing they are. How little they anticipate. Even in 1992, to photograph a stranger's half-naked children might have been considered strange. To send it without explanation to a London newspaper while the story was raging on every front page?

Jess doesn't know who took that photo, and maybe it doesn't matter much who it was. What matters now is the message, because that's what lingers.

One day even paradise will fail you.

That photo was endlessly reproduced, along with the words they liked to use – 'Nightmare', 'Hubris', 'Hippie', and the name they had for Jess and Ro: 'The Orphans on the Beach'. For the duration of their front-page fame, Jess and Ro had a monopoly on orphanhood. Later, she would encounter others, of course: Victorian wards, little match girls, governesses who would never know love, children in faraway orphanages rocking at the bars of their empty cots. From the start, she was determined not to be that kind of orphan.

While Jess turned her head away from orphanhood, Ro searched everywhere for orphans on which to model himself. And when he found that Superman had been an orphan, and Harry Potter too, he would fantasise about the unique powers the status might confer. The orphan tag gave Ro's life a certain meaning, even an emerging destiny when he was sent off to school – though he discovered soon enough that it wasn't Hogwarts. He gave up on orphans after that. Between one exeat and the next he had switched his focus to the paranormal, the unexplained. He couldn't have been more than ten when he became obsessed by spontaneous combustion and alien abduction. But while Ro looked for answers in Roswell and the *Mary Celeste*, Jess simply tried to close the book.

As for the other picture, in which she and Charlie look ridiculous – smug and super young – she can't remember it being taken, but it could easily have been one weekend soon after they bought the house and were showing it off to friends invited for old-fogey Sunday roasts before she became aware of acting crassly, before she grew nervous about all that debt. And though every instinct urges her home, where it might just be possible to slip in through the back gate unnoticed and take to the duvet, she knows that her salvation lies the other way entirely, at the office, with a pile of contracts to fillet and skewer.

There is no one reading the *Daily Post* on the Tube, but by the time she arrives in the office, she is exhausted by the agony that someone there might have read the piece. And she realises that to have lost two parents in such a way feels shameful. Mel at reception hands her a baby wipe. 'Right shoulder,' she says.

On the glass coffee table between the sharply contoured Italian sofas, a copy of the paper is cast at a casual angle. She extracts the Business section, lays it on top of the *FT*, then removes the remainder and drops it in the bin.

In her inbox, there is an email from RENNIE, Miles. It is curt, and to the point. She is to handle the Grosvenor deal on a fixed fee he has already firmed up with the client. Right away, she knows the sum agreed is ridiculously low, that she will need at least two junior associates working on it with her. She emails back to tell him that, and then she goes to work on the documents that have already begun arriving, direct from Grosvenor's in-house lawyer. She manages to skim one contract, to find the flaws in a couple of the obvious problem clauses, the usual sticking points. Around mid-morning, she feels suddenly cold. The air con perhaps, or a window seal gone. But as she tries to rub the chill out of her upper arms, she starts to realise that it is coming from inside.

Charlie calls to ask if she's OK. He's seen the paper. And though she can tell he's rattled by it, he hides that very well.

'That's the shock,' he says when she tells him about

feeling cold. And she remembers how kind he can be, how kind he is really, deep down. 'Make yourself a milky coffee, lots of sugar. Maybe have some chocolate. Or take some time out, go home and rest.'

When she puts the phone down, she buries her face in her hands. She wants to forget. Is that so bad? Just forget. She wants to gather her walls around her, and finish trawling through this document, neutralise the danger zones she knows by heart. And sure enough, even though her heart is pumping so loud she can feel it in her ears, the text calms her as it always does. However chaotic and uncontrollable the world, she can always manage the words on the page, massaging them into shape, closing off ambiguity, freighting them with established meanings only another lawyer will recognise. Belt and braces. Making things safe.

She works on undisturbed till lunch, which she spends in the canteen with Sarah.

Sarah smooths her linen shirt down over her six-month belly and sighs. 'Another one of those bloody NCT classes yesterday. Those earth mothers, God. Just give me the drugs. All of them.'

Jess decides not to mention the conversation with Miles. It's the last thing Sarah needs to hear. Besides, they have dug one another out of many a hole.

'You left in quite a hurry the other night, Jess. Everything OK with Ruby?'

'Oh, she was fine. I just missed her, that's all.'

'Missed her so much you left your laptop behind? That's not like you.'

'Maybe I've changed.'

Sarah makes a face. 'But you're my best hope, Jess. The one who has it sorted.'

'Am I?'

'You've got me worried now. I don't fancy losing my marbles once Junior makes his exit.' She sits back in her chair and rests her folded arms on her bump. 'By the way, what did you do to Miles Rennie? Someone said they saw you two, deep in conversation.'

'Who told you that?'

'Intense, that's what I heard.'

'Well you heard wrong.'

And even as she says the words, she knows that she has burned a bridge here, and put herself beyond help. That she has made the wrong decision.

'Oh, you know Marcie, that new PA. Probably just Bellini brain, not that I can talk, the way my head is at the moment.'

There is a chance here to raise the subject of things Sarah might have forgotten to do, but she can't bring herself to do that.

'I mean, on Saturday, I actually went to a baby-clothes show. Can you believe that? I never even knew there were such things. What a world! My mum wanted to buy a little cardigan in three different colourways, even though she's refusing to be called Granny. She doesn't want the tag, she says. And actually, Granny Annie, can you blame her? What does Ruby call your mum?'

'My mo— mum? I'm not really sure.'

'I don't like Nana, do you? As for Gran – that's just dreadful.'

She feels an intense sense of shame now – it is an insult to the friendship that she has never told Sarah about what happened on the beach. She would like Sarah to know, but she can't bring herself to tell the story, partly because she has no idea how to start. There is no easy entry point.

'What's your mum's name? I guess some names are more grannyish than others.'

'Sophie. Her name is Sophie.'

'Not remotely grannyish,' Sarah decides.

'You're right,' Jess says. 'Not remotely.' And it hurts so much that she has to make her excuses and retreat to her office.

Back at the desk, Jess's phone is blinking – a voicemail from Hana on her direct line. 'Call me,' she says.

The secretary from the conference floor rings to say that the guests have arrived and that she has them in 4C. Should she serve coffee right away or wait for Jess? Jess gathers her papers together, a pen and a spare, the reading glasses she needs occasionally when she is tired. The next time the phone rings it is Hana again. She sounds agitated, borderline peevish. Jess recognises the mood at once, and moves to quash it.

'Hana? Is everything OK? Where's Ruby?'

'Ruby is fine,' she says. 'This is not about Ruby.'

'OK . . .' Jess opens the drawer and retrieves a mint from its crackling wrapper. She doesn't even like mints but she needs something.

'There is someone outside the house. I had Ruby in her buggy and we had just been to café for pain au chocolat. We came back and he was at the back gate.'

Jess has always hated that gate. 'Probably just someone having a nose around. He's gone now, is he? And the gate is locked?'

'I think he is gone.'

'Look, don't worry. There are all kinds of people on the Common. Most of them are perfectly fine.'

'You think that it's OK, that some strange man can just stand at gate to wait for us?'

'Well, I doubt he was waiting for you. And the gate's locked now. Right?'

'Right.'

'Why don't you take Ruby to the swings, and we'll talk when I get back. I shouldn't be late tonight.'

'Shall I call Neighbourhood Watch?'

Hana seems to think that Neighbourhood Watch is some sort of militia.

'No, no. No need to bother them. Don't worry, I'll be back soon.'

She picks up the newly printed pages, and rushes to the meeting. Just inside the door, the attendees are clustered around the tea trolley with its plastic flasks of hot water and coffee and its shallow china dishes containing tea bags that remind her of the lavender bags her granny used to make each summer. In fact, the silky little pouches – chamomile flowers, hibiscus – put her off slightly and she usually sticks to coffee. The men look up at her expectantly.

'Feel free,' she says, then smiles to take the edge off it. It's enough that she drafts their documents. They can pour their own coffee.

The meeting begins, and very quickly they are snagged on one of the clauses that never give anyone any trouble. She can feel her patience ebb. In her pocket her phone buzzes. Once, twice, three times. She excuses herself and steps outside. Hana again. 'Oh for God's sake, Hana.'

'For God's sake? Why God's sake? This man, he actually came into the garden. He saw Ruby and spoke to me and—'

'What?'

'He follows the man with wine for party into the garden. And then he asks about the party. When he leaves, the deliveryman tells me he is a weirdo, and to lock the gate. But he is still outside the house. What am I supposed to do? If I move shutters, he disappears. But then when he thinks I don't see him, he comes back again. What you want me to do?'

Jess's heart clenches. 'Where's Ruby?'

'She is upstairs, with naptime.'

'She's OK? You've checked?'

'Of course I have checked.'

And then she forms the question she has been dying, but not daring, to ask.

'What did he look like, this man?'

'I suppose you think he must be black. That all trouble is black.'

That is the last thing she thinks, but she knows too that there is no point in fighting off the personal slur, and so she waits for Hana to continue.

'His hair is like it doesn't have any colour to it. Not blond exactly. Just kind of nothing. And then there is this place on his arm that he keeps scratching. And it is like he might tear himself. So skinny and pale.'

So skinny and pale. She visualises him, with his milk-white skin, his shadowed eyes. Nobody knows why Ro scratches that arm. That's the thing with Ro. Nobody knows.

Another message from Hana, this time with a photo attached. It's fuzzy and she can't quite make it out. It could be him, she supposes, standing just outside the back gate. But then again, it could be almost anyone.

When she returns to the conference room, she finds it hard to concentrate. The meeting starts to drag. It occurs to her then that her client has no intention of doing this deal at all. He is putting up unreasonable barriers, sticking on points that he knows the other side can't possibly agree. Meanwhile, the clock on the wall behind the client is jerking slowly towards seven. Somebody needs to get back to the house to relieve Hana. She steps outside the room again, puts a call in to Charlie.

'If I could, I would. You know that, babe. But that's why we have Hana, yeah? Hey, I've gotta go.'

'Oh, and I think Ro is—'

But Charlie has already put down the phone. She sits and stares at the blank wall in front of her. Babe?

'Fuck this,' she tells the corridor.

'That bad?' One of the associates from Environmental raises his eyebrows as he passes by.

She looks in at the meeting through the glass panel on the door. The in-house lawyer for the other side is jabbing his finger at the document and gesticulating. When she tries Charlie's number again it's busy. She glances through the window into the meeting room. This is ridiculous. What was she thinking? She needs to get home.

She walks into the meeting room, where voices are raised now. Her client looks to her as if she has the solution, but she is about to break it to him that she isn't staying. She presents it as a fait accompli. 'I've just had an emergency at home, I'm afraid. I'm going to have to leave.'

'What? Right now?' The client clearly doesn't believe his ears.

They all look up at her in astonishment.

'Look, why don't I ring down for Carl and see if he can stand in for me. OK?'

'Carl?' says her client, investing the name with maximum disdain. She is beginning to like him less and less.

'You've met him, Geoff. He was at the last meeting, remember?'

'The articled clerk?'

Has she suggested an orgy? She doesn't think so.

'He only needs to take a few notes. I'll be on to it as soon as I get in tomorrow.'

And with that, she simply backs out of the room, leaving them all open-mouthed. In the lift, she feels strangely liberated. She has never done anything like this before, and yet the sky hasn't fallen. The plaza outside is unchanged. The silver and gold mime artists are still magically held aloft, and the same wet-weather gear is flapping its pessimist's charter outside Mountain Warehouse.

She feels herself crumple as she gets on the Tube. She

isn't sure which she hopes for more. That it's Ro, so at least then it isn't someone else. Or that it is anyone but him. Because she doesn't think she could cope with Ro. Not just now.

She can picture him standing there, still strangely child-like, waiting for her to solve all the problems that have no answer. When they were brought home to London by Auntie Rae, Sparrow would slip his hand inside hers and sometimes not let go of it for hours. She has often tried to imagine what being Rae was like. She was probably only five or six years older than Jess is now when she took them in. She already had her own daughters – orderly, piano-playing types who liked Brownies and patchwork – when she was suddenly put in charge of two bewildered, semi-feral children who had no notion of bathtimes and multiplication tables. When, at the insistence of their father's family, who had firm ideas about abstract things like discipline and tradition, Ro was sent away to school, Jess was the one he blamed when it turned out not to be Hogwarts, even though it broke her heart too, even though she'd had no say.

When Jess walks through the gate, Hana is already at the window, peering out over the plantation shutters. As Jess puts her key in the door and steps into the pale stone-flagged hallway, the squat, wide-hipped Swedish clock that stands there like a distressed babushka starts its din. Hana is already pulling out the sleeves on her jacket that she always hangs, annoyingly, on the banister at the bottom of the stairs. She must have a date.

'I need to have more support from parents,' she says,

like a schoolmistress dealing with a recalcitrant mother. Jess can read the warning signs; she has been here before. She can't afford for Hana to leave, not just now.

She tries a gentle 'I really appreciate the care you—'

But Hana shoots right back at her. 'This man, he was interested only in this house. Every time, he was outside this house. Right there.'

She tugs at Jess's sleeve and leads her out along the carefully gravelled path to the back wall.

'Come, open,' she instructs. When Jess has pressed the buttons to release the gate, and they are both standing looking out at the Common, she points.

'This bench, right here. This tree. And sometimes he is over by these new exercise things. I told you about that? Pulling up and looking over. Yes?'

Jess nods, but open-air exercise doesn't exactly sound like Ro's thing. She hadn't noticed the appliance before, though she's embarrassed to admit that. It looks like it might have sprung up out of the ground. Wood and metal, parallel bars for swinging like a monkey. Now that Hana realises she has Jess's attention, she goes for the jugular.

'If he returns and you are not here to give support, then I will find better family.'

She has no intention of apologising to Hana – not for the presence of a stranger outside the garden wall, even if he might yet turn out to be her brother. But she is disconcerted by Hana, who makes her feel larger and clumsier than anyone else does. She finds herself shrinking inside, growing self-conscious. Hana never makes an excess movement. Everything is just enough, and performed with aesthetic care.

When Hana leaves, plucking her coat off the newel post, jabbing delicately at her phone, Jess feels a sense of relief, as if she is gathering the house around her again. Reclaiming it. But someone wafts in to fill the gap left by Hana.

After they returned to London, Ro grew silent. He would look up at them all from under his long blond fringe, but he said nothing. No one was allowed to touch his hair. He was impossible to bathe. Auntie Rae used to have to carry him into the shower where he would cower against the tiled wall and slip slowly to the floor.

Now that she is a mother herself, Jess can see how difficult it must have been for Auntie Rae to cope. In the beginning, she had been determined to keep the two of them together, though Sparrow had been difficult from the start. She seemed to think that she would break through eventually, that he would come to accept her affection instead of jerking away from her each time she attempted a hug. But she was already a widow, with a full-time job as a nurse.

'I can't do it,' Jess overheard her at one of the weekly kitchen gatherings of local mothers. 'I just don't have the skill set.'

Jess, sitting at the top of the stairs in wait for snippets of information, didn't know what that meant, skill set, skillet, kill it, but she already knew that Auntie Rae had had enough, her cousins had said as much. The girls had parroted back to Jess all kinds of things she preferred not to think about. That Sophie was selfish, with a penchant for useless men. That her father was a disaster. As for Ro, Auntie Rae said that the trouble with Sparrow was down to his jeans.

Jess had puzzled over that for days, until she realised that she was thinking of the wrong jeans, that the right genes get passed on to you by your parents. But stop right there, she thought. If Sparrow is troubled by his genes, why does she not have that trouble too? When she asked that question, straight out one afternoon, Auntie Rae had flushed scarlet and said she had no idea what she was talking about, that she was sorry if Jess had been worrying about something as trivial as that.

Later the same day, Jess had found Ro curled into the corner of his bed, sucking noisily on the corner of his red plastic truck.

'Please talk to me,' she said. 'It's not fair that you don't talk to me any more. I'm afraid of what will happen if you don't start to try to talk.'

She reached out and tried to touch Ro's arm, but he pulled away from her, and then he began to whine. He shook his head. Whip whip whip whip, back and forth, his fringe flicking his forehead, his neck stiff. And then she took him by the shoulders and shook him until she was shaking him in time to the whips of his head.

'*Why Don't You Say What You Saw?*'

He screamed, high like a girl, and when he threw back his head, that scream hollowed out into a howl. Jess heard footsteps thudding up the stairs, and then the door was flung open and there was Auntie Rae.

'What on earth are you doing?'

She pushed Jess away and took Ro in her arms. She'd do anything for Sophie's children, she said, she really would. All she wanted was to protect them and make them happy. She just didn't know how.

Right then, Jess decided that Ro had seen something on the beach. She also decided that she didn't want to know what it was, that it was better not to know, that she would never ask him again what he had seen.

On the night of the beach, in the hours after their parents disappeared, everything had moved in slow motion. At first, there was no one who could speak English and, while people offered them pieces of fruit and sips of water, nobody seemed to be taking responsibility for them. By the time Eddie arrived, with his familiar accent, they were pathetically grateful. But even Eddie, acting as translator for the anxious-faced policemen, asked the same thing over and over again, until the question turned into a statement.

'You must remember something.'

But Jess hadn't been in the habit of remembering, not then. She hadn't realised that barely noticed details could attain a dark significance, that remembering might be important one day. But she has learned to remember.

6

Ro has been back at the café for a while now, watching Nefertiti over a single bottle of beer. The mother-and-baby, dog-walker shift is long gone and the atmosphere is mellowing.

He scans the competition clustered around her as she doles out beers to men who have taken their ties off, back-slapping and bantering, cruising along on London Pride. He guesses they're from the insurance company up the road. One of them asks her to turn the footy on. And she does, but she keeps the volume low. Nefertiti concentrates hard, he notices, asks the right kinds of questions. For a man who needs a bed for the night, she is promising.

She will focus on a detail of his story, like they always do – the temperature, the time of day, the distance to the nearest town. The mango. Everyone loves that mango. And that's just as well, because the only things Ro has are details. He has lost the big picture. And so the contours of his story stretch and sag until he's never really sure which version he will use – with Aussies who are only passing through, Irish girls with bluish skin, Brazilians in the Portobello Gold. He tends to pick the girl out early on, and then just bide his time. He doesn't do the obvious. No cradling of whiskies at the bar. He doesn't ever get drunk. He likes to focus when he slips his story in.

'Quiet in here tonight,' he says, but she doesn't answer, just looks at him neutrally, and on the screen the final whistle sounds. The players drift across the pitch and there's a close-up of the goalie, shoving his face into the camera, roaring. Right now, Ro could roar. Right now, Ro could stand at that bar, throw his head back and roar his story out.

'Football and beer,' she says, half to herself. 'Paradise.' And then she does a double-take, and it seems she remembers him.

He smiles at her. 'Ever been there? Paradise?'

She looks at him like he's a Scientologist, so he laughs to show he isn't serious, or might not be. She clinks his glass with a spoon. She licks her lips. He thinks she likes him.

He starts by describing what it was like at the water's edge under the hot sun, a child with a bucket and spade. She turns to look at him, and there it is – the moment when the story takes or fails. Many times, in many different places, the story hasn't taken. Once, in a Young's pub, he chose badly, a brunette with an overbite. Who did he think he was? she had said. 'Coming round here talking shite. Jesus. If that's what you need to do to get a shag.'

He has a sudden flashback to the laneway afterwards, the blood and broken glass, and fights it off.

Nefertiti is swiping a damp cloth across the bar. Where Pia jingles, Nefertiti's sound is a more sonorous one, with all those hollow bangles. And she has feelings too. 'That's awful,' she says. 'That's the worst thing I've ever heard.'

He gives her his modest look. She takes the order of a couple of girls – two large glasses of Sauvignon Blanc. The girls are regulars, it seems, and the three of them start to discuss a scheme to close off a road to traffic. And she's interested in that, for some odd reason, and the mad thing is that he could lose Nefertiti to a traffic consultation. But no, when she turns back to him, she is arranging herself, settling in for more. And he knows then that he's done enough. She is deep in his story. And it is a true story, that's the beauty of it. The best stories come from the heart. As for the telling, there are certain rules he always follows – never seem destitute or ruined or desolate. Keep the self-pity out of your voice. Don't beg.

'What a terrible thing,' she says. 'You couldn't make it up.'

But he hasn't. That's the power of it. OK, the trees might not be right – he wings it when it comes to the trees.

'Don't you remember anything else, though?'

Here we go again. He bristles at the hint of accusation, the whiff of doubt.

When he doesn't answer, Nefertiti does it for him. 'But your mum, she can't have just left, can she? I mean, who does that? Something happened, that's for sure.'

He doesn't like to have to talk about his mother. He doesn't like the stale words he's always forced to use. Free spirit. New Age traveller. Hippie chick. He has no idea whether they fit the bill or not. Those words belong to other people; they make him feel disloyal.

He remembers a guitar, a long blonde plait, the coloured scarves she folded around him when he slept outside. He thinks she smelled of peaches, or maybe that was just the fruit he used to pick out from the palm of her hand. Gentle, he thinks. But who can tell? Afterwards, they called her selfish, irresponsible, rash.

Nefertiti is cling-filming the cannoli, the little cakes. She is cleaning out the filters. And when it hits him that the café is about to close, he realises that he needs to crank things up.

'Actually – there is something else . . .'

She doesn't seem to hear him at first, but he keeps on going, throwing it all in her direction in the hope that some of it will stick.

'Sitting in the wet sand, by the water's edge, I turned—'

'And she was gone.' The girl is biting her lip. She comes and sits next to him, crosses her legs.

He doesn't like his sentences being finished for him, but she talks as if she knows about this kind of thing. He keeps on going, so as not to give her room to interrupt again or just to keep her with him, he isn't sure. 'And all that time, the sea just kept advancing until our tunnel was flooded with water. She'll come back, my sister said.'

'There was a sister?' she asks, as if he's been keeping something from her. She homes in on a splodge of something on the table next to him and rubs hard.

But then he sees a change in her. She is putting herself on that beach, imagining how it might have been to be that sister.

It always seems to Ro that some day he might tell a version that unexpectedly reveals the truth. Some day, he might hear the rustle in the questionable trees, or spot the person who wasn't there before, or simply see his mother walk away. Some day, he might solve the puzzle.

'After a while, I was so thirsty that I tried to drink the sea. My sister took me to the other end of the beach where there was a lady with a huge bottle of squash. She was reading a book. For ages, she just kept on reading, like she hoped we'd go away.'

The girl's mouth is moving soundlessly. She is looking for a way back in, but Ro doesn't want to stop.

'In the end, she put her book down and offered us slippery chunks of pineapple from a Tupperware box. Soon there were other people there, too. And when we'd finished the pineapple, they gave us little spicy pies. Samosas, I suppose they were, but we didn't have a name for them then.'

The girl puts her hand up, like she's holding up the traffic. 'I'm not being funny,' she says, 'but you probably need to see someone, yeah?' Her teeth are raking at her bottom lip, and she tightens her crossed legs, jiggling her foot.

Excuse me, Ro thinks, but you have some cheek to tell me what I need.

She runs her finger through a little pool of spillage on the bar, and the shape that she is making might be a flower or a cloud or just a scribble.

She needs to watch that lip or else she'll end up drawing blood. The white-wine girls are leaving now, the man with the beer too. He looks up past her at the dark outside, the top deck of the 137 just visible above the wooden shutter. He wonders if she lives nearby or if they'll need to take a bus.

He turns back to find she has set another bottle of beer on the table in front of him.

'That's not enough,' he says, so softly he isn't sure she'll hear him. He struggles to contain himself, but the memory of the laneway shames him and he manages to keep himself in check. She cocks her head to show she hasn't understood.

It's not as though he needs to spend all night with her. A quick one up against a tree would do. But she does need to give him something worth his while, after all she's had from him.

'You'd rather have a pint?'

She sits down again and her foot is going mad now. At least she's got the right idea. Every story has its price. One woman wanted to make a documentary. She rummaged in her pocket for a card, then scribbled down her home number on the back. And Ro considered that to be a compliment, and proper payment made, even though he never called the number. Plenty of women have wanted to feed him or give him poems. Occasionally there is a consolation fuck. Nefertiti is disconcerted. He can tell by that foot of hers. He watches her fingers tighten at the hem of the floral dress she is wearing over a pair of leggings. She sits up a little straighter. There's something she needs to say. He understands that need, can smell it miles off.

And then she stretches out her hand. 'Amanda,' she says.

The name gives him a start. It's a blonde-streaks-and-bare-legs kind of name – rich man's wife or teen starlet. She is not Amanda, not to him.

'Got one yourself?' Nefertiti asks.

He tells her his own name, though he doesn't go the full bird.

'As in "Row Your Boat"? Or as in some French thing?'

He has no idea where she got the French from. 'As in row of houses,' he says.

'Bit weird. But I guess your parents—' She doesn't continue. Maybe just as well.

'Something happened to me, too,' she says.

He is tempted to say that something happens to everyone. It's called Life.

'It's a long time since I've told anyone,' she starts, then glances at the clock. She moves to the door, flips the sign from *Open* to *Closed*, and locks the door.

'It's just . . . I know you'd understand.'

He approves of her technique – suspense, flattery – she's good. And he's intrigued to hear what story she imagines could possibly come close.

She is stacking chairs, whipping away half-finished glasses. When she's finished her work, she shrugs on her coat and he knows that the night is finely balanced. He might be walking her to the Tube, or he might be coming home with her. He's banking on the latter. From the look on Nefertiti's face, he can tell she's struggling. He knows that one well. Desire to hide versus need to tell.

'Something happened to me, round here in fact. You coming? I never walk across the Common on my own. Will you walk with me?' she says. There's no one else. She'd been banking on him all night. He didn't see that one coming.

Outside, it has grown surprisingly dark. Overhead, a helicopter with a search beam is stirring up a racket while a 137 blunders on. The Common is vast, and scuffling with life. Night creatures have come out – the streaking fox, the tangled lovers, the homeless people huddled in a circle by the drinking fountain. Further in, lamp posts blast down energy-efficient light. In the distance, he can hear the muffled engines of a plane that is winking its final descent towards Heathrow. She walks a little bit ahead of him. He'd have been happy with her bright kitchen, her warm bed. But the way she's leading him – this uncharted territory, her unexpected confidence. She glances over her shoulder. Stops a moment to allow him to catch up (almost, but not quite). And then she's off again, confident of her direction. It's like she's done this kind of thing before.

She avoids the well-lit paths, draws him towards the shadows. Silently they walk, circling the copse of trees beside the pond. At the water's edge, a lone angler crouches in his tent and, overhead, bats switch and flit.

She waits for him to catch up. And then she starts to speak.

'I was just a kid. Back then, I didn't realise there are places on the Common you shouldn't go.' Ro is already guessing where this story leads. He hardly needs to listen any more. And so her story doesn't mark him quite as deeply as his own, with all its fluctuations and uncertainties, its black holes. But he does feel something – the tang of complicity, perhaps, a twinge of loss. As they approach the clearing at the centre of the Common, it occurs to him that he has never had a woman on a bandstand before.

For a moment, he loses track of her. It's hard to concentrate on what she's trying to say. It's all too breathless, too tentative and indirect. There is something about a lift home, a van parked on the cut-through. Something about feeling herself to blame. He has lost the thread, and he can't ask her to unspool it for him again, that would be a fatal insult. Besides, stories like hers are two a penny. He can guess the ending.

Somewhere on the A3, there is a siren, and through the trees he spots a streak of blue that ruins the particularity of this. This story – hers, theirs, whatever – is spoiled. He is suddenly aware of all the other stories bursting to be heard. So many stories that must find their endings somewhere – in a helicopter overhead or in the clack of late-night skateboards at the half-pipe, in the meeting of two people at a bar.

They are almost at the bandstand now, and the girl is waiting for his reaction. He realises suddenly that she has finished whatever it was she had to say.

'What now?' she says.

And then it strikes him – perhaps her story didn't end the way he thought it would. Every story has its price. And because he hasn't listened, Ro has no idea what she's expecting him to pay.

The helicopter is closer now, clattering in the air above them, a searchlight stuttering its way among the trees. It's impossible to compete with it, so they both stand and watch. While it moves off, he starts to say that you can check these days what those helicopters are up to. That they put it all on Twitter now – suspect apprehended in alley, vulnerable misper talked down from roof. She looks at him blankly. And he knows for certain now that, whatever she was telling him, he missed the most important bit.

The helicopter is making the treetops shudder. The girl looks up at it, transfixed. And under the energy-efficient light, she does look strangely beautiful. As the beam staggers away, she stretches out her hand and steps towards him. And in that moment he sees that he has lost control of this encounter. And maybe he has also lost his bed for the night because he didn't listen to what she had to say about being young and ruined and lost. But it's not over yet. They walk together in silence, side by side, almost touching. They pass along the over-lit path, then into the dark section of open ground between the bandstand and the road.

They are just leaving the Common when he notices a couple, old yet spry, crossing the main road towards them. They are tall, thin people with a stiffish gait who look like they've hiked through life together and share a single thumping heart. The man has a small grey ponytail. The woman, a greyish plait worn over her shoulder. Something seems familiar, and when the man glances over, it clicks. Instinctively, he ducks away, off the lit pavement and back into the shadows. He is not ready yet for Eddie Jacques.

Nefertiti grips his sleeve. 'What's the matter?'

'Just let him pass,' he says.

And then she realises who he's talking about. 'I know him,' she says.

He hasn't seen Eddie since the row about the baby. He'd been staying with Jess at the time, after Flora threw him out, and she was still on maternity leave and oversensitive about Ruby to a ridiculous degree. She'd said she was popping out for a moment, a loaf of bread perhaps. He'd said that he would watch the child, but he hadn't realised that Jess expected him to watch her like she was a television. It was a lovely summer evening, so he'd cracked open a beer and gone to sit in the garden.

Somehow, upstairs in her cot, Ruby had found a tiny plastic monster that had hatched from inside the Kinder Egg he'd bought her the day before. Kinder Eggs were not allowed, apparently. And when Jess returned to the sound of spluttering on the baby monitor she raced up the stairs, two at a time, and found Ruby with a purple dinosaur in her throat.

She was still screaming at him when Charlie got home, and then Eddie arrived and they all ganged up on him on the back of a purely theoretical disaster.

'I get it,' he'd said. 'No more Kinder Eggs.'

But on they went, on and on about his utter irresponsibility, his criminal negligence. My God, she's not a lawyer for nothing. Eventually, they seemed to have talked themselves out and someone went to make tea. Meanwhile, Eddie began performing his brotherhood-of-man act, and lit some disgusting herb 'to clear the atmosphere', which pissed everyone off, especially Jess, who hates any kind of smoke in the house.

'You're a troubled soul, Sparrow,' Eddie told him.

'And you know what you are, Eddie?' he shot right back. 'You're a cunt.'

Charlie, who has no time for Eddie, at least not usually, was suddenly his staunchest ally. He leaped up on his high horse, and rode it hard. 'Guest in my house . . . old friend . . . will not tolerate.'

And that was when Ro snapped. He bent down to the open dishwasher and began flinging plates against the wall. It felt good, and soon he had found his stride and was spinning them like Frisbees until Charlie and Eddie, all boys together now, threw him out. He waited outside the house for a while, but no one came to ask him back in, not even Jess.

Nefertiti and Ro stand together on the pavement and watch the greyish couple disappear beneath the street lights.

'How come you know Eddie Jacques?' he asks.

'I don't,' she says. 'I mean, not really. He's got this van on the Common, funny-looking thing. Sells ice cream in weird flavours.'

'Just after the beach, he was the one to take me in.' And then an idea forms. It comes from nowhere, and he goes for it. 'Did you say ice-cream van?'

'Yeah. Ice cream. Why?'

'Kiddie magnet, isn't it? Probably up to his old tricks again.'

She doesn't say anything for a moment, but the shock on her face says he's crossed a line.

'Seriously?'

He enjoys landing Eddie in the shit. Besides, he's stuck with it now.

'And he's selling ice cream next to the playground?'

She looks furious, murderous even. Maybe he's gone too far, so he tries to lighten things a bit. 'Oh he'll probably be off again in a month or two. And anyway, what's it to you?'.

She glares at him, and for a moment she looks as if she might hit him. 'What's it to me? I just told you, didn't I?' She pulls her hand from his. 'Which is why I'm not too keen on paedos, yeah? Next time you're here in the daytime, take a look. It's not even a proper ice-cream van, just an old red banger some mate must have converted for him. You must have seen it. Real crappy home-made look about it. "Ed's Organic Ice Cream". Hippy-dippy stickers, and a window cut into the side. Fucking paedo, I'm gonna get rid of him, you wait and see.'

They walk in silence along the road. And now that he knows her story, more or less, he needs to make a gesture. They reach a bench facing back into the Common and he sits with her there a moment, guiding her head on to his shoulder and stroking her hair. Ro has lost the taste for Nefertiti after that, but there is still the problem of a bed for the night, and so he lets her take him home. Her flat is on the third floor of a council block with a reconditioned stairwell faced in glass bricks that are lit ice-blue. There is a warm kitchen and an even warmer bedroom – an orange and purple flowered duvet and a big wicker chair. It's surprising, he thinks, how little her flat resembles the face she gives the world. She is a Goth with a coloured nest.

In the morning, she seems eager to be rid of him. There are no scrambled eggs like there would have been with Pia, no little sweet cakes. Just a spoonful of instant in a china mug. Take your pick, she says, presenting a selection. Bleeding Heart, Boy Racer, Silver Fox. But he couldn't care less about any of that because his mind is fixed on Eddie. Eddie is no paedophile, but he knows more about what happened on that beach than he has ever admitted. And that's enough to damn him in Ro's eyes. As for the woman with him, she is the right age, the right height. His heart skips when he thinks of how close she is to perfect.

7

Charlie has gone to collect the hired glasses while Jess and Hana prepare the garden for the party. She has been keeping Hana away from Charlie. An intuition for self-preservation. A precaution.

Meanwhile, Ruby seems to guess that something is happening that isn't focused on her. Each time a piece of food is put on the tray of her high chair, she swipes it off, or rubs it in her hair, or flings it grandly to the floor. And then the rain begins. It batters at the gazebo, lashes the pale blue wall they had painted specially.

Jess turns her back on it all, and clatters down the cellar stairs to count the cases of wine. Two of red, three of white, two of Prosecco. When she comes upstairs with a case of white to be put on ice outside, the sky rumbles and sighs and the deluge starts.

She inspects the drenched garden through the French windows. There are puddles developing all over the gravel, and the gazebo they installed bang centre, with the four little parterres squaring off it, is almost swamped. She wonders if it will survive the night. But then the rain stops and a little slice of blue splits the clouds.

Hana is helping Jess set up the garden tables they hired from a place on Wexboro Road. They are laying each one with a white cloth, a candle in a hurricane jar and a disposable camera, bought cut-price from the bridal range, when the doorbell rings. Eddie is standing on the mat with not one but two tartan shopping trolleys trailing off behind him. There is the usual awkwardness when it comes to the number of kisses.

'I've come to bring offerings,' he says.

'You look so domesticated, Eddie,' she says, trying not to make fun of him.

He ignores that, and walks into the hallway. 'Maya says to tell you there are four different fillings, all veggie, no nuts. She'd have come herself, only she has class today.'

'Meditation?'

'Yeah. I walked her down to it. She hasn't been so well this week. Had a bad attack last Thursday, and it helps to calm her down. I've got an hour or so. Thought you might need a hand.'

'Another asthma attack? Oh, Eddie, I'm sorry.'

'She's fine, really. Just so long as she has her inhaler and doesn't rush around the place too much.'

She nods. 'I hope you don't smoke in the house, though. Seriously, Eddie.'

'What you take me for?'

'Maybe I should do Maya's class,' she says. 'Do you need to be some sort of expert?'

'I doubt it,' he says. 'It's not a competitive sport.'

When he is seated at the kitchen table, she looks at his hands. Slotted together, veined and age-spotted, his fingers look like ancient roots.

'Cup of tea? I got in some of that peppermint and nettle stuff. Just for you.' She lowers a tea bag into a mug and passes it under the boiling-water tap.

She hopes they don't have to pussyfoot around the article in the *Daily Post*. She hopes that he's seen it and that they can talk about it openly. And sure enough, he goes straight there.

'About the passport,' he says, 'I'd hate to see you get your hopes up.'

With Eddie, there is always the sense that he knows more about her than anyone else, except for Ro. After all, he was there when the sky fell in and there was no one else to comfort her. Eddie saved her, she still believes that.

And as she glances across the table at him, she takes another sip of water before tackling it head-on, the question she has asked him many times over the years.

'What do you think really happened?'

He looks away, and she knows he has no intention of spelling out his theory, if he has one. 'Your mother would never just have left you.'

'How do you know, Eddie? Did she tell you that?'

The hesitation is only momentary, but she notices it.

'No, but—'

'But what? That's not what women do? That's not what *she* would have done?'

'Think about it, Jess. Just imagine what it would cost

you to change everything, cut all ties. Then, think of that on a day-to-day basis over many years. It would be so hard. And it's much, much harder to disappear than you realise. The lies, the constant pretence. The psychological strain is so great that sooner or later . . .'

He sounds like he's speaking from experience, and she has a thought she's had before, but never let herself pursue. What if? What if the link went deeper than she'd thought? Eddie and her mother? What then?

'You knew a lot of those Scandi guys, didn't you? The ones who used to hang out down on the beach all night?'

'They were from the Balkans, actually.'

'They left soon afterwards, though, didn't they? I mean, I wonder is that something worth pursuing? I just thought, if you knew them.'

'I knew them a bit, I suppose. But they were techno-heads.'

He loves to talk about the golden days when acoustic was everything, before the dark shift that came with the craze for techno and the arrival of the huge speakers brought in from Delhi, before the advent of the harder drugs.

'A little bit of noise,' he says on cue. 'That's good. But all these new people – things were never the same again.'

'But could my mother have left with them? Because Ro has always been convinced that she did come back here, you know that. And now with this passport, it seems he might have been right.'

He's on the verge of saying something uncomplimentary about Ro, and she watches him think better of it.

'Look, we've been through all this before.' He has taken off one of the heavy rings he wears and is clinking it on the marble top. 'I wish I had something new to tell you, Jess. Because your mama, your papa, too – they were good people.'

Were they? Good people? Because she's not sure about that. They sound infuriating to her, maddening. They sound like interesting, mad people.

His blandness strikes her very much like insincerity. She hadn't noticed that about him before, and it disappoints her. Despite what he says, she has never really rehearsed all of this with Eddie. She feels like she needs to do that. Right now.

In the few pictures of her parents in Goa, they are surrounded by people. Europeans, mainly. Fellow travellers, burned brown by the sun. People with plaited hair and long skirts and hennaed hands and twists of fabric in their dreadlocks. But who they were and what they thought of any of this is anyone's guess.

Hana is busying herself with transferring bottles from their cardboard boxes onto the trestle tables. She is just outside the French windows, and she might well be listening, but Jess doesn't think Hana would be interested in any of this. Even so, she can't help lowering her voice when she turns back to Eddie. 'So, what's your theory?'

'My theory? It hasn't changed, Jess. They got into trouble with dealers, I'm sure of that. Your father was insatiable. There was no way anyone could feed that hunger of his. She tried, of course. But it was hopeless. She was the one to negotiate with them, and she was lovely and charming and sweet. My guess is she was used to getting her way. But she was naïve. Know what I mean? She was just foolish. She made promises she couldn't keep and that your father had no intention of keeping.'

She bristles at that. 'You knew him that well?'

The change in his face is only slight, but she knows that he has seen her notice it.

'What is this, some kind of cross-examination?'

'Never cross-examined anyone in my life, Eddie. Boring old contracts, that's me. You don't blame me for asking, though, do you?'

'You know I knew him. I've already told you.'

'But didn't like him.'

'Oh I wouldn't say that. There was a bit of a frisson between us, I suppose.' He gives the word a flourish, as though he wants her to know he's only half serious. 'Class war,' he says. 'All that.'

He throws his head back, but she can tell there's a grain of truth in it. And that he's dying for a smoke. Jess doesn't let anyone smoke in the house, so it's a mark of Eddie's status that she almost opens a window and tells him to go ahead. After all, what would it cost her? But she doesn't, and he plucks a crayon from the tub she keeps for Ruby on the kitchen table. He flicks the crayon in and around his fingers.

'Well, we came from different planets, didn't we? I was a working-class boy from Nottingham.'

'Just like Paul Smith,' she says.

'Not at all like Paul Smith. No talent. Just a notion I was a bit special, that's all. Took myself off and became somebody else. Those days, there were always people passing through. Folk with hippie notions about discovering themselves. People taking time out of their lives. Full moons and weeds and roots and tie-dyes. And they would do that, quite happily, for a couple of months. And then the call of convention would come and they'd be off. Your father – he was like that.'

'My father was a heroin addict.'

'That's what he became, Jess. It's not who he really was, though. He would have ended up in yellow cords and brown suede loafers, just like the rest of that family. He was a boomerang. He wasn't a conviction traveller.' He says this without a hint of irony. She is amazed and somewhat disappointed. She has often wondered what version of her father she would have preferred. Not that it matters, when he's no longer here. Not that she will ever really know what he was like now.

She gets the feeling that Eddie is enjoying this, that it matters to him that she should have a low opinion of her father. She is becoming emotional, and she mustn't let that happen because it skews things. She strives hard to keep the emotion in its place because she knows from experience that it will weaken her, make her less. But the tears are sitting fat on the rims of her eyes and she doesn't know if she can keep them there. And there is still so much to do. For tonight, but not just for tonight. There is all the stuff she hasn't done anything about yet. Ro, and all the rest of it. Meanwhile, at the office, Miles has begun to pile on the work. It seems overwhelming.

'Hey hey hey,' Eddie says, and she knows from the way

he is gripping on to the side of the table that he is about to get up so he can give her a hug. But she fends him off.

'No, Eddie, I need you not to do that, OK? I need you to tell me what you remember.'

There was a time during her teens, and living in a family of women and girls, when she wished that Eddie was her real pa. She doesn't wish that now.

'About your father? About William?'

And the way he pronounces the name – with three whole syllables – she can tell he despises even that. She fixes her father in her mind. The wild, joyful way he would carry her on his back and point out the most ridiculous things he could find. He was adventure. Until his light went out, that's what he was. And that was good. She knows she is not adventure. There was that brief period of wildness in her late teens and early twenties. But she is certainly not adventure now. She would not want to be what he was. But she wonders at it all the same.

'You say you want the truth, Jess, but you don't. Even if I had it, you wouldn't want to hear.'

And right now, the only person she wants near her is Charlie. Because Charlie wouldn't take this bullshit. Where is Charlie when she needs him to be here with her and hear the truth?

'Did my father kill my mother?'

'And then kill himself? That's a brave question,' he says. 'And one I'm afraid I can't answer.'

'Can't or won't?'

'I don't know what happened, and that's the truth. Of course, who says it didn't happen the other way round?'

The thought's occurred to her, of course, but she's shocked to hear it said. Spoken aloud it sounds brutal, and yet there is a look of satisfaction on his face when he says it. She doesn't know how to reply to that. All the things that spring to mind seem equally disloyal.

She is relieved to hear Charlie's key in the front door, the scrape of his leather soles on the hallway tiles. When he enters the kitchen, he crosses the room to kiss her.

'Sixty wine, sixty highball,' he says. 'They're in the boot of the car.'

At first, he doesn't seem to have seen Eddie. And then it's apparent that Eddie simply wasn't the priority.

'Hey, how are you, man?' Eddie says. As if they are old friends, not adversaries.

'So, you heard the news,' Charlie says. 'What's your take?'

She can see Eddie recoiling at this. Your what? But Charlie doesn't wait for an answer. 'What struck me was that they bothered telling Jess. I don't see what good it does unless they're suggesting that—'

'Nobody said that,' says Jess. 'They never once mentioned that she might still be alive. And anyway, it wasn't an official visit, I don't think. Only afterwards, I realised that one of the guys had been to see us at the time of the original investigation. I think the visit was just kindness on his part. To let me know, before I heard some other way.' She glances up at Eddie but he isn't reacting. He has lain back against the bench and his eyes are closed. He could be dead, or meditating, or just removing himself.

'They must think it's significant in some way or they wouldn't have bothered telling you about it,' Charlie says.

'I don't buy that,' Eddie says, which doesn't mean much because everyone knows that Eddie would never buy anything that Charlie has to offer. With his striped suits and his shiny shoes and his unspeakable allegiances, Charlie is everything that Eddie professes to despise. They are all silent for a moment, and she can tell what the others are thinking. The single trip from Delhi to France. The fact that the passport surfaced some place Sophie Considine might well have hidden for a while, if she'd run out of options. And why did she have two passports anyway? The old name and the new, that's odd too. She imagines Ro as a little boy, making an imaginary circle with his hands, so large it nearly toppled him over. She could be *any*where.

The night before she married Charlie it was Eddie who had a message for her. Don't think you have to go ahead with this. Nobody will think less of you if you decide to walk away. He had come to Auntie Rae's house. Auntie Rae didn't invite him in, and he stood in the porch to deliver his message, then walked back out into the rain. Jess stood there and watched him leave, slightly stooped, his shirt pulled up at the neck to shield him. She tried to process what it was he was telling her, but it made no sense. She wanted somewhere to belong, a safe haven. Someone who was certain about things. And she loved Charlie, she did.

Whether he intended to or not, Eddie had taken the shine off the day, which had been a fine day, come to think of it. All high drifting clouds and streaked sky and whiffling showers of confetti, with champagne prickly on the tongue and the frozen-face aftermath of a battery of cameras. All that, and yet an unsettling sense that she might be making a mistake, that she might not have seen the signs she should have done.

Even though it had its impact on the wedding day itself, she tried not to think about what Eddie had said during the three-week honeymoon they had in a small open-top car – a Fiat something – racing along stomach-clenching roads on the Amalfi coast. It was only later, the first time Charlie didn't come home, that she remembered. And, though it didn't make her think she ought to have done things differently, it did make her think.

Charlie joins Hana in the garden, and together they use the garden gate to bring the glasses in from the car. As he slips past Hana he places his hand at the base of her spine. Jess notes that, but she doesn't pursue the thought. She finds herself assessing Eddie instead. She likes to evaluate things, to gauge their extent, the likelihood there is that they might spring an unpleasant surprise. Eddie is wound up today. His movements are staccato, almost clockwork. She realises then that she hasn't seen him without Maya for a year, maybe more. He seems restless without her.

Eddie gets up to go. 'I'd better be getting on,' he says. 'Maya's class will be finished soon. Anyway, we'll see you later, yeah? And if you really want to know what I think? The best thing you can do is just ignore that passport.'

She doesn't say anything to that, and it's as if Eddie interprets her silence as a challenge. One way or another, he seems to feel he has to state his case.

'She might well have applied for a second passport. She was planning on travelling, wasn't she? A second passport can come in useful. Maybe it was a form of insurance for her. If the worst came to the worst, a passport in another name could be currency, her little nest egg, something she could sell if she got desperate and needed to get out. Perhaps she took out a passport in Mary Callan's name with that possibility in mind. Perhaps she'd already sold it on by the time she disappeared. Maybe the sale of the passport was what financed her disappearance. Who's to say she was the one to use it to fly to Paris? And why would she be flying to Paris anyway? There were no French people in the Yellow House. There are much more convenient places she could have gone. You know what the local police are like about carrying ID if you're a foreigner. Well, you probably don't, but take it from me, it made things simpler if you did. Just supposing she still had Mary Callan's Irish passport, it's quite conceivable that on that day, on the beach, she was carrying it with her because that was the one she felt she could afford to lose. If they were attacked by someone on that beach, or if your father was attacked and she went to see where he'd gone, the passport would definitely have been sold on by whoever got their hands on it. Passport like that, it's worth a lot of money. So, we have no idea who used that passport. None.'

'And yet somehow it found its way back to Curramona. At the very least, that's an extraordinary coincidence, isn't it?'

'We'd need to be able to ask the dead woman in the caravan, wouldn't we? Pity.'

There is no answer to that, and he knows it. She is on the cusp of mentioning Ro and then she stops herself. She doesn't want to spread around the news the policeman told her over the phone. She doesn't want to cast any more suspicion onto Ro. And she doesn't want to conjure him up either. Not until she's feeling stronger, more able to withstand the onslaught of his enthusiasm.

'Try and enjoy the party, Jess. You give such great parties.'

Around five, she realises there are no cocktail sticks and that they're short of paper napkins. She could ask Hana to go, but she feels like getting out of the house to try and clear her head. She walks over to the Tesco Metro on the edge of the Common. When she finds they don't have any cocktail sticks and that their only napkins are translucent scraps of two-ply, she proceeds to the Waitrose a little further down the hill. After the rain, the grass already seems greener than it was last week. It is the kind of expanse you rarely find in the city. It makes her breathe deeply, as if she's on a perfectly manicured piste, at the start of a ski slope she knows is well within her abilities.

When she returns to the house, Charlie and Hana are sitting together on the kitchen sofa, Ruby cooing happily between them. Jess enters the room and Ruby looks up and then flings a little plastic bus at the door, at her mother, at whatever has interrupted all this. The child looks back at Hana and Charlie and they all laugh, and Jess's heart clenches because in that moment it feels like she could lose everything, that nobody would mind if she vanished, right now, and never came back. She opens her mouth to say something.

But it's Charlie who breaks the silence. 'Don't be silly, Roobs, come and cuddle Mummy.'

And even though Ruby doesn't resist or turn away, Jess feels shamed. She buries her face in the back of Ruby's neck, in those silky blonde curls, that baby skin. The child pulls her tight, and for a moment that is all that is necessary, to stay there, skin to skin.

There will be a mix of people at the party. Work and school and nursery. Charlie's old rugby friends and their willowy wives. A neighbour or two invited for reasons of politics. Another few for kindness. There will be two long trestle tables, and a barbeque she borrowed from Martha. And there will be light: tea lights on the terrace, a magic ball trained on the newly painted blue wall, and those thick plastic ropes of LEDs that never look quite right, coiled around the cherry tree.

There is a rush of early arrivals, and the teenage sons of a neighbour, hired to do the waitering, seem to be doing OK. As for Jess, an early glass of Prosecco takes the edge off. While Charlie is at ease from the start, Jess doesn't feel relaxed with the small knot of neighbours who know one another better than she knows any of them. There is Reg from across the road – or Real Reg, as Charlie calls him – who has never hidden his yearning for a golden age when Riverton Street was home to Real People. Jess glances at the brace of intimidatingly black-clad blondes who waft in with their respective broods of wispy girl children in Docs and fairy dresses. Oh Reg, she feels like telling him. I know what you mean. She is looking forward to the arrival of Sarah from work. Although Sarah, being pregnant, might come primarily out of curiosity, it will be a relief to have one foot in that other life where she still feels competent and worthwhile. She hopes the house doesn't look too forbiddingly perfect. She wants it to look perfect, of course. That's the trouble. She just doesn't want to chase people away.

The evening darkens, and the Common recedes. As the day goes down the volume goes up and there are lights glancing off that pale blue wall. In the gazebo the wan light emitted by bunches of LED balloons falls short of the promise on the pack. The air is thick with the smell of meat and booze and sharp-sweet wafts of Jo Malone.

Once she has seen people in, and they have formed little groups, and it all seems to be going fine, she feels the need to be with Ruby. When she reaches Ruby's room, she finds that Hana is already up there, Ruby on her hip, walking back and forth attempting to soothe her. 'That music is too loud for baby ears.'

'Oh it's fine, Hana. You can hardly hear it up here.'

'No? You don't think what it sounds like to baby ears? Torture, that is what.'

How is it possible to be so sanctimonious when you are still only twenty-four? There is a fight to be had, but she doesn't have it. Instead, she tells Hana that she's a star. Even Hana seems to find that a bit of a stretch, but she takes it.

'Don't worry. Just go downstairs now and have a drink.'

Once Hana has gone, Jess draws the shutters and the curtains, and the nursery becomes a little padded cell. The music is muffled now, and she suddenly feels exhausted. She eases herself on to the floor, where the carpet smells a little sour, and closes her eyes. Gradually, Ruby asleep in her cot is all there is. Jess starts to match her own breath to her daughter's. This harmony, this unison, she could stay like this all night. Downstairs, someone has turned the music up, but Ruby doesn't stir. And there, into the space Jess has made for her, comes Sophie Considine, who was Mary really, and who, it seems, will never go away but linger uselessly at the margins – a reminder of the traps life lays for the unwary, and of the numerous ways a mother can fall short.

Would she be frail by now, osteopenic? Would she have run to fat? Would she have loved her grandchild, been bored by her, both? Jess tries to hold on to an idea of her mother, but it's a brittle thing. There is little to admire, still less to emulate. In an attempt to conjure up some substance, she resorts to the game she used to play with Ro.

If you had Mama for a day, what would you ask her?

If you had Mama for a week, where would you want her to take you?

Jess's answers were simple ones. She would ask Mama to stay, and she would want her to take her home.

The game had lots of other questions, of course, and the answers have changed over the years. She used to write them down each year, on her birthday, in a special book that must have got thrown out when she went to university. Presents she would give her mother, presents she might be given in return.

Ruby, for the first one. And a grandmother for Ruby who isn't Renée, for the second.

She would ask her mother to teach her how to play the guitar, whether she has a recipe for apple tart, what it was like to have a husband she couldn't control. She would ask her to stay in the guest room, and never to go away again. She would ask her whether she loved Dejan with the big moustache, whether she loved Papa, whether her life has been a happy one.

She wonders who has the home movies, now that Rae is gone. Poor Rae, so different from Sophie and yet so careful of her memory – she deserved more than just the three months of retirement her cancer allowed her. Out of nowhere, Jess has a longing for Rae, for the reassuring smell of her chicken casseroles, for her clean plain pine and cream house. But the stronger longing is for Sophie. What she wouldn't give to see Sophie move across a screen, flicking her long plait over her shoulder, turning back to the camera and then looking away.

The music has taken over now, some stadium anthem she half remembers. Even up here the rhythm buzzes deep in the floorboards. She wishes she could stay here all night, but she can't. Before she leaves, she eases the blanket up over the round of Ruby's back, folding it down across her small shoulders, and closes the door behind her. One storey down, the house still feels familiar, safe.

But when she reaches the ground floor, the skin of things is broken. There are half-finished plates of food, a battery of glasses stained with this and that, handbags tucked in under chairs like sleeping pets. In the kitchen, one of the hired teens is tying up the cords on a clinking bin bag. He has worn black for the occasion and looks startled to see her. Now that the weather has cleared, everyone is in the garden, where the rain has enhanced the smell of the flowers.

'Hey, Jess.'

Sarah. 'God, am I glad to see you!'

Sarah draws back a little, as if surprised at the strength of her reaction. 'Why? What's the matter, Jess?'

And then she remembers that she hasn't told Sarah about the passport, that she is trying to pretend it's not important.

'Oh, it's nothing. Just hassle. You know, stressful.' She gestures to the garden.

'Yes well, Charlie is having fun anyway.' Sarah raises her glass of orange juice in his direction.

Charlie is trying to encourage a conga line. Jess wonders idly who's manning the barbeque. Maybe she should be doing that, or is it supposed to be Hana? She can't remember what they agreed.

'Hey, Hana?'

Hana is talking to one of the black-clad mothers, a woman with a long neck and a thick flood of hair. 'Well, if you change your mind,' the woman is saying.

'Thank you. I will think about it.' Hana turns and smiles brightly, falsely at Jess.

'Where's that guy from the butcher's, Hana? I thought we were paying him to serve up some of those herby burger things he charges through the nose for.'

'I don't know where he is.' Her look is challenging. I dare you, she is saying. Make a scene, have a row, bring things to a head. This is your party after all. That is your husband over there. Get him to help you with the barbeque. Jess hasn't got the strength to fight. There are bowls and bowls of salad and cold cuts and all the rest of it. There are piles of booze. It will do.

8

It's after eleven when Ro turns into Riverton Street. He can hear the music from the end of the block and follows it until he reaches the laneway that leads onto the Common and the path along the back of the houses. Most of the other gardens are dark, but Jess's is lit up like Christmas. As he follows the path, the occasional motion-sensitive light clicks on, but not outside Jess's place. Jess trusts in the height of her wall, the sturdiness of her gate, and she is right. They are good enough. He stands outside by a line of wheelie bins, new for the party, and waits.

Listening to the laughter, the uncontroversial retro music – some Beatles, some Brazilian bossa nova elevator shit – he feels a twist of jealousy. It's not that he envies her the big house. He wouldn't know what to do with one of those. He doesn't envy her the idiot husband either, or the baby in the pram. At least, he doesn't think he does. But he does feel something. His blood feels harsh, acidic. Nefertiti is wearing off already.

He's not outside for very long when the gate opens. He ducks out of sight like a pantomime villain behind a sturdy tree trunk and watches as the ice-blonde comes out, opens the lid of a recycling bin and drops in a clanking bin bag. And then Charlie appears. He looks a little drunk. He is not exactly swaying, but his gait is loose. If a passing stranger were to venture along the path with malice in his heart, he might easily prod Charlie with a finger and topple him over like a skittle.

Ro stays in the shadows for the moment while something small and feral runs across his foot. Charlie is waiting for the blonde, and when she heads back towards the gate, he catches her by the bottom. The blonde shrugs him off, but then she stretches out her hand and leads him back inside. It's a kind of tribute to how well he understands his sister's husband that Ro is not in the least surprised. He is so very predictable, is Charlie.

Equally predictably, Charlie forgets to close the gate. Ro can hardly believe his luck. And yes, Charlie could be waiting to trap the unwary in among the lavender pots and the gravel and the murky-coloured door. But he doubts it. And that's when he edges himself in. And there is Charlie, one hand on the potting shed and the other on the blonde.

If Charlie is down at the shed, transgressing blithely, then where is Jess? Out on the Common, there is movement in the sky, the trees, but the back of Jess's garden is matte, motionless. Once he moves past the larchlap fence that conceals both the compost heap and his rutting brother-in-law, the garden is full of people. The music has been turned down now, and it seems like someone edgier has taken charge. The garden has been transformed. Trestle tables have been pushed up against the old walls, their feet sinking into the soft ground of the flower beds. There is enough food to feed an army, and he suddenly realises that he's starving. It's refreshing to feel the nip, to know there could be privations he hasn't even dreamed of yet.

Lying in wait has taught him that tentative movements are the ones to catch the eye. If you move with a sense of purpose, you look like you belong. He heads for a table laden with insubstantial morsels, stuffs some circlets of salty fish two-handed into his mouth, then pours himself a glass of tart white and downs it in one. He picks up a disposable camera from a nearby table and pockets it. In the kitchen, whose doors are folded right back so that the terrace forms part of the house, people are talking quietly now and the music is just a low pulse in the background. A couple of young guys in black shirts are sitting outside looking dazed. And there, just inside the kitchen, is his sister with an older couple. *The* older couple. He sees Eddie first, because the woman's back is turned, an embroidered scarf draped around her shoulders. And before he's even seen her face he knows who that woman is.

She turns towards him, and her expression alters. Oh so slight, that change – a kind of mist in her eyes. But he isn't ready. His heart has grown hooves, racing up against the wall of his chest. Eddie hasn't recognised him yet, and Jess is deep in conversation. As for the woman, she is concentrating on her sleeve now, flicking something from it. He busies himself with another glass of lemony wine while, over on the other side of the room, two guys are larking about with plastic cameras just like the one he has in his pocket, clicking at the kitchen cupboards, the ceiling, anything. Eddie and the woman on the sofa glance towards them, then look away. Kids, they are thinking. Idiots.

There is a moment when he has the perfect view of her face, tilted up into the light to speak to someone, and he can't resist. He reaches into his pocket and feels for the camera's smooth carapace. He itches to capture her so as to examine each angle of her later. Right now, his head is too full of jagged wishing to be objective. He needs to click and click until he has made a record of each aspect of this woman, until he can match her to his meagre recollections of his mother. Before he knows it, he has taken her profile, the top of her head and the sweep of her nose. He curses when a couple in mid-step barge into him and knock him off his stride. She glances up, and this time the charge of recognition in her eyes is unmistakable. She knows now, he can see that. And she knows that Ro does too. But then, somehow, Eddie is shouldering in between them. Eddie has interrupted things. Just as he interrupted things back in Goa too.

His memory of Eddie back then is of a man who wore wide cotton trousers in bright, clownish colours. The memory brings with it the blurred sensation of sunburn, an itching on his forearms, a belly swollen from too much spicy food. He and Jess were in a large, clanging place with hard surfaces and bad smells, and then they weren't. And they weren't because Eddie had taken them out of there and was trying to be Pa. Soon, maybe only a couple of days later, Auntie Rae turned up and there were tears and more tears, and then there was a plane. All too soon. All too eager to be gone. Ro has often wondered whether, if they'd hung around in Goa a little longer, they might have found out something that would have spared him this life of endless wandering. Back then he felt that he was abandoning his own mother, who would never have abandoned him if she'd had any choice in the matter.

Eddie opens his mouth to say something, but it's Jess who greets Ro first. She has a dark crust along her bottom lip, and he remembers then that the only wine she ever drinks is red. Her speech seems slurred, which is not like Jess. All she says is his name, the whole bird. 'Spaaaaa-rohhhh.'

He toys with the idea of blowing it all open – the husband by the potting shed, the return of the prodigal mother. But it's early days for that.

And then she starts again, better this time. 'Hello, Ro,' she manages. 'It's good to see you.'

She must have more than that to say, but nothing else comes out. She presents Eddie and the woman silently, with an open palm. Eddie doesn't react right away. And then he jumps to his feet. Well, he gets perfectly efficiently to his feet for a man of sixty plus. Eddie and Jess exchange a glance. It's a phrase he has never really understood, but now he gets it perfectly. It is collaborative and destined to exclude him.

He makes the casual shift from maybe to definite. Just a flick of the mind does it, and when he looks back again at the woman on the sofa, he is examining the side of his mother's head. Her greyish-blondish hair is worked into a bun that, while not quite elderly, is not glossy enough to belong to a younger woman. She looks up at Ro and, just as they are about to exchange a glance of their own, Eddie puts a stop to it.

'This is Maya,' he says. 'My partner.' Mine.

But the woman on the sofa, who moments ago belonged to Eddie, she's not ready to pull away from Ro. Not yet. She raises the bottle on the table next to her, as if offering to fill his glass. And in that moment he feels something that isn't just an exchange of glances. He feels a surge of recognition, something that might even be love. In all the years since that beach in Goa he has never experienced this before. As she stretches her hand out to pour for him, she displays the inside of her wrist. And there it is, a pinkish scarring. In the delicately veined skin where perfume is applied and cuts are made. There it is.

When she looks into his eyes, he imagines a long tough cord strung up between them, and pulls it tight. She tries to yank it away from him but he isn't letting go, until at last he weakens and lets her have her rope. Her eyes leave him, and she doesn't stay long after that. But as she leaves her daughter's kitchen, she kisses him goodbye. One cheek, then the other. As she moves towards him, he can smell the sweetness of her flesh like a memory of toddlerhood. And for tonight, that will do. But this is not the way things will be left. This is not the way it's going to be.

Jess sees Eddie and Maya to the minicab, placing a stack of empty Tupperware in the boot. Returning to the house, she is already attempting to work out what happens next. Ro is not in the hallway, nor in the kitchen either. The guests have almost all gone. A small cohort attached to the teen barmen are sitting at the low wall of the terrace and making short work of the pale ales, while further down the garden knots of people she can't identify from this distance are talking quietly. The music is over now, and there is an air of hushed content. She has always found that Ro's reappearance betokens crisis. The episode with the blood on his shirt, for instance, when he refused to explain what had happened. And the last time, of course, the ugly row, the insults.

'I know he's your brother,' Charlie had said, 'but I don't want him anywhere near Ruby.'

On the other side of the terrace, the glowing tip of a cigarette pulses brightly then dims. Whoever is smoking it is facing her, looking straight at her perhaps. She faces the little disc of red, fixes her eyes on it. As he walks towards her, Sparrow tosses the cigarette away in a skimmed orange arc and steps into the light. Later, much later, she might ask how he got in, whether the gate was open. Later still, she might even ask why he doesn't stay in touch, why he couldn't just have walked up to the front door like a normal person. Right now, though, his return seems supernatural. A single magpie defying gates and walls. She loves her brother, or at least that's what she tells herself. But that love is tinged with cooler colours, with apprehension and distaste.

'Funny time to have a party,' he says. When he crosses in front of the pale blue wall, the projected bubbles dapple him so that for a second or two he is the main feature, top of the bill.

She stretches out her hand to him. His grasp is soft and weak and slightly clammy, as it always has been. He performs the clench and raise manoeuvre he favours over a handshake or a hug. It used to feel conspiratorial, but tonight it just feels weird. She is shocked at herself, because already she is wishing he would leave. As she turns to walk back with him into the house, she spots the three women friends she loves most – Sarah, sitting in a chair nestling her bump, Martha and Alice, all laughing together, though they won't have met before tonight. She realises then that she doesn't want to introduce them to Ro, that she doesn't want the old things to reoccur – the oversensitive ego, the endless retelling of the story of the beach as if it is his story alone, as if he deserves something in return, the inevitable embarrassing scene. And so she moves him back, deeper into the garden, while she tries to think what to do next.

She needs to manage the meeting between Charlie and Ro after the last, disastrous visit. From the start, though, the history between them has been fraught. Even at her wedding, Ro was frail and overwrought, snatching glass after glass from the trays of passing waiters, then tumbling down the feature staircase at her in-laws' house before the speeches had begun, like a child fed booze too young. Charlie was furious with embarrassment, and on a day already clouded by Eddie, this had seemed like another omen.

Ro didn't turn up again after that for another six

months or so. Then, one day, he appeared at the office, dressed as if he'd just come from an ashram. She took him for coffee in the Prêt on the corner where he berated her for her career, for Charlie, for her navy suit, her bob, her pearl and gold drops, for the life she had chosen, all that. She sat there and took it, for the sake of harmony. And she was glad she did, because the rant seemed to soothe him. And what did it matter to her? She was stronger, more capable. But it did matter, because it made her sadder, a little less able to cope with Charlie and the tiny acts of undermining that had started even then.

The hold Ro has on her is something she will never be able to shift. From the moment on the beach when he tugged at her hand and tried to pull her over towards the trees, she has failed him. If she had only coaxed him into speaking instead of trying to shake the memories from him, if she had refused to abandon him to the insistence of her father's family that he attend the prescribed schools, if she'd had a heart, then maybe things might have been different.

'Too late for the food, I suppose?' he says.

That's one thing she can provide, and she jumps to it. 'You must be joking. The fridge is heaving with the stuff.'

She takes him inside and shows him to the table where Hana has cling-filmed two platters of leftover canapés. 'Eddie's partner made some little veggie tarts, too. There should be plenty of those.'

The only things he seems to want are the tarts that Maya made. He piles three or four of them onto a plate and sits at the breakfast bar to eat. She watches him as if he were a child who might choke on a pine nut.

'No sign of Charlie, then?' he asks. His eyes display a scorn she wishes he had the grace to hide, at least for now.

'He's around here somewhere,' she says. 'Look, Ro, I've been trying to contact you. I wish to hell you'd get yourself a phone. But maybe you're the one who should have been trying to contact me.'

As soon as she says it she realises it's too early for any of this.

'Well I'm here, aren't I?'

'We need to talk about—'

'The passport? It proves I was right. What more do we need to say?'

She is surprised, but she doesn't show it. 'It doesn't prove anything. Not a single thing.'

'Easy for you to say, when you see her every day.'

His eyes are hard, the pupils pinprick-small. She remembers then that Ro doesn't think like other people. 'What are you talking about?'

His mouth is working away at one of Maya's tarts as he leans back, his hands behind his head. 'Can I stay, Jess? Just a few weeks, that's all. I need to sort myself out.'

There is no room for him here. None. But she doesn't know how to say that, when there is so much room here for anyone but Ro.

'I'll have a chat with Charlie,' she says.

'You need to ask your husband if your own brother can stay?'

'Of course not, Ro. It's manners, that's all.'

'Manners? God, Jess, you are boring.'

The old jabs are the sharpest. She feels it. 'But you still want to stay, right?'

'Right.'

She catches sight of Charlie, further down the dark garden, where the only light comes from a pair of flaring candles that smell of verbena. He is standing in the shadows, talking intently to someone who barely reaches his shoulder. She blinks and strains until she sees a white-blonde head tilted up to him. Hana and her husband are lingering by the shed, just where Jess planted the amaryllis the year before. Instinct tells her to keep away, and when she sees the open gate, her heart whizzes. On the Common side of the wall, the trees are blacker than the sky, tossed by a wind that hasn't yet managed to invade her sheltered garden. As she stands there, she feels a bewilderment of breached defences but she hasn't the courage to shore them up, not yet. And so she retreats.

She is keeping Ro topped up with wine in the too-bright kitchen, when Charlie appears on the terrace and starts regaling the teen barmen with stories of beer-hall escapades in Munich a decade or more ago. It hurts to see Hana standing barefoot next to him, her little glinting mules fallen rakishly together on the floor.

Noticing Ro for the first time, Charlie makes a face. 'You really know how to choose your moment, Sparrow.'

Hana puts her hand up to hide her smirk, and Jess feels the blood rush to her face. She glances between the two men. Charlie, so filled out with confidence and food. Ro, so very lean and pale and washed away. And that's when she decides to take him in and keep him, her own blood for better or for worse.

'He's here because of Mum,' she says. And then Hana looks away, as if unsure how to react. 'I'll put him in the spare room.'

Ro still hasn't said anything. And then he approaches Charlie and does the same touch, clench thing he did with her. And though Charlie is flinching even more than she did herself, he lets it pass.

Carrying a bottle of wine and a couple of glasses, she ushers Ro into the empty drawing room with its gleaming floor. They must have under-ordered on the red, which has run out. She rarely drinks white, and it tastes like a pear drop, both tart and sweet at once. Already, it is beginning to gnaw at her stomach.

There is no baggage, just a grubby backpack. There is little enough chat.

'You've been away a while,' she says.

She's aware that she uses simpler language than usual with Sparrow. It's not that she thinks he's stupid. She knows he isn't. It's that when she is talking to him she seems to be straining for a past that's almost out of reach – a time when she was the leader, and he was lost.

'Where have you been?' she asks.

It comes out a bigger question than she'd intended, a more visceral one, and he recoils a little in response. All she is hoping to ascertain is whether he has been to Ireland, though she isn't sure she wants to know the answer. Ro looks as if he's not sure either what she means, and then he answers anyway.

'I come and go.'

'You never used to tell me where you went,' she says because, after all, she should have known better.

She is thinking of the time just after they returned from Goa and went to live with Auntie Rae, when they were two skinny, blond kids grown tough in the hot sun and accustomed to foraging for themselves. Ro would be in the garden one moment, and the next he would have disappeared, and she would get the blame for not having kept an eye on him.

He catches on right away. 'Oh then? Yeah. There was a place behind the café on the Common, a kind of gap between two walls. I used to squeeze between them and just sit there, looking up at the streak of sky above. Sometimes I'd scribble on the walls and pretend I was writing hieroglyphics on a mummy's tomb, but mostly it was Batman's cave. It was nice. And no one would ever find me there.'

He doesn't say the place is still there, that he walked past it only yesterday. Meanwhile, Jess is thinking about the times when he came home from school and would take himself to the Common and hide away from all of them.

'At school, did something happen to you? Something bad?'

'Nothing has ever been as bad as that day.'

And of course he is talking about the beach. But she doesn't want to go over all that again, the fact that neither of them remembers anything at all. She looks down at the distressed table that is showing its wounds while she is hiding hers. She decides to tackle the subject head-on.

'The passport means nothing.'

'Who says? Eddie, I suppose.'

She is taken aback that Eddie is the first person he thinks of.

In the hallway outside, she can hear people leaving. She doesn't want to have to talk to anyone, not right now, and so she goes and turns the key very quietly in the door.

For the first time tonight Ro smiles, and she can feel something of the power that smile still has for the women who let him tell his story.

'We'll find her, Jess. I know we will.'

She is suddenly overwhelmed by the huge effort it seems to take to keep your loved ones safe and warm. By work and care. By not knowing and needing to find out.

'I'm sorry I didn't protect you, Ro.'

'That was her job,' he says.

Upstairs, Charlie is drunk.

'How the fuck did *he* get in?'

He is cleaning his teeth, spitting into the basin.

'You hadn't checked the gate was locked, Jess? Really? You're obsessed with that bloody gate.'

She doesn't tell him what she saw. Doesn't say he must have known about the gate being open, had probably opened it himself. She needs to think first. Decide what she wants to do about whatever she thinks she half perceived, down by the potting shed.

In the meantime, she has put Ro in the room at the back, the bedroom looking out over the garden, the one that is painted yellow in case there is another baby. When she gets into bed, Charlie has already turned away from her, deep in sleep. She lies on her back and listens to the sounds outside – ragged laughter from the bus stop, a cry from somewhere in the middle of the Common. She is sure that Charlie is frightened of Ro – his frailty, but maybe also his unpredictability. Because there is no doubt that Ro can be unpredictable.

The idea of Ro under her roof makes her anxious too, and she feels guilty about that. The truth is, she is afraid that he will swamp everyone with his preoccupations. Or rather, his preoccupation. There has only ever been the one.

9

Jess is up at five, way before the rest of the house, and right away she can smell the aftermath of the party. Charlie looks like he hasn't shifted position all night long. She goes to the en suite to pour herself a glass of water, and then another, until the sour taste in her mouth is almost washed away. She likes to watch the Common come to life, and the dog walkers heading in the direction of the bandstand, where they will congregate for coffee. It makes her safe to witness these rituals, to survey the Common stretched out in front of her like a calm green lake. But there isn't time for that today.

Downstairs, the kitchen is a mess. The agency cleaners are booked for seven, and she hopes they arrive before Hana comes down. Wrestling sleepily with the coffee machine, she is berating herself for having agreed to a party on a Sunday night, birthday or no birthday, when Ro appears. She's never known him rise before ten, but he looks full of energy, his eyes shining.

'Well?' he says. 'Did you see the tattoo?'

For a moment she is confused, and then she realises that this is something he must have been thinking about all night long. There is an agenda here, and he is right in the middle of it. She should stop him now, but she doesn't.

'What tattoo is that, Ro?'

She is managing to keep her voice steady, but Ruby will be awake any minute now and she is impatient to get a move on.

'You're not telling me you missed it? She has a tattoo, just in the right place.'

She knows that Ro has drawn up an inventory of characteristics that, even now, might identify their mother. Among other things, Auntie Rae had told him that their mother's habit of wearing heavy earrings had stretched her piercings low down the lobes. And she confirmed the tattoo, of course. Sophie had no scars, but inside her left wrist there was a big blowsy purplish rose she'd had done one Saturday when they were both still at school, back in the days when a tattoo was the ultimate act of rebellion.

Ro is poking in among the cookery books. Next thing, he has found a pad of paper. Pulling out a page, he starts to draw, working with too much detail as he always does. She turns away and busies herself with warming Ruby's milk. By the time she has turned back again it's clear that he is drawing a rose.

'You don't remember?' He is pointing to the tender part of his wrist, the place he might cut, if he were that way inclined. He traces a circle there with his fingernail. 'Just here,' he says.

She is tempted to nod because perhaps she does remember. She thinks she might remember, but she knows too that memories are treacherous, that they can implant themselves and feel authentic without the reality having been anything like that at all.

'Are you talking about Eddie's partner?' she says cautiously. 'About Maya? I don't remember seeing a tattoo.'

His face falls. 'Well, you're simply not trying hard enough. She's had it removed. It's obvious. I've seen that kind of scar before – you can tell exactly where it was. That pale patch on her wrist. It's a ghost.'

She has vowed not to get mad with Ro. At least, not so early on. She is not going to get riled by him, by his willingness to bend the facts. But she doesn't want to join in. She doesn't want to subscribe to these theories of his. The week has started again, and it will be a fraught one. She needs to keep a clear head at work, to tie things down. She needs to think about Charlie, about Hana, who will still be looking after her child this week. As for the passport, it is easier by far to let it all go.

Ro reads her mind, of course, as he always does. 'Let sleeping dogs lie, Jess. Yeah? I don't think so.'

'But Maya? You're being ridiculous now, Ro. Maya is Swedish, she's been with Eddie for – I don't know – years now.'

Jess has never given Maya much thought. She has always been kind, and ready with advice and little treats for Ruby. She runs the nursery Ruby has just started to attend, and everyone there is crazy about her. Jess can see where this is going, and she won't have it. Besides, she likes Maya. She reckons Eddie has lucked out there. She recognises that expression on Ro's face, and it makes her queasy.

A tattoo is bad news, because a tattoo is one of the core tenets. Along with the overpierced ears and the rosacea and the chipped tooth. Things that might not be easy to conceal. All she knows is that she doesn't want a week where her brother believes that the mother who disappeared on a Goa beach twenty-five years ago has just attended a party in this house.

Upstairs, Ruby is crying. She has started tentatively, but in no time at all she can wind herself into a rage.

Jess puts her hand on his arm, then points to the ceiling. 'Help yourself to granola or whatever. I need to hold off an earthquake.'

He has no idea what she's talking about. He looks confused, and for a moment she wonders whether he might have forgotten that she even has a child.

When Hana appears, Jess feels her throat tighten, her face burn, but she busies herself in gathering up the throwaway cameras she bought for the party and putting them in a plastic bag to drop off at Snappy Snaps on her way to work. She's been warned not to expect much. Alice said she left cameras on every table at her wedding, but there had been practically nothing worth retrieving – feet, floor tiles, wild swipes of fuzzed colour.

Once she is outside the house, she finds that last night's events have lodged inside her like a splinter. She keeps replaying in her head the image of Hana standing barefoot in the kitchen next to Charlie, her glittery mules kicked away. It is an intuition, that's all, but perhaps intuition is everything. The day is such a beautiful one that she pushes the thought away. Perhaps nothing will change, and the significance of this will fade, just as all the other things have faded too – the sightings at unlikely branches of Tesco in the North East, on top of a bus in Rotterdam, in Nepal.

She is barely in her office when Miles's face appears at the glass panel. He doesn't open the door, just points to himself and raises five fingers. Five minutes. She recognises a summons when she sees one. She is waylaid by a call from Grosvenor, requesting a meeting at their offices, another from the PSL about a precedent she requested the week before.

As she walks into Miles's office, she can tell right away that the few minutes she has kept him waiting have allowed his temper time to stew. He is standing with his back to her, his fists clenched at his sides, looking onto the market below where a queue has formed outside the falafel stall. She notices the creases at the back of his knees, and wonders idly if his wife has thrown him out.

'You wanted to speak to me, Miles?'

He acts as if they're already mid-conversation and she knows exactly what this is all about.

'Know what? The client doesn't give a shit. He doesn't care that you've had a bad day. He doesn't care that your nanny's walked out or that your husband has left you. And if your kid is wandering down the A3 with the local kiddie fiddler, he doesn't really give a shit about that either. All he cares about is that you document his deal to his best advantage. That's it. Nothing more.'

She knows now, of course. He has found something, a small thing that he will blow up into something big.

And then he turns to her. 'They were on to me this morning and They Are Pissed that you walked out of that meeting. They Are Even More Pissed that you didn't draft in anyone to take your place.'

She opens her mouth, mumbles something about Carl. But he puts his hand up to stop her.

'Carl isn't qualified, remember? You might as well have had the girl from reception in there.'

She tries again, but he isn't listening.

'You'll have your chance. In the meantime, I've instituted disciplinary procedures. The email should be with you later. But you'd better call the client and do some serious fucking grovelling.'

She feels a flash of hatred for him. The strength of the emotion surprises her, frightens her a little. Often, her working day feels bland and impersonal, as if the climate control has done its work too well.

'This is ridiculous,' she says.

'Oh yeah? What about the Trentino contract? That could have cost the client dearly if I hadn't caught it. As for Grosvenor, you're clocking up billable hours at a rate that just isn't sustainable, given the fee we've agreed. Besides, I don't think it's desirable to have a senior associate's private life in the papers.'

He pokes his pinkie into his ear and vibrates it.

In the silence, she can hear the rapid clip of a printer outside the room.

'I'm hardly Katie Price,' she says quietly. 'I'm surprised

you'd try to use that against me.' She is outraged, actually, but she is just managing to stay calm.

'It's not the image we—'

'I didn't ask to be abandoned on a beach. I think you'll find that I'm the victim here.'

'And clearly stressed.'

His signet ring glints under the halogen and she concentrates on trying to work out if they will still be able to stay in the house if she loses her job.

She walks over to his desk, where a nauseatingly overblown rose is propped up in a tumbler of water. Miles is a gardener? She can't think how he finds the time. Someone is a gardener, but probably not Miles. As she passes it, her hand flicks at the glass. From the expression on Miles's face, he isn't sure if she's done it on purpose. She isn't sure herself. The water bubbles on the gleaming surface of the desk, a little stream of it inching its way towards a pile of paperwork. The rose looks like it's been spat from between the teeth of a passing gypsy. The image almost makes her laugh out loud. She grasps at the flower, her fist full of petals. It feels moist and slightly human. She gasps, and he does too, and then she drops it on the floor.

The email about the meeting arrives just as she has settled herself deep in the subclauses of a distribution agreement. It is to be held on the Sixth Floor, on Friday. The floor is the giveaway. She knows what's coming, and it's still only Monday. She can't wait till Friday – she'd be tumbled in anxiety for days. And so she emails HR and asks them to bring the meeting forward. They need a certain partner in attendance, the woman says, but so long as they can rustle him up at short notice, she sees no reason why that can't be done.

Jess really doesn't need to ask which partner will be attending. She thinks of Delia, who is, after all, the person she should talk to about these things. She has often said to Sarah how lucky they both are to have Delia rooting for them. No better mentor in the whole firm. Someone with clout. She does what she now knows she should have done the morning after the Summer Party, and calls Delia's direct line. But there's no reply. She goes to try and find her, but the PA says she's in Dubai. 'She's convening the Middle East group conference on the seventh, so I'm not expecting her back for a fortnight at least.'

She has to stand all the way home on the Tube, her document case wedged between her ankles. She is determined to work all night, if need be, to secure her job, to make it up to the client. But, wary of putting any of this in writing, she has decided not to email Delia in Dubai. Besides, there are so many other things jostling around in her head that the prospect of the Sixth Floor seems like a detail. Charlie and his late nights, the passport, Ro.

Up ahead, a dog is leading his owner on the end of a taut chain. Magnificently white, its tail rests on its back like a boudoir puff. Despite yesterday's rain the path of beaten earth is dry and dusty, and chestnut trees crowd out the sky. A man in a business suit is sitting on a little clearing he's made. No rug, no reading matter, just himself. There is another business suit, over by the fitness area. Standing motionless, alone. And it seems to Jess that they are the silent heralds of some disaster she hasn't even begun to perceive yet.

Ro has spent the day with Hana. He has eaten bowl after bowl of cereal, drunk mug after mug of strong tea. He has conducted a thorough search of Jess's room for images of his mother that will prove they are in constant contact. He has been through the bottom of the wardrobe, the bedside drawers, the row of cupboards beneath the windows where he found some Christmas decorations and a violin, together with what must be every note Jess has ever taken for every lecture she has ever attended. The photo albums were in the living room on an open shelf, and there seemed to be nothing to hide. While Hana popped out to the shops, he took the precaution of Sellotaping the keypad on the garden gate, just in case he might some day need an alternative way in. By the time Hana returns, he has trawled through three years' worth of Jess's emails, checked her Facebook photos as far back as he can go, but he has found nothing.

Ruby is at nursery, and there is still nearly an hour until pick-up time. Hana is slumped on the leather sofa in the TV room with the shutters closed. She is watching music videos and painting her nails a violent shade of green. He'd thought she might be Finnish on account of the hair. He knew a girl from Rovaniemi once with hair like that, and the same slightly slanted eyes. In fact, her colouring reminds him of a winter sunset somewhere in the Arctic Circle. All that pink and ice and blue. But she laughs at Finland, and tells him she's from Brazil.

'It's not like you probably think it is – all football and samba,' she says.

That isn't what he thinks at all. His image of Brazil is way more apocalyptic. It involves unfinished tower blocks inhabited by knife-and-needle people, the laying waste of areas as big as Wales. He wants to keep in with Hana, though, so all he says is that he's always fancied Carnival, all those long-legged black girls in feathers. She shrugs, takes a puff or two at her nails, then turns on the hairdryer next to her and waves her absinthe fingers in the hot air. The motor is too loud for conversation, and he wonders how much longer this is going to take. He has wasted a whole day here already, and he is still no further along.

'I suppose it's nearly time you picked up Ruby,' he says as she gets up to leave the room.

'I suppose.' She is wrestling with the buggy in the hall, her hands held straight and stiff so as not to spoil her nails. She bends to yank some lever that will make the contraption unfold. When she doesn't succeed, he takes over from her, then finds he can't manage it any better than she does. She laughs at him, showing her little white teeth. As she dips the front wheels of the buggy down over the front step, she turns to him, and there is a sly look on her face.

'Why don't you come with me to pick up Ruby,' she says, and he hopes she hasn't guessed because that's exactly what he had in mind.

He is stoked up now, and finds he can't stop talking. She can't stop talking either, all about the boyfriend who fucked her best friend back in Bauru and how she got her own back by reporting him for tax evasion.

'I got all the evidence they needed. Easy. He was so fucking stupid.' She shrugs again. It seems to be her default setting. 'I'm going to train as a lawyer when I get home,' she says.

'I can't stand lawyers,' he says. Why not test her out, is what he's thinking. See where the boundaries are, if she has any sense of humour. See if she dares mention Jess.

She barely reacts, just keeps on pushing the pram.

'Rules, that's more like it,' he says then, backing off. 'I hate rules, and forms and small print.'

'Oh, I wouldn't worry,' she says. 'Most lawyers hate those things, too. For me, I want to know enough about the rules so I'm smart enough to fuck the system real good.' And she turns towards him, in her chilly way, and smiles. There is nothing warm in that smile. She is not the kind of person he would let take care of his kid, if he had one.

'See much of Eddie?' he asks.

For a moment, she doesn't seem to recognise the name. And then she nods. 'Oh yeah, him? I don't think of him as Eddie,' she says. 'He's just the old hippie to me. Eddie, is that his name? Your sister calls him Dad,' she says.

At first he thinks she said Dan, which would be odd enough when the man's name is Eddie. But the way she looks at him shows that she realises she has planted a bomb and is quite prepared to walk away while it explodes behind her.

'Could you just repeat that?' he says.

'Which bit?' And then she realises. 'Oh yeah, the Dad bit. Pretty weird, huh?'

As she walks ahead of him, he has a chance to take a really close look at her arse. She is wearing leggings, if that's what they're called, or maybe those are yoga clothes. He wonders how long she's been fucking Charlie.

They pass a fallen tree that has rooted itself again. A squirrel flits along its length, darting, twitching, darting. As if nervous of putting its faith in a dead tree, the squirrel streaks up into a living one instead until it is lost somewhere in the high foliage. A line of young birches casts wavery stripes of shadow onto the scuffed lime of the football pitch as Hana turns the pushchair towards the café.

The idea of the café at this time of day is a nightmare. It's not just that he would rather not run into Nefertiti with Hana around, it's the combination of tiled floor and bare walls, the clatter of cups and glasses and the mad chatter of attention-seeking kids worn out by playground exertions. Today, the place is crammed with truffling dogs on rattling leads, with children falling over scooters or peevishly struggling against the restraints on their pushchairs. But at least there is no Nefertiti.

'We could always have a coffee after the pickup,' he says, because that's the only reason he's bothering with this, to have her with him, a kind of alibi to allow him to stand outside the school and view his mother.

But Hana seems determined to extract her coffee first. He buys her an inky espresso made by the Sicilian woman at the counter who is so proud of her work that she delivers a personal flourish to everything she does, a drizzle of honey on a cake, an extra piece of chocolate with your coffee.

'I wonder why she calls him Dad, though,' Hana says, once they have taken their seats and pulled Ruby's buggy alongside. She is looking at him, wide-eyed, clearly not willing to let this one go.

'We don't *have* a dad,' he says. Actually, they never *did* have a Dad, that's the last name their father would have selected for himself. She doesn't catch on at first, looks at him blankly over the rim of her tiny cup. 'Maybe it's a joke,' he says. 'A lawyer's one.'

'She might be sleeping with him, of course,' she says in her blasé, seen-it-all way. 'It might be some weirdo sex-game thing they have going on.' She fixes him with her cold eye.

I've seen it all, too, he thinks. But that's a very odd thing to say.

He watches her quick fingers as they grasp the spoon and give the coffee a vigorous little whirl.

She drops in two ancient-looking sugar lumps and tips her spoon against the side of the cup as they melt. 'Strange, though, to call him Dad.'

He agrees. 'Strange all right, if it's true.' And he smiles.

The girl from Brazil looks at him, and her eyes narrow. She knows she has hit her target, but she can't be sure if the dart will hold.

'How long are you staying?' she asks. 'You're the older one, right?'

He is not the older one, but he doesn't bother to put her straight on that. One question at a time, that's his policy.

'Like me, until the wind changes?'

And he supposes that's as good an answer as any.

'Or until they throw us out.'

He isn't sure when me changed to us. But she smiles at him, and he can tell she wants him to notice the change. OK, he thinks. This is interesting. Let's run with this.

As they leave the café, he notices a girl with bright pink hair who is filling a plastic beaker with juice and handing it to an angelic-looking toddler. Their eyes meet, and she smiles up at him, warm and wide. His sister would never have employed a girl with bright pink hair, or with tattoos either. She would never have looked twice at Nefertiti. Whereas Hana, with her perfectly adequate English and her neat jeans and her fake Burberry raincoat – she fits the bill exactly. He looks at the back of Hana as she disappears out the door, tipping the buggy up to negotiate the threshold. He might help her with that, he supposes, but she is more than capable. He knows that. She is capable of a lot, he thinks.

Outside, she stops a moment and takes a look at her phone. A small smile on her face, she taps at the screen before putting it away. There is never any reception here anyway. It's one of the annoying things about the Common. Perhaps she's gone to the trouble of signing up with the only service provider to cover this place. That would say something about her, he supposes. He wonders if Charlie has competition. Some biker dude. Some bit of rough.

'Come on,' she says. 'We need to go.'

It seems his mother stands at the school door at home time, shaking hands. How ridiculous. How unhygienic. And how heartless to shake the hand of every other mother's child, with no thought for her own.

His mood nosedives as they stride across the open prairie of the Common, where the little boys in red are being marshalled together, where a big net is being filled with footballs, and stakes are being pulled out of the ground. They cross the thundering road just behind the kids, at a spot where the lollipop lady is being ignored by a Sainsbury's juggernaut. He sits outside on the wall. And he waits. A little boy in a pirate outfit with jagged trousers and a cardboard parrot fastened to his red plastic belt is play-fighting with his brother, over in the tousled blond grass that fringes a path of beaten earth.

Ro hated school. Soon after arriving at his boarding prep, he had been locked inside a cupboard by an older pupil, his eye welded to the crack of light that ran the length of the door. Outside, the sound of squealing boys, the punt of a football. Inside, the rush of hot piss down his leg. And at that moment, he realised that he would always be locked in or out. One way or the other, real life would be taking place somewhere he couldn't access.

The people waiting outside the school are nearly all women of about Jess's age. Some are wearing gym gear, others look like they've rushed here from a meeting.

Hana goes to speak to one of the other nannies while Ro stands at the back of the crowd and waits for the double doors to open. It reminds him of bunking off school for a Radiohead gig, when he can't have been more than about fourteen. He stood popping pill after pill as the air turned flamingo pink and burning orange and the music flowed like honey in his head. Afterwards, he waited at a side door for Thom to appear, hour after hour until the colours faded and the music did too and he felt himself shrivel and the world go grey.

His mother seems more confident than she did at the party; here in Toddlerland she might even be commanding, in a kindly sort of way. The good witch, maybe. But, witch or not, she still doesn't look like the kind of woman who would abandon her children on a beach. She stretches her hand out to each child, then bends to their level to hear whatever it is they're saying before pressing them on their way.

Hana waves over to him to say that she's going down to Ruby's classroom, and to wait for him there. Most of the older children have left now, and Hana disappears into the depths of the building with an exaggerated swagger, palming the empty buggy through the double doors. By now, the choke of parents waiting to collect has eased, and there are only a few people still hanging around. His mother is deep in conversation with an emaciated woman who looks as if she rarely sleeps. As the numbers thin out, Ro walks straight up to her, lingering round the back, waiting for the moment to approach.

The badge hanging around her neck on a laminated

lanyard says *MAYA* . . . The surname is in a smaller font, and he can't decipher it. Above the name, there is a thumbnail photo and, dominating it all, the Maltese cross of the school. He scrutinises the movements of her hands, to catch the ghost on the inside of her wrist. Her hands move a lot, he thinks. Doesn't that mean something? He can't remember if it indicates a lying nature or just an airy-fairy one. He'll google that when he gets back to Jess's place. Overuse of hands. Meaning. He is beginning to feel light-headed, tense and out of breath from the effort of following those hands. But when he finds what he's been looking for, he feels like yahooing. Her watch slips and reveals a stripe of holiday white, and there it is. The little round scar he saw the other night, on the inside of her left wrist, just where he thought it was.

In all the acres of newsprint devoted to speculation about Sophie's possible whereabouts, the tattoo was the thing. If she were still alive, perhaps suffering from memory loss, perhaps lying low, the tattoo would be the sure-fire identifier. But nothing lasts these days, not even an inked-on rose. The sight of the scar feels even better this time around, without the alcohol and the noise. But when she still doesn't look at him, let alone acknowledge his presence, he feels the void open up again, along with all those other voids: the emptiness of a Sunday afternoon away at school, sitting alone on a bench on the side of a windswept playing field, the voices of the other boys like screeching gulls, the rain pelting his face. And the fact that she has felt the need to hide herself from him empties him out.

Hana reappears with Ruby already strapped into the buggy. The woman who is her grandmother bends right down to the child and squeezes her fingers. And he is so engrossed by that sight that he doesn't quite realise that Hana is making introductions. His wayward mother looks up, but it's clear she doesn't remember him. How could that be, when she was reunited with him only yesterday? How could he not be at the very forefront of her mind? His hand is stiff in his pocket while hers appears to float in mid-air as it moves to greet him. He is transfixed by that hand – its pearly nails, its silver moonstone ring, its weathered skin. Just in time, he recovers himself. He stretches out his fingers, and lets her shake them gently once, twice. Her hand is warm, and softer than it looks, but there is a burr to it, too – perhaps a callus at the root of a finger or a tiny plaster.

He is entirely unable to tell if this is how his mother's hand should feel. Everything has stopped. His heart, the clock, the movements all around him. And then someone nudges him, and the world cranks up again and takes off without him.

'This is Jess's brother,' Hana is saying. 'Just staying for a few days.'

And when he realises that it is Hana who has spoiled the moment, he almost spins around and thumps her.

His mother's face is blank. He wants to find excuses for her. It was late, after all, and everyone had been drinking. He tries to say that his name is Ro, but he is afraid that even the shortened version sounds infantile, and he can't afford to be a little boy again. Instead, he uses the name his father's family insisted upon, the name they used at school. Even then he was always told that using his father's name made matters easier. It was simpler all round.

'My name is William,' he says, but it's clear that means nothing at all to her, and so he adds, 'I'm also known as Sparrow.'

There is no one else in the whole world called Sparrow. She can't hear that name and not know who he is. And yet she doesn't comment, her eyes don't even flicker. She just smiles at him, then addresses Hana, as if he's one of the toddlers, 'Oh, but I met him at the party.' And there's a tiny bit of an accent in the way she says party, *paa-teh*.

'And how do you like London?' she asks, as if he's a commoner and she's the Queen. She doesn't even look him in the eye, but gazes blankly at his forehead, or his hairline maybe. And she doesn't wait for his reply either, not that he has one.

'Well, I hope you have a good visit,' she continues. Before she even finishes the sentence, she has moved to greet the child behind.

This is the moment when he should walk away. Travel somewhere far from here. He could go towards the sun. Somewhere they are looking for people to dole out aid or build things. Famine. Disaster. War. There is always somewhere, after all. There is no real need to stay around. He has survived twenty-five years without her, why prostrate himself before her now? Because an alternative scenario, playing out in one of those awkward corners of his brain, has him flinging himself at her feet and tugging at her skirt and begging her to . . . what? Begging her to what, exactly? Because it's all too late for her to be a mother now. Acknowledge? Atone? Hana pulls him by the sleeve and he wants to push her away, and tell her just to let him have a moment to grieve. What? The end of dreams. What? The loss of hope. What? The cruelty of mothers.

They walk out the gate and stand at the zebra crossing until someone has the decency not to mow them down. He turns to look at Hana, breaker of spells and of homes. Her face is too small for the rest of her, he thinks. It is perfectly regular, but somehow meaner than it ought to be. She seems to be lost in thought, and even though Ruby is grizzling, stiffening her body in an effort to capture Hana's attention, she doesn't react. It's extraordinary how certain she seems to be of the security of her position in Jess's house, in that room of hers she rarely seems to occupy, while insisting to all and sundry that his is the temporary stay. He takes her up on that as soon as they leave the school grounds.

'That's what Jess told me,' Hana says, perfectly matter-of-fact about it. 'And she should know. I think she needs the room.'

'For what? She has plenty of rooms. And even if she does, I could always sleep in the cellar.'

She screws up her nose at that. 'Down there with Charlie's precious wine? With the mice and the spiders?'

She has no idea the places he's been. None.

And now that he's been told his time is short, he feels like running back through the school gates and shaking his mother by the shoulders until the truth falls out.

He is scarcely aware of Hana now, he is thinking so hard about how to do this. The little boys in red are still trickling back and forth across the green, but the light has turned to acid. Leaving the Common, they pass a circular pillbox building. He'd almost forgotten about the deep shafts to the old air-raid tunnels. The building seems newly painted, and he wonders if they do tours now. Anything is possible. There must be some way in, some way down. But how terrible to spend any more time than necessary underground.

They say that everything works its way to the surface one day. Long-lost mementos uncovered by a plough working a grassed-over battlefield, Frechen pots or mammoth bones unearthed by Crossrail. She must want to be found out; she wouldn't have come here otherwise. And he wants desperately to be the reason for her return. But Mags is in his ear again. Jess, Jess, Jess. And the likelihood that her return has nothing whatsoever to do with him lodges in his heart like grit.

Who knows how things might have turned out if she'd been half the mother she should have been? As for his father, he is just a ghost. There is scarcely any memory of him at all. Except now and then, a certain manly, oaky scent of sap and fibre. If that was his father, Ro can't imagine that he could ever be that kind of man.

At the duck pond, they pass someone in a yellow

singlet who is doing a funny walk. His arms are like wind-mills, his stride ridiculously wide.

'Idiot,' Hana says, loud enough for the man to hear, and laughs, and for a moment she looks as if she might be about to ram him with her buggy.

There is a malice about her that sets him on edge, and excites him too. He wonders what she values most, power or money? He wonders if he might make use of her. How far she can be trusted. He can feel her eyes on him, but he doesn't turn to face her. He wonders what she's going to say.

'I heard all about the newspaper at the one o'clock club. That new au pair of Martha, she told me all about the missing mother, the beach, the woman who was hid-ing her passport. I think this is the kind of thing you should tell me, Ro, now that we are friends. This is the kind of thing I need to know. If the house where I am living is in a newspaper – it is something I should be told. You were cute little boy, Ro . . .'

If she keeps on going she will put her finger on it. And he isn't ready for that.

' . . . And your mother was beautiful. But I hope Jess is better mother,' she says. 'That right, Rooby Roobs?' and she bends to ruffle Ruby's soft blonde hair. 'We hope that Jess is good enough for Ruby, because we don't think she is good enough to keep Papa.'

On Jess's behalf he hates this girl. But there is no doubt that a girl with such balls might come in useful, down the line. To prepare the ground, he starts to tell Hana his story. What he tells her, though, is quite a different version from the one he usually tells, a very different one from the story he told Nefertiti just the other night. In this scenario, he is not an abandoned boy at all. He is a man with a mission. At the centre of the wrong that has been done to him, he places Eddie. Eddie who took them away to the Yellow House so that for two days the police in Goa didn't even know where they'd gone. Eddie who knows more about what happened than he's letting on. Eddie who is not what he seems, with his ponytail and his organic ice cream. Unlike Nef, Hana is non-committal, only half interested. But as he nails Eddie like this he feels a sense of satisfaction. This is not the paedo crap he fed to Nefertiti. It is something half remembered in his own past that is being honoured here. He is edging towards a kind of recollection that might lead to more. He turns to look at Hana and the little catlike moue of satisfaction on her lips, and he can't help thinking that Hana is the kind of person who might very well end up in a black plastic bag at the bottom of a lake.

As they turn in off the gritty running track that skirts the back of the house, he sees her look around her as she presses in the code.

'I guess you've got to be careful,' he says. 'You don't want someone coming by and rushing you as you enter the garden.'

She looks at him, astonished. That possibility hasn't even occurred to her, and even now that he has articulated it, she clearly finds the thought ridiculous. 'Oh no,' she says, 'I just like to see their faces as they trudge the long way round. The look when they realise that people actually live here and can walk straight out onto the Common like it's theirs.'

She smiles over her shoulder at him, and he wonders what could have possessed his sister to have employed someone without tattoos and pink hair but with so much spite in her.

10

Hana is sitting at the bottom of the stairs playing with Ruby when Jess gets home. Her eyes are edged with greater definition than usual, and she has painted her nails a strange shade of green. On my time, Jess thinks.

'Date?' She tries to keep the sarcasm out of her voice.

'Kind of date.' Hana glances at the door into the kitchen. 'Ruby is Superbaby today. She has eaten up all her broccoli.'

Ruby clenches her hands up over her head like a tiny prizefighter and shows her perfect little bud teeth as she reaches out for Hana. In three deft movements, Hana kisses the child, untangles herself, and is gone. Jess tries to ignore the hand outstretched in the direction of Hana's departing figure, the turned-down mouth. But as soon as the heavy front door slams shut, Ruby begins to cry.

She is taken aback to find Charlie in the kitchen, and then she is deflated. Charlie looks a little sheepish in return to have been caught playing house. He is wearing a butcher's apron she hasn't seen since the period early on in their marriage when he specialised in curries with extensive lists of arcane ingredients that he would leave strewn across the countertop in a dozen unwashed bowls. Today, he has a stack of clean plates in his hands, and appears to have emptied the dishwasher. She adds this to the growing list of hints and clues that she will have to force herself to face. But not now. Later, sometime soon, when she can bring herself to confront this.

'Where's Ro?' she says.

'Out having a smoke. That's why I'm here, in fact. My meeting in the West End was cancelled, so I decided to show up unexpectedly, see what he gets up to. I don't want him feeling too settled. The last thing we want is him turning into a permanent fixture.'

'Relax. He's only just got here.'

'I was only in the door when he and Hana arrived back with Ruby. Poor mite was starving, so I made her a bowl of pasta. She's just sitting in her high chair, happy as Larry, when he comes and sits down opposite her. And then the little bastard starts to mimic her. Even poor Roobs seemed to realise there was something odd about it. But, you know, good girl and all that. So, she laughs along with him anyway, though she's puzzled, you can tell, and cautious. He pushes it then. You know? Push, push, push, the way he does. Takes the bowl up to his face and starts snorting into it like a pig. He keeps on and on and on at her, way past the stage when that feels funny or even normal. And next thing, she's bawling her eyes out.

Because even though she's just a kid, she can sense, you know, that he's being bloody weird.'

The word puts her hackles up. 'Oh come on. I'm sure he didn't mean to make her cry. At least he's joining in. He's just trying to play with her. I think it's quite sweet, really.'

'I don't find him sweet,' says Charlie. 'I just find him weird. And I don't want him hanging round Ruby.'

'He's her uncle. The only one she's got.'

Charlie's face looks grim. She is sure that when they first met he was set differently, more loosely. She doesn't know where the clip and clamp of him came from. She has no idea how he got to be like this, and how she failed to notice it happening.

'For Christ's sake, Jess. This isn't helping him. You know that. He's got to learn to make a life for himself. He can't just come and piggyback on us. He has an allowance, after all. Let him find a flat. He's not destitute, is he? Well, is he?'

She doesn't know. He might be, she supposes. He might have spent it all, be in hock to someone. In fact, it's quite possible that he owes someone money, somewhere along the line. It's happened before.

'In fact, he bloody *has* a flat. Didn't he buy a studio in Balham when he got his lump sum from the trust? What's happened to that? Is it rented out? Jesus, Jess. How long is he going to be here? I mean, what's he planning on doing?'

'For God's sake, keep your voice down. Try and be a tiny bit sympathetic.'

When Charlie goes upstairs, she looks for Ro in the garden. The evening has turned cool, and the wind has caught the high leaves of the chestnuts on the other side of the gate.

She finds Ro leaning against the blue wall, and goes to stand next to him. It feels companionable, and they remain there for a while, side by side like in the old days, until Sparrow is the first to move away. She broaches the subject casually.

'Have you thought about what you want to do, Ro? A course maybe? You could take the bus to Wandsworth and see what they're offering. A guy I used to know, he—'

He levels his eyes at her, and she is reminded how very pale they are. Paler than hers. Paler than almost any eyes she's ever seen. Swedish eyes. Maya drifts across Jess's mind until she blinks her away. She wonders where those eyes came from. What dalliance with the invader. She wonders what else has come in with the blood.

'You could think about woodwork, maybe. Remember that thing you made? The little house?'

'It was a kennel.'

'Oh yes, of course it was.'

'For Puzzle.'

Puzzle was Auntie Rae's dog, a wild little mongrel. She remembers Ro struggling home from school one holiday, a thick green bin bag over his shoulder. He spent the entire weekend assembling the sections he'd cut in woodwork class, then painting the little kennel in carefully applied stripes from dregs of old paint he found in the shed. He's probably never had a dog of his own.

He can't have done, with all that travelling. Maybe she should get a puppy, with the Common just outside. Ruby would love that. But Ro has turned away now, and she can't tell if she's insulted him or if it's just the wrong suggestion.

'Or a cocktail course, maybe? In case you wanted to take up—'

'It's not the right time,' he says.

'I'm pretty sure they do summer courses, too,' she says, but he keeps on moving.

'That's not what I meant.'

'If it's about the passport—'

He stops then, and turns around.

'It's not about the passport. It's about my mother.'

'Ah,' she says.

'I mean, it's obvious now. With her living around the corner.'

'What are you talking about? *Who* are you talking about, even?' And then she gets it. 'Not Maya, I hope . . . Oh, you are kidding me. I thought that was just a passing whim.' And though she is showing him frustration and disbelief, not worry or fear, she is much more fearful than she's letting on.

'It's her, isn't it?'

'Of course it isn't her.' She won't get anywhere with him while he's in this mood, so she changes tack.

'What happened to the flat on Stinton Street? It *was* Stinton Street, wasn't it? You had it with some agency, didn't you?'

He mutters something about people kipping there.

She doesn't ask him why he doesn't kip there too because that would be unkind and she doesn't want to be unkind to Ro. She knows that she's the lucky one. Despite Charlie and his secrets, whatever might happen on the Sixth Floor, she is still the lucky one.

'But you'll want the flat yourself, Ro, won't you? If you're planning to settle back in London.'

He looks sheepish, then defiant. 'I got rid of it.'

'You sold the flat?'

'How else do you think I manage to live like this? Keep on top of things, follow sightings halfway round the world?'

She is teetering on the brink of saying something she regrets. 'Look, Ro, I've had a really shit day at work. I'm just going to go upstairs for a while. OK?'

In their bedroom, Charlie is propped up on a pillow and scrolling down his iPad.

'Did you tell him his days are numbered?'

When she doesn't answer, he looks up, then throws the iPad to one side. 'Oh Jessie, you've got to tell him he can't stay. You've got way too much on your plate. One toddler already, you don't need another one. As for work—'

'That's another thing we need to talk about. I'm in the doghouse, Charlie. I mean, in the shit, really. I had to leave early because Han— oh, it doesn't matter why. A meeting, a client. It wasn't good. And now it's disciplinary procedures, all that.'

'Is that Miles Rennie again?' he asks. 'Anyone would think he had it in for you. Prick.'

She should have told him. But it is too late to bring it up now, the garden full of fragrance, her terrible disabling fear.

'I think they need me, though. That's the thing. I don't know how they'd manage if they lost me.'

'He's a bastard, Jess. I'd watch him. Doesn't fancy you, does he? Because it sounds like he's getting off on putting you down.'

That takes her aback, and for the first time she wonders what Charlie is like at work, how he is to women. She's never considered that before, and she'd rather not go there. Instead, she adopts a lighter tone, as if none of this matters, as if her job is a frippery she can afford to cast away.

'Oh, you know what it's like. If the client complains, well—'

'I'm sure you're overreacting.' He pats her leg. 'You don't make mistakes.'

His eyes have shifted back to the iPad and she can tell he's trying to find the right moment to get back to it without being rude.

She reaches over his knees and hands it to him. 'Here. Check your emails.'

He has the grace to look embarrassed. 'Have you eaten, by the way? There's some of that pasta bake Hana makes. I left it in the oven.'

But she doesn't feel like eating, and certainly not Hana's pasta bake. She glances at the clock radio. It's not even nine yet. 'It's OK. Thanks, though.'

He stretches out his hand and takes hers, but his eyes are still on the screen. 'New York's going ahead. God knows how long that will take.'

She is reckoning on as much as a fortnight – two weeks away from Hana – and feels a little twinge of satisfaction. 'We'll manage,' she says. 'Ro might even be a help.'

'Dream on.' Charlie is tapping out something on the iPad. He pauses and looks up at her. 'I'm going to have to take the red-eye tomorrow. You'll be OK, yeah? Just get Hana to do overtime whenever you need her.'

'I'm not sure Hana's that keen on overtime.'

'I'll have a word.'

'*You*'ll have a word?'

He doesn't catch her tone, or if he does he chooses to ignore it. 'Sure. I'll tell her we'd appreciate it if she could be extra flexible while I'm away. Anyway,' he says, 'the one you really need to sort out is your brother.'

She ignores that remark. They both work on their laptops for a while and later, when it's time to sleep, he kisses her chastely on the cheek, then moves as far away from her as possible into the vast white tundra of their bed. In the silence and the dark, she realises she is jealous of his trip. Before she had Ruby, travelling was something she did too, zipping herself into other lives, seeing places she'd never have thought of visiting were it not for work.

On her last trip to Algiers before Ruby was born, the afternoon meetings cancelled, she decided to leave the artificial sphere of the hotel, with its orange trees and carefully whitewashed walls. She walked up the avenue lined with clumps of oleander and just as she reached the gate one of the staff, uniformed in Arabian Nights garb teamed with an unlikely purple fez, stepped in front of her and asked if she was leaving. He mentioned that most guests took a driver who could bring them to all places of interest within the city.

'No,' she'd said. 'I'm fine. I can walk.'

The road deteriorated quickly and soon her unsuitable business shoes were kicked over with a reddish dust. Down below, the city spread out like an intricately stacked puzzle of whitish squares and oblongs interrupted now and then by a narrow tubular minaret. The bay was generous and blue and she knew there would be a corniche along it. There was always a corniche. There would be men standing aimlessly here and there in clumps, or playing backgammon at bars that weren't actually bars at all but cafés selling small cups of strong, gritty coffee. She imagined there would be a pastry shop, some French patisserie where she could buy a gift to bring back to the office. Tiny fruits made of marzipan, buttery little biscuits.

As she walked further from the hotel, she realised that she wasn't used to being shut out from the sense of a place. She had no idea what the signs said, for instance, no idea where she was going other than that she was heading towards the sea. But it was really only when the streets grew narrower that she began to realise it wasn't the custom here for people to wander about on their own, by which she meant women, of course.

She was out of place and vulnerable. She started to think about her mother, and to allow herself to skirt the worst fears that had plagued her once. By the time she heard the car pull up next to her and realised that this wasn't someone come to lock her in a cave but one of the costumed flunkeys from the hotel, she was pathetically grateful. On the way back, his eyes glanced up now and then at the rear-view mirror. He didn't say anything until the gates swung slowly open.

'What if you had been taken?' he asked. 'What if you had disappeared out of sight?'

He couldn't have known, of course, and the poor man was horrified to have caused her such distress. She found herself weeping uncontrollably, submerged by an image she had spent much of her childhood attempting to shift – her mother in a basement somewhere, chained to a wall, and men who came now and then and did things to her that she didn't understand other than that they were terrifying and unspeakable.

It had been humiliating to become so terrified by a walk into town, to have fear lie so close to her skin. She was not the kind of orphan Sparrow was. She wasn't freed up by it like a boy with a raft on the Mississippi or a book of spells or a cape. She was made diligent by it, cautious. She had been turned into a locker of doors.

As she lies there, with Charlie just out of reach, her mind helicopters between the back gate and the Sixth Floor and Ro's obsessions. She thinks about Miles Rennie and how he has a mission now. It's intolerable just to lie there doing nothing about any of these things, and so she forces herself out of bed and up the stairs into the attic room where her desk is.

As soon as she is up, she realises that there is nothing

that can be done. All she can do is displace her worries for a while. She sits in front of the blue screen of her laptop, and it soothes her, that screen. It presents her with options, pleasant situations in which to place her little family, new versions of herself brought to possibility by a random purchase. Tonight, it is a picnic rug, some place in Scotland that weaves in limes and heathers and soft pinks, new colours in the old tartans. She clicks, and is calm. But unease follows her back down the stairs and she is still awake, flat on her back in the dark, an hour later and an hour after that.

Someday, she wonders, will she look at that rug laid out on the crisp summer grass of the Common or flung over the arm of the sofa, and remember this night? Will she remember today as a day on which she bought a lime and pink rug, or as the day she crushed a rose in her fist?

Ro is up just after dawn. He passes silently through the house, then out the door into the greyish light. As he reaches the Common, a small, bent man in overlong trousers is picking out his path as if selecting things to spear with his stick. Overtaking him, Ro has the sense that he is seeing his ancient solitary self.

They are renovating the bandstand. Overnight, a sign has gone up. Lottery funding. Friends of the Common. Two rows of crash barriers surround it, and there are sheets of thick plastic draped over the structure itself to keep the rain off the ridged, jelly-mould dome. Already, someone has taken a pneumatic drill to the concrete paving.

He strides on past the shuttered café across the flat expanse of green towards the school. He wants to get there long before the teachers arrive, to find the best vantage point on the forecourt, the narrow in/out drive. There is a bench opposite the school and that's where he waits.

Slung over the railing that separates the Common from the busy road, he notices a workman's abandoned high-vis gilet. He tries it on and immediately he belongs. He remembers then about the camouflage there is in being obvious. If only he had a prop with him – an attribute for this new persona he has adopted, for Sparrow Considine, road sweeper. One of those grippers, perhaps, for picking up litter. But the nod he gets from a man with a backpack, the smile from a woman with a pram, makes him realise the gilet alone is enough to transform him from a loner loitering outside a school to a man who's paid to be there.

Bolder now, he breaks both his rules on visibility. He stands stock-still in the middle of the pavement and waits. He almost misses his mother in her small, silver woman's car with its comical sad face. When she slows down for the entrance, however, he spots her long blondish-greyish plait, the soft sweep of her face. She has pulled out from the side road onto the main drag, her hand flapping out the window to show that she's about to pull in. There is a bracelet on her wrist. And he thinks he might remember a bracelet – a cool slide against his skin.

Now that he knows the reg of her car, and where she parks it, he can keep tabs on her. And keeping tabs is the start of action. The thought of action makes him light-headed, delirious. Soon, his spirit is rising high above that boy of a man in his high-vis jacket, way above the level of the roofs and even the oldest chestnuts. From up here, the little world down there is child's play – the white-fronted school with its Smartie-box columns and its red and white toy minibuses, the bandstand with the high-vis ants – it all seems manageable for once. Up here, he is Superman and Batman and any number of orphans turned superhero. He is both avatar and player; as he soars above the 4X4s, and the Waitrose lorries and the number 35 and 37 buses, he can see the future begin to play itself out.

He can discern the matrix of streets he knows by heart from summers spent patrolling on a bicycle, practising his navigational skills for all the journeys he would one day make – Renoir, Sisley, Stuckfield, Renishaw, Stubbs. He can see the football pitches and the skate park and the café. And, over on the very edge of the Common, something he'd forgotten about – the old half-derelict changing rooms. Boarded up now, what, twenty years? And, like the superhuman it's become, his avatar swoops down again to join his high-vis self.

It takes Ro about ten minutes on foot to reach the place, past rectangles burned into the grass by disposable barbeques, through a double row of trees whose arms are stretched in supplication to the dusty sky. The building itself is surrounded by a fence made of fragile larchlap strips, degraded by weather and lack of maintenance. At the far corner, three or four of the boards have fallen away to leave a hole just big enough to let him through, should he dare. Next to the fence is an antiquated contraption equipped with rotating brushes for cleaning boots. He stands there a moment, gazing at the stubborn, yellow head of a dandelion while he decides what to do.

A girl comes jogging past. She stops just next to him to take a call, and he can hear her talking macarons, and how come the pistachio ones are such a weird shade of green. She sees him standing there and, though he doesn't think he looks as if he's listening, she turns away. He decides then that if he doesn't make himself part of the scenery, she will remember him. He can't afford to be remembered and so he gets up on the contraption, which looks like something you might find in the Torture Museum, and scrubs his trainers back and forward on the brushes. She nods at him before jogging off, as if she's mistaken him for a member of her club. The club of healthy participators. He stays there, scrubbing away, until the girl is out of sight.

When he takes a closer look, he realises there is work to do. He would have to create a proper entrance; you couldn't ask a woman of her age to squeeze herself through a gap in the fence. And she would be afraid of things. Of rats and spiders. Of hobos hiding out in the undergrowth. Of people pressing flesh under the chestnuts. She might even be afraid of him, at least at first. He would need to kit it out, make it into a reassuring, homely place.

The building might be a derelict changing block, but

whoever designed it made it look like a red-brick cottage, borderline gingerbread, its central door flanked by four-paned windows that might be made of barley sugar. Were it not for the absence of a chimney, a curved path up to a shiny front door, this could almost be the house that all kids draw, that perfect haven. But it is not that house; the brick is stained and there are flourishes of graffiti around the windows, with love hearts and WOZ HEREs scratched into the brick. There are certainly no roses around the door. The roof looks like it is made of corrugated metal beneath a battened-down tarp. He pulls back the loose slats in the fencing and squeezes himself through. On the other side, a patch of long grass and dandelions surrounds the building, the cottage that is.

There are two entrances – that central door and another one to the side. The main door is secured by a stainless-steel bolt, too large and brutal-looking for the task. Although perhaps such things are necessary, since some-one has plainly tried to wrench it off. On the side entrance there is just an old-style lock. When he puts his shoulder to it, the wood comes away in sodden lumps of splintered pulp until the whole door gives. And it's as easy as that to find a place to put his mother.

Once inside, he thinks spores, asbestos, poisoned air. Little light penetrates, although the grimy windows have not been boarded up, but are covered in a thick plastic film, yellowish, with a criss-cross pattern, as if the cottage was only shut up temporarily and then forgotten about. The single room is lined with pegs and benches, the main source of light a gaping hole in one flank of the building where a wooden hatch cut into the brick has rotted away and fallen into the weedy grass.

He can just about make out something in the middle of the floor. At first, he thinks it might be a dead rat, but it turns out to be an ancient football boot. Further in, there is a jumble of empty cans – Red Stripe, Stella – and bottles of Lidl whisky. Outside the wooden hatch, there are the remains of a fire, or perhaps of many fires, corralled inside a circle of rubble and brick. For obvious reasons, he won't build a fire, but he will need to find some way of generating heat, light, food. He will need to make the place safe and warm. Warmth will be important.

He senses something move behind him, a kind of shifting sound, but he turns and there is nothing there, or nothing visible, at least. He feels a whisper at his neck, the shallow wheeze of Mags, come to pour poison in his ear. He turns his back on her, light-headed with the sense that he is standing on the threshold between how things are and how they might turn out to be. This is no changing room. Despite the lack of roses, this is a cottage. His cottage, not Mags's. Theirs. Leaving it, his mind is so full of images that it's like leaving a cinema in the middle of the day.

He powers across the Common without any thought as to where he's going until the world rematerialises around him and he finds himself on a road that heaves ahead of him with its own sense of destination – surging down into a valley, then sweeping up into a matching hill on the other side. From where he is standing, there is no way of seeing to the end of that road, no way of discerning what might lie beyond its sink and swell. And the fear of never knowing seizes him again. Unless he acts, he might never know what happened on that beach.

Down in the valley, the road is lined with the kinds of places where Jess likes to shop – twenty different kinds of olives, tasteful black and white photographs of local landmarks, focaccia with *fines herbes* frittata and Camembert. He looks in through the window of a craft beer place, and for a moment he can't quite work out who is outside and who is in. A dark shadow moves across the glass like a floater on an eye – a silhouette of a woman on a bike. His rational mind assures him that a woman on a moving bike could not be inside the restaurant and yet he has no idea where the membrane might be that separates this space from that. He wonders if it exists at all or if everything is permeable, and all things possible. They are all there, more or less, and they are all in some way real, but which is his reality and which belongs inside that burger bar he really has no idea. In fact, he is beginning not to care about such distinctions. He is starting to discern that letting go of what the world calls reality will be a kind of liberation.

When he first went away to school, he used to comfort himself from the deep well of his imagination in which he was a boy alone in the world whose magic powers were as yet undiscovered. He conjured up a kind of Dumbledore with a large ragged book. Inside that book, images of his mother could be animated at the touch of a finger – an iPad before such things existed. And this wizard promised that one day he would allow Ro to see his mother, though she would not be able to see him. He would be able to watch her eating, for instance, perhaps with a new family. She might be dancing or playing a guitar. He would even find out where she was. The story would be told and it would be true and it would be up to him to act on it or not. But he had to promise not to flinch when he heard the truth, no matter how hard it was.

He remembers the feel of his mother's hand outside the school, and the little rasp to it. It reminds him that she already has a life among everyday things that she may not want to change. It tells him what he has always suspected. If he wants his mother back, he is going to have to take her.

His throat is parched at the thought of all that lies ahead, and he stops off at a corner café with blond wood shelves bearing rows of oils and biscotti and teas. How could there be so many teas? The ceiling is a tangle of taut copper wires that bloom into an overgrowth of Edisons. The tables glow with Apples. A crying child distracts him, and the next time he looks up, it's as if everything has changed up there, the lights striking glints from different bottles. He slurps the dregs of his coffee, and as he tilts the cup back and sucks in the foam he feels as if those bulbs are trained on him.

The girl is small, blonde. She is wearing high heels and a pale pink sweater, and looks a bit like Pia. Her hair swarms on her shoulder as she settles herself on the long bench to his right. He wonders how heavy she is, how determined she would be to put up a fight. Her thin bum hardly covers half the width of the bench. He could take her, but not without attracting attention. The girl would cry out, she might even scream. But he plays the moment in his head anyway.

He imagines crossing that stained expanse of oak flooring, past the jam jars with their caps of paper lace and the clustered flasks of tap water by the till. The girl is engrossed in the blue glow of her phone. He imagines knocking against her as she's getting up to leave and hustling her out the door. Or just scooping her up with one arm around her waist, and making off with her. But where would he take her? He is Jack without a beanstalk and she is surrounded by allies – boys with beards and beanies, girls with retro tastes plugged, one ear only, to the Smiths. When the girl has finished her coffee and gets up to leave, Ro is ready for her. She slings a backpack up over her shoulder with one hand as she thumbs down through Facebook with the other.

He exits just behind her. When she turns right towards the Common, so does he. They pass the copse of trees where everything darkens. Although she doesn't turn right around to check him out, he thinks her glances to the side are deep enough to take him in. Once they're out of sight of the road, he launches himself towards her. As she whips around, he perceives the glint of metal in her hand. And as the key makes for his eye, he dodges. But not quite quickly enough. She jabs at him, just the once, and then she runs.

He turns his jacket inside out as he's seen done in the movies, and walks smartly off in the opposite direction. His eye is stinging, but the damage is slight. He can feel where she's scraped a wound into his eyelid, but the eye itself still functions. He feels strangely blank about it. He's glad he didn't hurt the girl. He's almost glad she got away. What would he have done if he'd got her? He feels no anger towards her, no desire. He has nowhere he could take her. He hadn't even covered his face. It was an experiment, that's all, and he's lucky that it failed.

The siren probably has nothing to do with him, but he tacks off across the Common anyway. On a dog-free paddock of mown green, a woman has set up a trestle table with an old-fashioned flowery tablecloth. She has hung pastel bunting from the trees, pink and primrose yellow and the palest of blues, and fat bunches of balloons trail ribbons onto a corral of cool boxes and picnic hampers. He looks at her for a long while. She catches his eye, and keeps busying herself with removing paper cups and plates from a large wicker bag. He knows she's aware of him, that he is making her nervous, but he doesn't look away. He feels a tide of envy for this woman's children, two tiny blond boys in Chelsea shirts, tumbling over a football. He is heartbroken never to be a child again.

As he turns away, he realises that smash and grab is the wrong method for capturing a mother and her love. He needs a pretext tailored to the target. *Can you help? There's been an accident or a mother looking for her child or a mother looking for a child who's had an accident. Do you have a heart?*

But even if the pretext worked and he was able to persuade her towards the Common, she isn't likely to let him lead her all the way. What then?

He'd need to knock her out, that's what. No blows to the head, not for his mother. No violent assaults. He needs a kinder method of oblivion. He's thinking nineteenth century, a hankie to the mouth, a swoon. Can you purchase chloroform online? Do they even make it any more? He doesn't know but he means to find out because that would be the gentle, silent business.

11

It is mid-morning when a message beeps in on Jess's phone.

'Happy to accommodate your request to bring the meeting forward. Miles can make three. Would that suit? Don't forget that you're entitled to have a friend in attendance.'

A friend? The word alarms her in its assumption that she will be otherwise friendless. In the belated realisation that she should be taking this much more seriously than she has been doing, she calls Sarah's extension, then her direct line, then her mobile. She messages her, sends emails to work and home, but Sarah doesn't answer. Out in the PAs' pod, there are *Bake Off* brownies, but she hasn't got the stomach. 'Anyone know where to reach Sarah Phelps?'

But it seems Sarah has gone home sick. She almost asks one of the PAs to come along, to bring the brownies while she's at it. But they all do occasional work for Miles; it would be putting them in an impossible situation. And so, when she heads for the lift, Jess is on her own.

When the lift doors slide open, Miles is already in there and she has to share the lift with her executioner. They stand in silence as a faint strain of piano music circles overhead. Chopin. She is almost on the other side without having had to mount the scaffold. She allows herself a smile and then she catches Miles's eye and it's clear that smiling isn't on the agenda today. She has come across as flippant. The abandonment of a client? The assassination of a rose? They are hardly capital offences. But smiling won't do.

In the Sixth-Floor conference area, the woman behind the desk exchanges greetings with Miles and looks straight through Jess, and it seems only moments later that they are walking down the corridor a foot apart and into a meeting room with a wall of windows looking out on St Paul's from behind a stretch of lavender and box hedging.

He has got it all – dates, times, stats. He is able to show that she is heading for a huge write-off on the Grosvenor deal, though of course that doesn't show the true picture, where the resources she was given to deal with the work agreed were ridiculously inadequate. She forces a defiant smile onto her face as she watches a blue-bottle move efficiently across the window. Because she will not show him how this feels.

'There will be a compromise agreement, of course,' says the woman from HR.

'Of course.'

Jess is calculating the value of a lump sum over the cost of trying to defend herself, not to mention the mental agony involved.

The woman from HR looks bemused. She pulls her skirt down over her knees. Jess guesses that people usually put up more of a fight, but she knows that she has given Miles the whip hand. The morning after the Summer Party, she should have nailed him for assault, sexual harassment, the lot. In a place like this, charity is weakness.

Miles has left the best wine till last. He has found the error she didn't even realise she'd made. A Sale and Purchase Agreement from earlier in the year in which the IP was worthless, and yet no disclosures were made to that effect. As it happens, it's a dead letter; the product in question is out of date, so the intellectual property would be effectively worthless now anyway. But it's the principle that counts. She made an omission that could have been very costly to both the client and the firm, and so her competence is open to question. Miles couldn't have known it, but this is his trump card. She would never be able to admit to Charlie that she was negligent, and so this is the very accusation she will never contest. She will take the pay-off and go.

Before the meeting is brought to a close, she turns to the woman from HR. 'I don't hope to call this in aid for my own case. But I'd like to make a statement for you to have on file about Mr Rennie and an incident at the Summer Party.'

The woman sits up in her seat and glances at Miles. 'Would you care to elaborate?' she asks Jess.

'It was an assault. Mr Rennie assaulted me.'

'Oh come on.' Miles is consulting his watch in an

exaggerated manner, as if to say he is much too busy for this.

But the HR woman looks concerned. In fact, she looks as if Jess has just ruined her week. 'Would you like to talk about it now, Jess?'

'No thanks. I'm just flagging it so you know to expect a statement.'

Miles's face has reddened. He sits forward in his chair as if he might launch himself out of it. 'Of course she doesn't want to talk about it because it never bloody happened.'

'Please moderate your language,' the HR woman says.

'How do you expect me to react when I'm accused of assault? My God, it's pathetic,' he says, shaking his head. 'Typical. If you're in the shit, cry—'

'I don't need to remind you of the seriousness of an allegation like this, Jess.' The HR woman cuts across him.

'No,' Jess says. 'You don't. I'm going to make a statement, and I want it put on Mr Rennie's file. But don't worry, I'm not intending to try to keep my job.'

'The compromise agreement will stipulate that you withdraw any claims against the firm,' the woman says.

Miles sits back in his seat, looking gleeful.

'In that case, I won't sign it.'

'Then there'll be no payment.'

'So be it.'

They don't leave the meeting together, Jess and her executioner. But he looks chastened, scared almost, as he sits on with the HR woman and Jess walks out the door. She had expected that someone would accompany her back to her desk. It has entered into office folklore, that walk of death. She is about to reach the end of the corridor when her escort finally appears. She recognises him from reception, a guy she passes the time of day with every other morning. But he doesn't meet her eye today, and she guesses he is angry with her for forcing this situation on him. He slips into the lift beside her, just as the doors are sliding shut. And so she has a chaperone after all.

Back on the Fourth Floor, she passes the pod of PAs. Kerry glances up at her and then at the security guard. She makes an 'eek' face and mouths 'Sorry'. Liz offers to come and help her clear her desk. But the security guard says that's what he's there for. He says it quite nicely really, and the women hang back. All the partners have vanished. She can't help thinking they are avoiding the area for the half-hour or so it will take for her to leave the building. Once they have passed the barrier at the lifts, the security guard leaves her. She hands over her pass to Mel on reception.

'You have got to be kidding me,' Mel says, grabbing a handful of tissues from the box she keeps beneath the counter. 'What a fucking shithouse.'

Jess hadn't even realised she was crying. She doesn't feel pain or sadness. She feels furious – with herself, with Miles, with Charlie, with Ro, with the whole world.

'I'm on my break in twenty minutes if you feel like a coffee,' Mel says. 'We could go across the road?'

But Jess needs to get away. She feels curiously ashamed to be here, where she no longer belongs. Walking across the plaza, the buildings all seem taller, more impregnable, than before. She's been banished and all she wants is to be somewhere she isn't reminded of that. But then the shame is blotted out by panic. Her heart drops in her chest when she realises that the worst has happened – unless she gets another job very soon, they will not be able to stay in the house.

Once she's left the Tube, she walks home past the bandstand café, but the Common is no comfort to her today. Groups of women are sitting at pigeon-haunted tables under the huge chestnut tree. Some are cooing over babies, shovelling puree into sparrow mouths. Others breastfeed ostentatiously. She tries to picture herself there, maybe even pregnant again, but the thought of losing an independent life terrifies her. And yet, that's all she has now. The bastion of Charlie and Ruby is all there is. She has a momentary vision of Delia, striding across the concourse outside the offices, and her cheeks flush. Delia is the person she always thought she would become. There is no other template, and she is bereft.

There's a sprinkling of men at the café, too, sitting singly with their toddlers. Men in open-necked polo shirts, their chinos worn high at the waist. They seem harassed, unmanned. One man is redder than the sun could have made him. He is like a scalded chicken. The baby with him doesn't notice the colour of his face. She doesn't know that green glass bottle he is necking doesn't contain juice. She doesn't smell the alcohol, but Jess does and Jess feels the man's desperation as if it were her own.

Back at the house, there is no Hana, no Ruby either. But Ro is there. He gets the look she normally reserves for Ruby, a sweeping glance that takes in everything. She notices a cut, just above the eye. No more than a scrape really. As a child, he was always covered in cuts and bruises. He blinks at her, bites his lip and she knows that he's remembering too. He leaves the room, and she can hear him pissing in the loo next door. A man all right. But still a child too.

She shudders to think of the harm he used to do himself. Poor little Sparrow, pale and blank-eyed at the remembrance service Rae arranged for their mother, soon after their father's funeral, to ensure that Sophie wasn't forgotten. Ro was standing at the granite ledge where they had placed the items they wished to remember their mother by – her guitar, of course, a tortoiseshell hair clip, a jar of cornflowers because she loved them. Rae had tried to get Ro to participate, perhaps by carrying up the little jar of flowers, but he turned towards a column, hooking his finger into the stone and scratching away at it. When nothing resulted from his efforts, he began whipping at the column with his knuckles. Jess understood what he was trying to do because he had whispered to her that he wanted to take away the bits of bright. But no matter how hard he picked at the shiny specks, they wouldn't detach themselves. When Auntie Rae began to read from *The Prophet* he started to burrow at the granite ledge with his forehead, as if trying to take himself away from all this and into the stone. Later, at their aunt's house, she found him picking bits of mica off the pebble dash on the sunny side of the house, the side that faced the flat green garden. He was picking off the stones and putting them in his pocket. When she asked him why, he said it was so that he would always be able to remember how this day had felt.

And then she realised he had come to understand that even sunny days might need to be remembered, that adults might expect you to recall a thousand random things that had seemed unimportant at the time.

When she came back later, though, he was at the wall again, working at the patch from which he had removed the stones, headbutting it as if trying to work his way inside. She pulled him away, and put her arms around him. And for a few moments he let her hold him. But even then she could feel his heart thrashing, the rush of his breath. It was like trying to still a bird.

Years later, she would hear of girls who'd slashed at themselves to feel a sense of release. And she would think of Sparrow, miles away in boarding school. She would worry about what he might be doing to himself, surrounded by boys who liked to run and shout, hitting out at balls, trees, whatever. How she worried about Sparrow, with his pale, vague eyes and his habit of banging his head on sharp-edged things.

The loo flushes, and he is back with her again.

'What happened to your eye?' she asks.

He looks away from her. 'What happened to your job?'

She feels her eyes smart, but he walks past her to the bread bin. The sky might just have fallen in, but for Ro it's all about carbs.

He draws up heels of half-eaten loaves and flings them away. 'Any bread in?'

'As a matter of fact, I've just been fired.' She feels her mouth begin to distort.

Ro looks at her steadily. He makes no attempt to comfort her. 'No tears for Mama,' he says. 'But a whole torrent for the job. Oh well.'

It's so unfair she feels like lashing out at him. And then she has another thought. And it's the one that's been lying there dormant under everything else. She should be telling the police that he's here. She really should.

'Have you spoken to Eddie?' he asks.

'Why?'

'We need to discuss my mother.'

'She's mine too, Ro.'

'Well, you don't believe in her, do you?'

'For God's sake, she's not Santa Claus. You've invited yourself here, Ro, but you're not telling me the truth. I know you're not.' She can't bring herself to take it any further. He starts to scratch at that arm of his, and then he turns away from her.

'You shouldn't ask me questions you don't want to know the answers to. You shouldn't do that.'

The horror she feels is really a kind of blankness. Everything has been erased. There is only this now. She needs more, she needs much much more, but she can't bring herself to ask for it. 'Hana and Ruby are at the shop,' he says then. 'I forgot to check the bread situation before they went.'

The kitchen door opens, and there they are. Hana

with bags of shopping, and Ruby clutching a little knitted alien. Hana's eyes narrow, as if she sniffs a kind of failure off Jess, a weakness she can work on. Once the shopping has been unloaded, the fridge re-stocked, Jess hunkers down next to Ruby who hands her brick after brick to be built into something unspecified. And then Hana joins them and, because Hana knows the game better than Jess does, she wins when it comes to the wall. She wins full stop. The kitchen feels too small for the four of them, and Jess moves into the hallway. But that feels too eloquently appropriate, and so she goes up to her room.

Upstairs, Charlie has left her flowers – three or four plastic-wrapped bunches of waxy lilies in a large white vase she hasn't seen for months. Funeral flowers. She peels off the uncomfortable suit whose skirt has worn a red welt into her waistline, the tights, the silk shirt with the thin blue stripe; their jumble on the bedroom floor is like the remains of someone she used to be. She thinks of the witch who shrinks until all that's left is a puddle. In the wardrobe, she finds jeans, trainers, a sweater. The person she is now. She takes the vase in her arms and carries it downstairs. She finds a bucket just outside the kitchen doors, transfers the lilies to it and leaves the vase in the kitchen sink. And she's off out the door before anyone asks where she's going.

Outside, the sun is knifing across the Common and, on days like this, it looks like the kind of place where nothing bad could ever happen. She wonders again if she should get a dog, now that she's to be at home. Don't kids like dogs? Perhaps everything would be normal if she had a dog.

She walks through one section of the Common, then another, and almost as far as a third. Right down a long road choked with traffic and back again. She goes as far as to call up Crowe's number on her phone, but as she rehearses her spiel, she finds she still doesn't know what to say. Ro would have told her about Curramona, if he had been there. He might be keeping something else from her, but she's sure he would have told her that.

She sits on a bench looking out on a playground as if she might decipher what kind of mother Sophie might have been from watching others. Her mobile rings as she's sitting there and she is immediately guilty when she sees that it is Charlie and hears the tension in his voice and realises that she'd completely forgotten that he'd gone away. The sound of his voice causes her to feel such a mixture of relief, embarrassment, shame that she isn't able to answer him at first.

'Jess? You still there?'

'More or less.'

'You OK?'

'I've been fired.'

She wonders if she'll be able to admit that to anyone else. It is hard enough to tell Charlie. She can't bear to be thought less than she should have been. It seems to confirm the seriousness of their predicament when she hears the catch in his breath.

She doesn't fill the silence, and he has the grace to do that for her. He quickly corrects himself. 'Well, I guess lemons, lemonade. At least Ruby will be delighted,' as if Ruby is a senior colleague who needs to show approval.

He is insisting on silver linings. No more rush-hour Tube journeys wedged into some bloke's armpit, no more fucking clients. 'We'll manage, Jess. Good for you. You deserve a bit of me time.'

'Me time? What planet are you on, Charlie? Do you think the tooth fairy paid the mortgage, or was that the fairy godmother?'

'All it takes is a bit of luck with the CFDs, and we'll be fine. I'll go large on sterling. Just wait and see.'

'Whatever fantasy you're clinging on to, we're still going to need my salary.'

He has now riled her in various different ways in just a few sentences. But he doesn't stop there. 'You know how you've always wanted her to have a proper mother? Now's your chance. You'll be freeing up a bit of Hana's time, too, so maybe she could take on a bit more admin. She'd still be good to have around.'

She cuts him off; she can always blame the Common and the terrible reception. No sooner has she dispatched Charlie than Sarah calls. 'I heard, Jess. One of the PAs called to tell me. God, that's grim. I'm so, so, sorry.'

She is almost expecting Sarah to be ringing to apologise for letting her take on more work than she should have done, which is unreasonable of course, ridiculous.

'Look, I hope you don't think this is a bit presumptuous, but I emailed Delia. She's absolutely furious about what happened. But, you know how it is, she's not in the office right now. She'll have to talk to Miles and to HR so . . . In the meantime, I've been in touch with a friend of mine who might be able to help. Just in case things don't work out with, well just in case. Sally has an agency. She's only just starting out but she's really good. I filled her in on your experience and she's pretty sure . . .'

And Jess decides that's what she'll do. She will keep moving forward. But because she is not ready to speak to Charlie again, she switches off her phone and walks herself into a state of calm. By the time she heads back home, it is dusk. The sky seems backlit, mobile. It is like an exquisite silk – fierce blue, shot with purple – bordered by a frieze of silhouetted trees. Earlier, the Common felt as if it had drawn right in around her. Now, with a meeting set up for tomorrow afternoon, it has stretched back out again.

The next afternoon, Jess leaves the house dressed for work in her navy suit like one of those Japanese salarymen who can't forsake the briefcase. She is only gone half an hour when the knock comes at the door. Hana is in the back garden with the child, and Ro stands there for a moment in the hallway, the stairs streaming up behind him, a rhomboid of multi-jewelled light cast through the stained-glass panels and onto the tiled floor. Whoever it is ding dongs one, two, three, four times.

'Lazy pig, Sparrowman,' Hana shouts in at him from the garden. 'Open door.'

Eddie is leaning against the wall, his elbow propped against it. He doesn't step forward from the mat, not immediately, and Ro just waits. Once Eddie has made his move, Ro follows him into the kitchen. He concentrates on the back of Eddie's head, and the straggle of grey-gold hair surrounding a bald patch the colour of day-old pasta.

'She isn't here,' Ro says, but Eddie keeps on walking.

'It's you I've come to see,' Eddie says. He doesn't bother with preliminaries. Doesn't even sit down. 'I've come to knock things on the head,' he says, which is an unfortunate turn of phrase, all things considered. 'This is not an easy thing to say, Sparrow, but there's no happy ending here. I'm surprised you don't see that. Chances are a dealer killed your parents. They killed your dad, we already know that – or at least that's the working assumption. And I'm telling you now, those guys don't believe in leaving witnesses.'

He feels like laughing in the man's face, but Eddie isn't laughing.

'Look, there's any number of scenarios when it comes to that passport. Lost, stolen, sold.'

'So how does it wind up in Curramona, then?'

'Life is full of strange coincidences.'

'Oh come on!'

'You really think your mother wouldn't have been in touch with you if she'd survived?' He knows he's on to something here, Ro can tell, and he moves to press home his advantage. 'Your mother would never have walked away from you and Jess. It's impossible.'

Ro feels a prickling high in his sinuses and his ears are ringing with the effort it takes to hold back the tears. He could cry a salty sea right now. He could cry like he used to when they first came back to England, when he'd felt like he was the one doing the abandoning, leaving his parents a million miles away.

'All Will really cared about was his fix. Sorry, man. That's just how it was.'

Eddie glances at the breakfast bar, then opts for a seat at the table instead. He sits without being invited, as if it's just as much his place as Ro's. 'But it's not really to do with the kind of people they were. You know? Maybe they would have pulled through. If she'd managed to get him back to England, put him into rehab, he could be here today. Some prick in Lloyd's, whatever. I suspect whoever killed your father, killed her too. In fact, I'd say her body is somewhere near that beach, and they just haven't found it yet.'

He is talking as if this is about someone neither of them knows, and that angers Ro. But Eddie doesn't seem to notice, or even care.

'There's always the possibility that she drowned. There are currents there, rip tides. It's treacherous. Why do you think you were the only people at that end of the beach? It's not safe to swim there.'

'She didn't swim. I was there.'

'Oh come on, Sparrow. You were just a nipper. You had no idea what you saw or didn't see. Believe me, I tried to get some sense out of you. Not a clue. So actually, forget what I said earlier. I guess maybe it was to do with who they were, you know? A little bit. That recklessness they had. And my best guess is they were down on that isolated end of the beach because that's where Will could get his fix.'

Ro feels bludgeoned by it all. Because he can't seem to find the certainties he had just ten minutes ago. He starts casting around for them, but there are only shreds now.

'I saw it on her arm,' he says. 'The tattoo.'

Eddie knows right away who he's talking about. 'Maya's from Sweden, Sparrow. And she doesn't have a tattoo.'

Ro laughs at that, and his spittle sprays the surface in front of him. 'Not any more, she doesn't.'

'Never did.'

'Go on then. Just ask her. See what she says.'

'What's wrong with you, man? You want to ask her about some imaginary tattoo, then do it yourself.'

'Don't you worry, Eddie. I will.'

And Eddie looks at him for a moment, really looks, as if he might be beginning to take him seriously for a change. But it doesn't last. He thinks he's won the argument now and he's off on his favourite subject again, how they all were in Goa. 'So you mustn't blame those people who were hanging out with your parents for leaving when the shit hit the fan. They didn't want to get mixed up with the authorities. That's the kind of thing they'd run away from. They thought they were in paradise, man. You know? We all thought that. We didn't want to be told about the flaws, the dangers. We just didn't want to know. All we wanted was somewhere that was perfect. And you know what? Even if we'd found nirvana, we'd have ruined it. Your parents, they had no sense really – even less than I did myself. They were so First World, such spoilt brats.'

Ro has almost stopped listening when, out of nowhere,

the suggestion comes to him. He has no basis for it, not really. It's just a guess.

'But you were there, Eddie, weren't you? You were on the beach that day, too. I'm sure I saw you. After they went missing. That was you, moving in the trees.' He can't interpret the look on Eddie's face.

'Hell, man. You were a kid. What would you know? You've probably imagined a dozen different scenarios. That's cool, I get the need for imagination when a kid is trying to make sense of a bum deal. But don't put me there because I wasn't.'

Ro has never seen Eddie shaken before, but he is certain now that he has hit the nail on the head. 'Was Maya there, too?'

'Don't be ridiculous.'

'When did you and Maya meet?'

Eddie shrugs, as if to indicate that they are old souls, that it's a crass question, that in relationships like theirs there are no beginnings, and then he turns away. 'Your parents are dead, Sparrow. You should let them be.'

Apart from the incident with Mags, which was down to sheer provocation and not his fault at all, and excepting the woman in the alleyway (also provocation), and a couple of other times out of sheer necessity, Ro has never attacked anyone. He would not wound or cut or thump. He would not slice or hammer or flay. He would not kick or punch or bite. But Eddie gives him violent impulses. There, on the other side of the breakfast bar, this man is helping himself to coffee from Jess's machine. Ro can see what he's trying to do. He is trying to neutralise them both. Feeding honey to one and jam to the other to put them off the track. Telling lies to both. He wants to take the hippie by the throat and make him admit that, however he has managed it, he has stolen his mother and remade her as someone else.

'Maya and I got together much later. A marriage on, in fact. Sometimes it takes a while to find your soulmate. Don't worry, Sparrow. Your time will come.'

And then he smiles. And the way he pronounces that childhood nickname turns it into an insult, plain and simple. There is a wooden mallet in the ceramic pot at Ro's right elbow. Tenderise. He thinks of the bald patch, the yellowish scalp. He runs his finger on the diamond-sculpted head. That would do the job all right. But he's not that much of a fool. He's not a fucking idiot. 'I hear you're a bit of a celebrity round here. Got a reputation, Eddie. Eddie's Ice Cream – great draw for the kiddies, right?'

Oh yes, Ro thinks. The tongue is mightier by far.

Eddie sits there, all puffed up with pride, and waits for the kind of flattery he gets from Jess. 'Mango, coconut, pistachio. Make it all ourselves,' he says. 'Wouldn't believe the hoops you have to jump through. Health and safety, all that.'

'A word in the wrong ear at the right time could ruin a business like that.'

He stops then, and is very still. 'What are you saying, Sparrow?'

'Oh, you know. Some people will believe anything you choose to feed them. Two days in Goa when anything might have happened. Not that anything did, of course. But it might have done, Eddie. It might.'

Eddie has never struck him as a violent person before, or not especially. But Ro feels sure that if he keeps on pushing, he will expose a nerve in Eddie that will drive him from that side of the kitchen island over to this. And he wants to push, push, push so he can see what Eddie is, so he can have that much revealed at least.

'Next thing, there could be mothers warning kiddies off your ice cream. Stay away from Ed's, they'll say.'

Eddie is on his feet now. As he heads towards the door it's clear that he's not biting. He turns to face Ro. 'They keep upping the hygiene regs, but I've got that cracked now. As for anything else, Sparrow, don't ever feel that lies will soothe your pain.'

And it's frustrating to have an adversary who is so at home under his own skin.

'Do you live together then, yourself and—' He isn't keen on using the made-up name.

'Maya?'

'If you like.'

Eddie shakes his head at that, more in mock sorrow than in anger. 'We live together, yes.'

And he wants to ask if he could meet her privately – just the two of them. But why should Eddie be the one who decides if a man has access to his mother?

Eddie walks over to the bifold doors that open onto Jess's gravelled garden. He stands there a moment and raises his hand to Hana, or pretends to – Ro can't see from where he's sitting. And then he turns back into the room.

'She's done well,' he says, 'your sister. Jess isn't always trying to remake the world. She's a realist. I'd take a leaf.'

It isn't clear whether he's making a recommendation or just referring to himself. He turns then and walks towards the door. 'People have second passports all the time,' he says. 'It's no big deal. Her birth name, so what? She had a perfect right to that name. And even if someone did use it to get into the country, so what to that, too? Maybe they realised it made sense to chuck it afterwards, just in case. Who knows how it might have found its way home?' He turns around then to face Ro. 'Whatever, man. I wish you peace.'

Ro watches Eddie walk the length of the dark stretch of corridor between the kitchen and the gleaming hall, sauntering along as if he's got a right to be there. But of course it's all an act. Eddie came here when he knew that Jess would be out. He came to put the lid on Ro's suspicions. Unless, of course, Jess is in on it all, keeping him like a mushroom in the dark as she's always done. How he wishes he could switch people off and find their resting face, the place where the truth lies, before they get a chance to rearrange it. How to disable his mother long enough? How to keep her there until she gives the answers?

Ro takes the meat mallet from its jug and tests it against the back of his hand. The wooden spikes feel medieval. He lifts it like a hammer, just an inch or two, then lets it fall onto the back of his hand. The pain is not exactly pleasurable, but it does produce a sense of reality. He will try to keep that in mind. He will try to preserve the clarity of the look she gave him at the party, which was a look of recognition, he is sure. Now that he's found the cottage, he can see a way through. But, parked right in the middle of the Common in a red van, there is a problem. Eddie. He will have to find a way to get rid of Eddie. He barely realises that Hana has come back in from the garden, holding the baby by the hand. She edges past him, her eyes fixed on the mallet.

'You look like something from a film,' she says.

She has already left by the time he thinks to ask her which film. And even if he knew the film, he'd want to know which part. The boy who walked into the path of the lorry? Or the lorry driver who didn't stop? The abandoned boy? Or the shadow moving in the inky trees?

12

On his way to find Nefertiti in the café on the Common, he encounters a couple with matching quiffs who have let their dogs off the leash. Their Afghan hounds, all long-haired seventies chic, lollop across the golden gravel between the café and the bandstand. His father's lot were doggy people – beagles and lurchers. As a boy, he'd imagined being companion to a St Bernard, digging people out of avalanches and offering them brandy from a little barrel slung around the dog's neck. Thanks to Lady-bird, he's a bit of an expert when it comes to dogs. He glances back, and the seventies dogs are chasing one another, round and round the bandstand like a circus act.

A pigeon lands in front of him, harrying a discarded muffin. He only knows the obvious birds. Crows and magpies and pigeons. And sparrows of course. He doesn't know what a chaffinch looks like, or how it sounds. But there were birds on that beach, or in the trees at least. He's sure there were birds, flumping up into the trees.

In the café on the Common, it is summer in Sicily. Bottles of greenish olive oil, filled on the premises, tourist posters of shimmering seas, a pyramid of oranges ripe for squeezing. A bearded man in glasses peers into the chill cabinet where home-made cannoli filled with pistachio cream are lined up like fat slugs. Ro glances around for Nefertiti, but she isn't there. At the counter, a kid is being held up to the glass to select from speckled cupcakes, iced in half a dozen colours. Ro looks out at the bandstand and conjures birds he has no name for, then imagines them swooping and pecking with sharpened beaks at Eddie, at that U-shaped patch of scalp.

The doors from the kitchen swing open and there is Nefertiti – the black swipe of her eyes, the thick ropes of hair coiled up on the back of her head, the thin arms tattooed with thick rings of pigment and weighted down with bangles. When she spots him she stands back a little, does a double take, then has a chew on the little stud in her upper lip.

'What's up?' She sounds offhand, and there is a cough in her voice.

'Big news,' he says. 'I think I've found my mother.'

Her wiry little tattooed arms are working away on stretching circles of mozzarella and salami over puffy oblongs of ciabatta, twisting and clanking and tapping at the coffee machine that is steaming and frothing by her side.

'Uh-huh?' she says.

He knows she doesn't believe him, which is a pity. He has imagined Nefertiti taking care of his captive mother. She would be good at that.

'You around later, Nef?' he says.

She does that double take of hers again. 'Amanda, remember? But yeah, I suppose I could be around.'

And with the surge of satisfaction that gives him, there are the beginnings of a plan.

He plugs himself into Jon Hopkins as he walks back towards Jess's house. But Jon isn't in tune with how he's feeling now, with this new mellow vibe. To match this heart of his gone green, he finds some piano music. Chopin, to make him float. And as he passes under the great avenue of chestnuts, his heart rises like freshly baked bread and he imagines himself a stork, not a sparrow. If he were a stork, with a sash in his beak, this is where he would take his mother. He would carry her up into the high branches, make a nest there for her. He would keep her safe from predators, out of reach of the grubby little world. And as he feels his better self begin to soar again, he doesn't try to quash it. Up he floats, up and up, until the whole Common is a flat pattern of itself. There are Velux windows glinting blindly up at him, neat squares of feng shui gravel around lily-padded ponds.

He is still light-headed when he returns to earth, still filled with bliss. He is just about to turn into Riverton Street when a man steps in front of him, and stretches out a hand in greeting.

'Sparrow Considine?'

'What's it to you?'

The man falls into step beside him. 'Mervyn Price, *Daily Post*. I was hoping for a word or two?'

'Fuck. Off. That do?'

'We've had a chat with Jess. It would be nice to chat to you. About the passport, your mum, what it's like to be one of the Orphans. Your take on it all.'

'My take?'

And there she is, Mags Madden. Back again and whispering in his ear, 'Have a little take,' so that he can no longer hear what the journalist is saying. All he can do is follow the flap of the man's mouth as he witters on. When he sees the second man, standing at the bus stop with a camera in his hand, Ro flips. He raises his boot and back-heels the fellow nearest to him in the thin skin of his calf. He lurches towards the other man, grabbing at the camera, but its owner is too quick. He is still click click clicking as Ro legs it towards the house.

Inside the door, Hana has her hand over her mouth. She has seen it all, and is laughing.

'Temper, temper,' she says.

Ruby looks at him as if he's mad. Her eyes are round, stargazy. She glances at Hana for reassurance, and Hana pulls a face at her. 'Silly Mr Boo Boo Man,' she says.

Ruby laughs, a trilling baby laugh. Not often you hear mirth of that quality. And then she lunges for one of her plush bunnies, and Ro is forgotten.

'You need a drink?' Hana says. 'Because I know I do. I don't want association with these things. It is way too much trouble for me.'

He ignores all that, and heads for the kitchen cupboards in search of booze.

'Wrong way, Sparrowman,' Hana says. 'In dining-room sideboard there is vodka, gin, whisky. Whatever you like.'

Hana asks for a large vodka with a dash of Red Bull. Ro has a gin. He doesn't even like gin, but the bitterness soothes him.

Ruby seems to be taking to him. He feeds her a cookie and she loves him for it. It strikes him then how easy it would be to steal the child's heart away from all the people who want only what is good for her. Ro doesn't believe in what is good for him, and never did. He believes in pleasure and results. Ruby has an instinct for those things, too, and they are getting on wonderfully well.

While Hana puts her feet up, Ro turns Jess's drawing room into the set from *Teletubbies* with a huge mound of cushions in the centre of the room. He and Ruby stagger-tumble in and out among them, and he lets her bring her scooter into the house so that they can be Laa-Laa and Po until Ruby exhausts herself and nestles between two of the cushions.

'Fuck this place and this job,' Hana says, as she pours herself another generous two fingers. 'Tonight you will have to put yourself to bed, Roobs. That right, Rooby Roobs?'

Ruby grabs her own bottle and sucks on it solemnly, her eyes passing back and forth between Ro and Hana. And then she fingers the little fleece blanket beside her. Her eyes stop moving then, and she looks like she is entering a kind of trance.

'She is pooh nappy,' Hana says. 'I can tell.'

'Well I'm not changing her,' Ro says, and suddenly this seems like the funniest thing in the world. They both start to laugh, and Hana takes the gin bottle from him and tops up both their glasses.

'I wonder when Jess will be back,' he says.

'Don't worry about Jess,' says Hana. 'You think Jess is going to do anything if she finds me having a little drink? You must be kidding. Even without job, she needs me, Sparrow. She can't do Ruby all by herself. Can she, Roobs? No. Mama no good. No. Mama bad mama bear.'

And even through the fug of gin, a chill passes through him when Ruby shakes her head along.

'That's right, baby,' Hana says to Ruby. 'Mama no good at all.'

They don't move Ruby out into the garden until Ro decides that he wants a cigarette. Hana points to the little walled terrace between the kitchen extension and the French doors of the dining room. 'That's where her "Dad" goes,' she says and throws her head back and laughs. 'I'm sure you can go there too. If you like.'

'I'm good,' Ro says. He strikes a match and cups his hand to save the flame.

Jess is twenty minutes early for the meeting with the agency. She is not familiar with the area near City Hall, where a whole new quarter seems to have sprouted up when she wasn't looking. She finds a Prêt and sits there with a double espresso, scrolling through her depleted inbox as she waits for the clock to grind around to four. The job is as close to ideal as she could hope to find. Right level of experience, partnership potential, in-depth knowledge of the sector required. There aren't many candidates around who have done as much energy M&A as Jess has. If there is a perfect job, come at just the right moment, this is it.

The agent is a woman in her late thirties. A former lawyer, she seems relaxed, almost carefree, and Jess can't help wondering whether this might be a less stressful way to earn a living. But the salary wouldn't be enough to service the huge mortgage they have on Riverton Street, so there's no point going there. Jess tries not to seem too anxious about salary, but even the small hints she gives that she is looking to be paid at least as well as she was before, that decent partnership prospects are vital, are translated by the woman on the other side of the desk into questions of competency and suitability.

'I'm sure you'll be up to the role. After all, it's still going to be contracts, more or less. When you boil it all down, what isn't?'

The agent sits back in her chair, moving her head a little as if to get a better purchase on Jess's face. She taps her hands on the desk in front of her and her rings clink. And, even though her rational mind recognises the extreme unlikelihood of the woman having any idea that she is one of the Orphans, Jess is gripped by a kind of panic. She is the new girl at school again, and someone has left offerings on her desk – an eraser in the shape of a teddy bear, a packet of Skittles, alms for the Orphan.

She reaches forward for the jug of water and it pours too freely, jerking the water out in splashes.

'I'm sorry,' she says. 'Stressful time.'

The agent doesn't react, but her eyes do. Jess decides that she must have read the *Daily Post*, and is matching name to name, face to face. The thought that someone she has never seen before, whose name is Sally Something, and whom she will likely never see again, might already know about the single incident that defined her childhood is devastating. She feels undermined, exposed.

'If you'd like to take a moment.'

The woman is perfectly nice, if that's the word. But there is an uncomfortable prickling of sweat on Jess's forehead. Her mouth seems to have dried out, and she can feel her confidence start to drain away.

Sally Something has her face to one side as if waiting for an answer to a question she hasn't asked yet. But Jess is suddenly incapable of speech, because the only thing she could possibly say right now is yes, I do, I miss her. I have always missed her. I am only a scrap of the person I should be. She manages to make an excuse about feeling unwell before sidling out of the room, but she has lost a golden chance here, and she knows it.

As she crosses the Common it feels as if there is a wind behind her, pushing her on and on, as if there's some urgency she hasn't discovered yet. She is sharp with anxiety, because she needs a job, and soon. The lump sum from the trust was enough to pay the deposit and it allowed them to do the place up, but that's gone now and the mortgage soaks up most of what she earns. Her mobile rings, a number she doesn't recognise. Crowe sounds more formal today, more official.

'I'll talk to Ro, Officer,' she says, and she can hear her voice hoarsen as she says it. 'Just as soon as I can contact him.' She clears her throat and starts again because she has never lied to a policeman before. She has hardly ever lied, full stop. 'My mother disappeared twenty-five years ago. I mean, it's not as if this is urgent.'

'Urgent means different things to different people,' he says. 'I'm sure what seems urgent to your clients makes not the slightest bit of difference to me.'

'Getting back to see my kid,' she says. 'That's urgent to me. Today, right now, that's what urgent means. Ro, well, Ro will show up when he does.' She hasn't actually said she hasn't seen him. She keeps telling herself that.

'I'm going to have to make myself a bit clearer here, I can see that. The Irish, you see. They'd like a word with your brother. Because Ms Madden didn't just keel over, you see. There's evidence of an assault.'

'Ro doesn't go to Ireland. He's got no reason to.'

'I'm not so sure about that. You knew there was a sighting of your mother recently?'

'I don't pay attention to sightings. There's always some nutter.'

'Well, you're right, of course. But this time? She was seen right near where you used to go on holiday. Right near where the Madden woman lived.' And now she's on alert, and dread sweeps round her like an old grey curtain. 'Local thing, really, though it did hit an inside column in one of the nationals. *Irish Independent*? Know it?'

She knows it.

'I shouldn't tell you this because it's not my case, but you need to understand how serious this is now. The night Mags Madden died, a local taxi man brought some bloke – young, with an English accent – out to the house. He remembered the fare because the house is a bit of a wreck. Odd place to visit, and all that. I suppose I just wanted to know if that young English bloke might be Sparrow. I suppose you might want to know that too. Because if Sparrow comes and talks to me before this all gets out of hand – if we can clear this up – then I'd like that and I know you'd like that too.'

She manages to bring herself to thank him.

'I want to help. I'm on the same side. Just remember that. So, you'll get in touch now, Jess, won't you? Just as soon as you've spoken to your brother.'

As she walks the familiar route along the edge of the Common, she follows a long, meandering crack spooling down the centre of the path. It must always have been there, but she's never noticed it before. It's as if the earth has undergone a shift that has only just become apparent. In the distance, she can hear the mechanical drone and thump of drum and bass. Nearing Riverton Street, the volume seems to rise. As she turns into the street, Reg from opposite is standing at his gate, hands on hips, scanning the top windows of her house. He gestures to her, and she nods, but the only word she catches is 'racket'.

Meanwhile, two kids she doesn't recognise are standing in the middle of the street, headbanging along to the music.

She smartens her step and slams the gate shut behind her. The air inside her house is sweet with smoke and booze. Ro is stretched out on the floor, propped up against the big leather beanbag she bought for Charlie last year. At first he doesn't answer and then he looks up at Hana and they collapse in giggles like a pair of naughty children.

Jess feels patronised, then suddenly panicky. 'Where's Ruby?' she says.

Ro looks more substantial than he'd seemed that first night, when he was just a flickering shape in the candlelit garden. Maybe she wasn't looking properly then, or perhaps was remembering him from before. He'd seemed like a child then, but he is a presence now. His shoulders have a heft to them. Even his face seems less ethereal. His eyes, always a little vague, are pinprick sharp and greener than she remembered. And when she notices that he is wearing Charlie's jumper, it makes her furious to think of Ro in their room, rifling through their things.

'I said, where's Ruby?' She's having trouble controlling her voice, and it sounds high-pitched, comical.

'She's in the garden, yeah?'

'On her own?'

'Because of smoke,' Hana says. 'Be cool. It's safe. She has her Wendy house. She is happy in her Wendy house for twenty minutes, more. We check her. If she falls over, if she gets upset, she calls me. No problem.'

'You can't leave a toddler alone in a garden.'

'Oh Jess, you are ridiculous. You worry always about what happens at that gate.' Hana sniggers. Jess knows exactly what Hana means by that, and it makes her so angry she could smack her.

Ro sits up, and it's almost as though he's joining them for the first time. 'What's wrong?' he says.

She doesn't scream or shout. That's never been her way. She just turns to Hana. 'You can go now,' she says.

'What you mean, go?'

'Just leave, please.'

Jess doesn't wait for an answer. She rushes into the garden where her daughter is sitting on the damp grass and playing with a whole regiment of the miniature plastic toys she has forbidden Hana to buy.

As soon as she lifts Ruby, who feels warm and wet, the child bursts into tears. So often, when presented with the option, Ruby has reached for Hana, glaring at Jess as if she is an intruder. But this time she clings to Jess, reclaiming her. And through her fury, Jess welcomes that. She presses the child to her and carries her in from the garden while Hana hovers at the door. Ruby blanks her nanny, gripping her knitted alien even tighter than before. Jess is surprised to see a tear poised on the very edge of Hana's lower eyelid, held in check by a clot of mascara. She doubts its authenticity, but it is satisfying all the same. The upper hand feels good; she should have taken it months ago.

'It shouldn't take you long to pack. I'll be waiting down here to see you out the door.'

'The thing is,' Hana starts, her eyes flickering as she swipes a finger under them. 'It was no big deal. You can punish me, if you like. But it was nothing. You can have, if you want.'

Jess doesn't ask her to explain. The inference is just about ambiguous enough to be ignored. Besides, her mind is on Ro now, and all those unanswered questions. She clutches Ruby to her like a warm, wet doll. Closes her eyes and glides her cheek across the child's silky hair.

It seems like no time at all has passed when Hana's bags thump down onto the hall floor. Jess straps Ruby into her high chair in the kitchen so she doesn't have to witness any histrionics. But Hana is perfectly calm, off-hand almost. Her house keys in her hand, she picks at the chain in a fruitless attempt to remove the pink diamanté key ring then tosses them towards the glass jar on the radiator. She misses, and the keys clank onto the floor. Hana and Jess both look down at them, pink spar-kles glinting under the halogen, but neither bends to pick them up.

Meanwhile, a slow wail is spiralling up out of the kit-chen. By the time Jess has reached Ruby, the crying has taken hold. And as the front door closes on Hana, Jess feels herself begin to crumble.

Ro has sobered up. He is lying on the sofa in the draw-ing room watching a programme in which a nerdish cou-ple are being shown around a converted barn in France. The ashtray has disappeared, but the place still smells of smoke so she sets the extractor fan in the kitchen to run full blast. With all the shutters closed, and the TV beaming out sunshine and vineyards and warm stone, it is almost possible to forget the hostages to fortune closing in around them. She gets between Ro and the screen, and clicks the TV off.

'Were you in Ireland before you came here?'

'I think you asked me that already,' he says. 'The answer hasn't changed.'

'Can you remind me what the answer was? Because I don't think you gave one.'

'I can't believe you even need to ask me that.'

'A woman is dead, Ro.'

'Women die every day. Men, too.'

'But the police want to talk to you.' Her voice weakens, as if her breath is no longer strong enough to power it. He gets up from the sofa and walks out into the hallway.

'Because a woman died? We've all got to go sometime.'

She follows him. How come she failed to notice this hardening in him? It terrifies her. 'What are you even talking about, Ro? This is mad.'

He turns and strikes a pose he often adopts when under attack, feet slightly turned in, arms hanging out from his sides. It makes him look vulnerable, too easy a target for the inevitable victory to be worthwhile. But she doesn't let that stop her, not this time.

'There's a man called Crowe. A policeman. He's from before, from when we came back from Goa. He was keen on football.'

'So were you.'

'He used to try to get you to play. Maybe you don't remember.'

'You're right. I don't remember.'

'Will you talk to him? If I make the call perhaps?'

'Why does everyone always want to talk?'

'It's a simple matter. You've nothing to hide – so just tell him that.' But even as she's uttering them, the words sound weak, unconvincing. She realises then that she is starting to doubt, and doubt is not who she is. She is certainty and clear purpose. And so she tries again.

'Where were you anyway, before you came here?'

He looks her in the eye, and for a moment she thinks he might be about to answer, but instead he shrugs and picks at the paintwork on the banisters with a fingernail.

'You're going to have to leave, Ro. I can't just hide you here. I can't just pretend. I mean, twenty people, maybe more, must have seen you at the party. If I keep having to lie on your behalf, we'll . . .'

He walks around her and out the front door, but he will have left his yellow backpack here, and she's pretty sure he's still got the key he never returned the last time – that horrible row, the plates, the screaming that stayed with her for weeks.

This time she's glad he's gone. But it doesn't bring her any relief, because she is full of apprehension for what he might have done. Her lost little brother. There are tears in her eyes when she thinks of that, the awful waste of it.

Outside, rain has begun pelting the gravel. He has always hated rain, and she allows herself the fantasy that he will be back, that he will see sense, that there could still be some innocent explanation for this belligerence of his. Two people banished in an hour, she is drained by that. She pictures Hana, sheltering under the tarp-covered bandstand, looking out onto the harsh lamps that now edge the paths through the Common. What kind of woman just casts her employee out on the street? She didn't even offer to pay Hana for the days she'd worked that week. She didn't even ask if she had her fare home to Brazil. Scrolling down the numbers on her phone, her finger hovers over Hana Mob. But then she remembers the party, the back gate. She remembers the two heads that seemed joined together in a kiss, and then she puts the phone away.

Upstairs, she reads to Ruby with the lights low. By the fourth reading or the fifth, Ruby is asleep. Jess is hungry. She is hungry and disorientated. She doesn't know how the days pan out when you don't have work to go to. She has no idea when Charlie will return, or how long they can last with just his salary, which is much less than it used to be, although they've never discussed that fact.

When she goes downstairs to make herself some cheese on toast, she notices a smell of curry from a ready meal Ro must have eaten earlier. She swipes a gloop of bright orange sauce off the work surface, and deposits the black plastic container in the bin. When she realises that all the bottles have been collected and packed into a recycling bag, the ashtrays emptied, she feels a momentary pang of guilt for pushing him away.

They used to talk about all kinds of things. He has travelled a lot, and so long as it's possible to get him off the subject of, well, off *the* subject, he is surprisingly well informed. He has certain obsessions, of course, and they are not always, or maybe ever, *her* obsessions. He knows the cast of every Hitchcock film off by heart, for instance, though she has no idea what started him on that tack. She isn't a list person herself, but it can feel like a kind of anchor, this mastery of fact, when reality is so difficult a thing to grasp.

But Ro doesn't reappear. To fill the silence, she sits watching the ten o'clock news on the TV she scarcely knows how to use. Now and then, a car swishes along the rainy street outside. She feels ill at ease in her own house, though she doesn't doubt that it's secure. Soon after they moved in, the local bobby made what he called an aware-ness visit. He arrived in full dress, complete with squawk-ing radio, to explain that it was sensible to have gravel out front instead of grass (so that an approaching intruder could be heard), that she should get rid of the hedge out-side that front window (so there would be no place to hide), that an alarm is worthwhile, but no guarantee, that keys must require ID for cutting, and so on. By the time he left, she was exhausted, bombarded by all this new potential for disaster.

Just for a moment, she wonders if ignorance is bliss. After all, disaster doesn't always hit. She has plenty of friends who lead charmed lives. Hana's sparkly keys are in the jar on the radiator cover. Jess might have lent her another spare set, but she can't remember. She should know for sure how many sets of keys there are for the house, but she doesn't.

The day has sucked the energy from her. Upstairs, she

closes the plantation shutters and the heavy drapes and lies down on the bed. It's a comfortable room, and she feels safe here. The rug, an abstract design in cream and black, is soft underfoot, and the bed is piled with Hungarian goose down topped with a throw whose weight makes her feel secure and whose faux-fur texture reminds her of a beloved teddy bear, long before the beach. Just as she feels herself relax, she has an image of Hana, crouched on the other side of the garden wall in the cold and dark, being pelted by rain. It is a vision straight out of Thomas Hardy. Even though she tells herself that Hana isn't the kind of person to find herself washed up against a wall, the image doesn't fade. And then an alternative anxiety develops – Hana, in secret occupation of the cellar, awaiting Charlie's return. She is half listening to *Book at Bedtime*, a gentle story about a family of girls in wartime Cornwall, when the bedside radio switches itself off. She is left alone in the suspended quiet of her padded room and soon she is asleep.

Later, she wakes. Or rather, something wakes her. She starts, sits up, pulls the covers to her throat. The sound is coming from downstairs, and her first thought is that at least whoever is down there is nowhere near Ruby. She doesn't move, not at first, but she listens hard, straining to hear beyond the dull thud of her own blood in her ears. There is the faint, hollow noise of feet on the cellar stairs, a clatter of something, a slow dragging sound. This is her house, and yet she doesn't have the courage to challenge whoever might be down there. As for her mobile, she left it in the kitchen to charge. She closes her eyes and prays to the darkness behind them that whoever it is leaves soon, that he doesn't mount the stairs.

Just then, she hears the bifold doors into the garden open and then shut again. Hauling herself out of bed and over to the window, she pushes aside the drapes and opens the shutters and is just in time to see Ro leave the back garden, Charlie's rucksack on his back. Relief washes over her, but she is furious with him too. He doesn't shut the gate, and that infuriates her even more. She knocks on the window, but he doesn't turn. He is walking with that strange gait he's had ever since he was a child – stiff, upright, slightly robotic, with his hands held a little way out to the sides. It looks more tentative than it is, that gait of his. He is not the willow he seems. He is used to getting what he wants when people have given up trying to stop him getting it. She knocks again, harder this time, then slides the window up.

'Sparrow!'

But he doesn't seem to hear her, and she realises then that he has probably got his earphones in. Her eyes are tired now, but she's determined not to lose track of him. The path he's following is a diagonal that leads in the direction of the copse of trees, almost a wood, that scratches up against the cut-through, close to where the burger van is parked. She is afraid of woods. She has never ceased to fear that big bad wolf. But that isn't where he's heading. He stops and seems to look back at the house, and then he steps off the path and out of the light. It's only then that she realises Ro isn't alone.

The fact that there is someone with him slides into her

heart like a chip of ice. How Hana would relish stoking his paranoia, feeding his fantasies. She runs down the stairs, slides her feet into her shoes and crunches out across the gravel of the back garden towards the open gate. There is a man on the bench out there, playing with his phone. He looks up when he sees her, and his thin face is lit by the electronic glow. She attempts to put a foot out onto the grass. What is the Common, after all, except an oversized garden? But she finds that she has become too afraid of such places. Besides, Ruby is alone in the house, and so she steps back inside her garden walls and shuts the gate.

13

The wet grass squeaks underfoot. By the time Ro and Nefertiti reach the cut-through, Ro's Converse are soaked and his toes feel gritty and cold. Eddie's van is parked a little way from the bright lights of the burger hut and the oniony smell of fried fat, but still too close to the idling cop cars for comfort.

'Fuck that,' says Nefertiti. 'We'll just have to wait it out.'

He takes the swigs she offers from a naggin of vodka. When he lowers his backpack carefully to the ground, she starts to giggle.

'What you got in there?' she asks. 'You look like a commando.'

Nefertiti's attention switches back to the cops, who don't seem to be in any hurry, over there by the duck pond, while she is wound as tight as her dreads. As the alcohol starts to singe his veins, Ro feels himself begin to change until he has become more than he was – vigilante, avenger, renegade. But the feeling doesn't last and, when the fat cops are still there a half-hour later, he grows bored. Their crackling radios disturb clusters of birds that whip up out of the high greenery and off into the night, and he wishes he could fly off with them. He's on the verge of going over there and getting a cheeseburger for himself, but she tells him not to be daft, that they have to stay incognito. It must be pub closing time before each of the three cop cars heads away from the cut-through.

'No breaking windows or fucking up the engine. We're delivering a message,' Nefertiti says. 'Keeping it dignified, yeah?' When she closes her eyes, she looks as if she's praying, and her black eyeliner has soaked into little black rays like cat's whiskers. He can see this escapade means a lot to her, though she swears blind it isn't personal.

'My own creepo fucking weirdo went to Australia,' she says. 'Nothing to do with him.'

Ro stands there, just looking at her, until her eyes flash open.

'Well, OK then,' she says. 'Let's get on with it.'

Nefertiti goes for it. Soon, she is doing it to the max, a spray can of acid yellow paint in each hand. She has left the bangles at home for reasons of stealth and, as they stride out together, he feels proud to have a project and an ally. Once he gets the hang of it, he starts to enjoy himself, spraying a bright yellow cock and balls on the bonnet of the van, and another one on the boot. He can see how this spray-can lark could get addictive. It makes him feel high, and he tells her that. Nefertiti laughs. 'Just don't inhale,' she says.

This daring, this breaking of boundaries, he'd forgotten he had the capacity for it. But then he thinks of the girl from the café, the one in the pink jumper, and how perfectly he judged the moment it made sense to let her go. It's all about keeping your head. He wishes he'd kept his head with Mags Madden. Losing the rag meant never finding out what it was she had to say. He looks back at the house, where Jess's light is still on. He feels sorry for her – always trying to shut things out, while he's discovering how exhilarating it is to let things in, to chase possibility all the way to the end of the line.

It thrills him to imagine Eddie arriving at his van tomorrow morning. Whistling, most likely, and fiddling with his ponytail. Ro pictures Eddie at the moment of realisation, when it's all about getting that van away as quickly and inconspicuously as possible. *Paedo*, Nef is spraying. *Paedo, paedo, peado.* She spells it right twice and wrong once and that annoys the shit out of him, but he says nothing. So what, if it gets Eddie out of the way? He is thinking about the next stage, about the cottage he can just about glimpse out of the corner of his eye, about the small haul he has for it from Jess's house (to add to the stocks he's already put in there), when Nefertiti reaches into the pocket of her jacket and draws out a stubby little steampunk knife. She was the one to set the limits of violent conduct, yet here she is, jabbing at the tyres with her little goth knife. It takes a surprising amount of effort to prod a hiss out of one of those tyres. The passion she displays is exhilarating, but he hasn't agreed to take this as far as tyre-slashing, so when the wounded van starts leaking air he tells her, no offence but he's off.

'Let me walk you to the main road,' he says, while she's still down on her knees wrecking the tyre. 'Before the cops are back for their chips.'

'You backing out then?' She gets to her feet and draws some posters out of a plastic sleeve. 'Here,' she says, handing him a roll of gaffer tape. 'Trees, lamp posts, whatever.'

He does the first six or seven, but the surfaces are soggy, so there's no guarantee they'll stay in place till morning. She's casting around her like some comic-book villain. 'We'd better split,' she says. 'You coming my way or not?'

'Not,' he says. 'But I'll walk you all the way to the bright lights.'

'OK then,' she says. 'I'm fine once I have the lights.'

He leaves her on the South Side, at the bus stop with the big, bright shelter, and then he doubles back onto the Common.

There must have been a match earlier. Clods of earth still litter the concreted area in front of the changing rooms, though the rain has turned them into mulch. He looks around to check that no one's watching. To the right, the broad road that skirts the Common like a gyratory around an oversized field is busy even after midnight with cars and buses and throaty black cabs hissing through the surface water. All around him, the branches are weighed down and sagging, and up in the higher foliage the occasional bird is still cheeping wildly.

He stops dead a moment when he spots a group of men walking steadily towards him, four abreast, their string bags slung up over their shoulders. He steps off the path, and they don't even look in his direction. Another couple of men overtake him from the opposite direction. They head for the undergrowth. And in that moment, with all this night-time activity taking place around him, he has a perspective on where he is and on the place that he's about to explore. He considers the copse of trees like a location. Let's call it woods, but not really. Let's think of him as babe in the woods, but not actually. Let's pretend this is a challenge, a task, a talent to be rescued. But no, this is his entire raison d'être. It's the day he's been waiting for. All his life, he has been awaiting the return of his mother while the father whose body was discovered in the trees was scarcely given a second thought. So much for fathers.

As he stands there, contemplating the hole in the fence, there is a moment when he could draw back from this. And he does consider consequences. Or at least he considers them as far as he can trace them, which is not that far. He looks at the fence and wonders if the hole has got bigger, if there might be competition for this hideout in plain sight. He has no home, equipped with all the homely things, though he held on to the flat for a while. His heart has roamed too widely to allow him to stake his claim to a single set of walls. He has found most of his requirements in Jess's kitchen, in her cellar, in the neat blue shed in the back garden. He has brought steel wool to stuff into any holes made by rodents, a sleeping bag, a soft pink and green throw he found in Jess's dining room. As for food, it's not as if they're in a wilderness. There's a Tesco Metro just down the road. He will feed her sandwiches and fruit and chocolate. He will bring her hot tea in a Thermos. His eyes smart to think of it. Once he's close enough to listen to her pulse, the bloom of blood around her veins, he will know if she's telling him the truth. And he won't berate her. He will be gentle. He will invite her back into his life as if she's barely grazed him.

Once upon a time, when he was doing casual building work in Berlin, he was painting a wooden fence under a baroque frieze still shot with bullet holes. When he saw a woman cross the street towards him, his heart flared, until he remembered that his mother would no longer be that woman with her long blonde plait, that he might no longer recognise the real Sophie Considine at all. His heart had leaped and fallen in the space of those few seconds, and he was somehow duller, sadder at the end of that day than he had been at the start of it. In his early twenties, that kind of thing was happening once a year at least, and sometimes more. In his middle twenties the frequency declined until, now that he was almost thirty, it was hardly happening at all. But then France occurred, and Durham, and then there was Curramona. He winces when he thinks of that. It's not that he's sorry Mags is dead, not Mags with her thin mouth, her taunts and jibes. But if he'd kept a cooler head he might have come away with something useful.

He reflects on tonight, and Nefertiti. Lovers are two a penny. What he's always been looking for is an accomplice. Someone who will accompany him to dark places, to rotten cottages or tunnels beneath railway bridges, to the bricked-up room beneath a bandstand or the unexpected space between two walls, to a damp hole in the ground. He thinks Nef might come there with him; she has the balls for it anyway.

He steps through the hole in the fence and into the wild garden where creatures scurry away from him. The building is silent, heavy with its own presence. He tries the door. It feels stiffer than before but, when he gives it a sharp tug, it opens so easily it almost knocks him over. He flicks at his ears to repel the sound of rustling leaves. And Mags is keeping away, right enough, at least for now. But he can't bring himself to stay, not tonight. Just inside the door, he dumps the things he crammed into the backpack earlier – the sleeping bag, the throw, the rope he will only use to keep her safe when he's not there. The cottage and Nefertiti and the red van, they are all part of a tomorrow that is already lightening beyond the black fringe of trees.

When Jess awakes, the sound of Ruby's breathing on the baby monitor is barely perceptible. The first thing she does is check Ro's room, but he isn't there. She thinks of Inspector Crowe and feels a surge of relief that she is no longer obliged to lie. She is just out of the shower and in her dressing gown when the phone rings. Charlie sounds very far away. It must be two in the morning over there and she is listening hard for anything in the background that might reveal where he is – music, traffic, the clink of glasses. But he is speaking out of silence, so perhaps he really is where he says he is – in his hotel room in New York, just before sleep. She reminds herself that he's away on business, that this is not something he's chosen.

'Has he gone yet?' he says.

She pretends not to know who he's talking about.

'Oh come on, Jess. Your fucking brother. Is he gone?'

And then it kicks off. Because she no longer cares if it was Hana with Ro last night. He is not her fucking brother.

'You know the history. Have a tiny speck of decency, if you wouldn't mind. But since you ask. Yes, he's gone.'

She can hear him swallow hard, and wonders what it is he's drinking, whether he has managed to find a Speyside malt to fit the bill.

'All I care about is you and Ruby and all of us getting mixed up in whatever fantasy is churning round his head right now. Because don't tell me he's taking this passport thing lying down. He's developing theories, isn't he? He's drawing conclusions and lining up the wild geese. Oh my God, I can't stand it.'

'Is that why you rang?'

She can hear him more clearly now. The slur of too much booze is not the same as the slur of sleep. He is pissed.

'I suppose it is really. Now that you ask. I suppose that's what prompted the call. You're sure he's gone for good?'

'Sure? Of course I'm not sure.'

'Did you confiscate his key?'

'Did I what? What did you expect me to do? Empty his pockets? Pat him down before he left?'

'Well, if he comes back, take his key. Please, babe?'

'Please, what?'

'Babe.'

'Oh for God's sake.'

'Whaat?'

'You don't have any empathy, do you? You really don't feel things.'

He makes a noise that might be a snigger. 'I feel. In fact, I feel lots of things.'

'I don't mean . . .'

She lies on the bed, that extraordinarily comfortable bed, and lets it comfort her.

'Is that what you want, Jess? To chase me away? Because if life is always going to be one great big quest. If you and your fucking brother are always going to be searching for the thing that nobody will ever be able to give you. The great big answer to the great big mystery. Well then, I'm sorry, babe, I really am. Because I'm not so hot on all that. I mean, it's even getting to me. I'm here in New York, right? So I go into a café, you know? It's just one of those regular Italian places you find every-where here, the ones with the trays of sandwich fillings and the flat whites. And even *I* think I see your fucking mother. There's this old couple behind the counter. And they're say sixty, sixty-five, and I have myself convinced that the woman is Sophie. I'm telling myself, it's her. I'm sure of it. In fact, I was so sure that I stopped and spoke to them just to hear the accents. Isn't that ridiculous? I mean, isn't it, Jess?'

She doesn't reply because she doesn't want to start bawling down the phone. She has to hold it together, doesn't she? Full-time mother. Full-time charge. Full-time strength. Don't waver. Don't lose concentration for one single second because if you do, you'll be punished for it.

'Jess? Jessie Jess? Look, I'm sorry for being a dickhead.'

She should hang up on him, but she doesn't. She wants to keep him here with her. Here and not here.

'What did you say to them? The people behind the counter?'

'I told them the truth. That she reminded me of someone who isn't here any more. At first that freaked them out a bit. And then I explained that it wasn't like that, or not quite, that the woman had disappeared from my wife's life, someone dear to her. And you know what they're like over here. Even the word dear is enough to make them cream their pants.'

'Jesus Christ, Charlie.'

'They said it was sad. I'm sorry, Jess. I should have been able to work that out for myself. It is sad. It's so terribly sad that one moment they were there and the next they weren't. And it's even worse that it's still going on, the not knowing, the maybe never knowing. That bloody passport, I wish we'd never heard about it.'

'Why not?'

'Because of what it means.'

'You think it means something? One thing? As in, one thing and not another thing?'

'Well, yes, I do. Don't you?'

'You didn't say anything about this before, Charlie. So, OK, tell me then. What does it mean?'

'I think she planned it, her own disappearance, and I think she might have disappeared your father too. Thank God you didn't get whatever twist there was in her. But that brother of yours, he's a fucking lunatic. You know? That scene in the kitchen last time – ridiculous.'

She has still got the phone in her hand but her other hand is clenching and unclenching the soft fleece of the bedcover. And all she can think is that it's just as well she hasn't told Charlie about Inspector Crowe.

'He's up there on Mars. I mean, you've thought that too, haven't you? You must have thought that.'

And she is afraid to answer because there is only one honest answer and it's not something she can bring herself to say.

'Look Jess,' he says. 'I'm not away from you because I want to be. I'm here in some miasma they call a hotel. I'm in a tiny bedroom with a porthole for a window and a light so dim you can hardly read the fucking room-service menu. It's not where I'd choose to be, Jess. I'd choose to be with you.' And he lets that line settle, and seep in.

But she doesn't believe it, and she is almost able to say that and risk the roof falling in on top of her, but he keeps on going.

'I wish I was some use to you and not just this joke who doesn't know where he put his feelings. Because that's what you think, I know. At least, some of the time that's what you think. Look, serious now, I love you.

Don't give up on me. I think things will be better for us, now that our little friend is gone.'

'OK,' she says. 'You're right.' And then she lets him have the quid pro quo. 'I'm so glad I finally got around to sacking Hana.'

He starts to laugh. Is it a laugh? Not really a laugh, no. More a hard crack in his voice.

'You sacked old Hana?' he says then. 'Well, blow me down but you've got nerve. She'll hate you for that, you know. In fact, make sure she hands over her keys. She's a feisty little minx.'

'Listen to yourself. You're like something from before the Flood.'

But his voice is serious now. 'Just be careful, Jess. My guess is she's a bad loser.'

'Oh yes? And what has she lost, Charlie?'

He doesn't answer that, just gives her one kiss, two kisses, three. Soft smacks against the earpiece. 'Don't worry, sweet. When I'm out of this shithole, we'll get back to normal. We'll be a little nuclear family again, and we'll forget all about that beach.'

And for the moment it takes him to say that, it seems like a plausible option. Forget the past and move on. Start again, just the three of them, secure and happy behind their garden wall. But as soon as she puts down the phone, she knows the moment for that has already passed.

She pulls on her old running shoes, and gets Ruby dressed for nursery. It feels like a novelty to be pushing the buggy across the Common instead of heading for the Tube. On the way back, she stops in at the newsagent's to pick up some milk. Asmita looks worn out this morning, and Jess can tell from her body language that something is wrong. She is talking, talking, talking. About her nephew and how his school just doesn't prepare them properly, about how his mother is determined to have his class changed. She is talking as if she doesn't want to let Jess go. Jess reaches for the fridge, takes down a dewy white carton of milk. But as she moves towards the newspaper rack, a look of alarm passes across Asmita's face. Her hand darts to her cheek. Jess is about to ask what's wrong when she looks down at the overlapping newspapers that stretch all the way along that side of the shop. The *Daily Post* is always the first one she notices these days. And there is Ro, his face snarled up, his body a flurry of limbs.

FROM ORPHAN TO BEAST.

'Your brother?' Asmita says.

We've interviewed one Orphan. The other one has been less forthcoming. We wanted a word with Mr Considine outside the home of his sister, City lawyer Mrs Jessica-May Clark (34). But Mr Considine had other ideas.

'Your brother is in trouble?'

Jess pictures Crowe and his kind face. But then she remembers the voice at the other end of the phone, the clear insinuation that this goes beyond old loyalties, that, when it comes to Ro, something more is required of her.

Suddenly, this ordinary shop feels like hostile territory, the rows of brightly packaged sweets obscene. Asmita is still talking, but Jess's ears no longer seem to work. She is trying to untangle the emotions. Anger, yes. Anxiety. Disgust. Fear for the future. Despite all these things, she won't ever abandon Ro, whatever he has done.

She imagines the questions they might ask. You must have known how dangerous he'd become. There must have been a sign.

And she'll say no. There was never any sign. No pulling wings off insects. No torturing the cat. And yet that answer wouldn't be entirely truthful. She did know that he had given his whole life to a single obsession, and how greatly he craved respect for that. She knew that his heart was a shrivelled thing, that his natural affections were blunted by disappointment. Outside the shop, she starts scrolling through the Cs. Cabot, Carpenter, Cathy, Centre for, Chiropodist, Crowe. But she finds herself unable to make the call, not without giving him a head start. She wants to scream it out so that somehow he will hear her. Run, Sparrow. Run.

Turning the corner into Riverton Street, she sees them. Two men propped against the low wall opposite her house, one smoking a cigarette, both weighed down with cameras. She quickens her step, then breaks into a jog. After all, who's to say she's not a jogger? But they have seen her now, and they are shouting out the name her mother abbreviated, but which Auntie Rae insisted on using in full. Jessica-May. The name swamps her like an old fog. And there she is again, a responsible kid holding her confused little brother's hand. She turns and runs. But they are after her. Grown men running up the road behind her. Out of nowhere, she hears a whisper in her inner ear.

Take to your heels and run.

And she is with Auntie Rae down at Clapham Junction twenty-five years ago. The man had been standing next to the flower stall until, like an assassin, he whipped a camera out from under his raincoat.

Take to your heels and run.

They ducked across the street into Arding and Hobbs and through its close-packed aisles full of old-lady clothes to a curtained changing room where they clung together until the danger passed. For a while after that she'd thought that's what a flasher was – a man in a dirty mac who stole something from you, then put it in a newspaper. She found a scrapbook at Auntie Rae's once. Press cuttings and photos and tickets pasted onto thick blue-grey pages. It was a record of such incidents, of theories and speculation, pasted in week after week.

Take to your heels and run.

As soon as her foot leaves the pavement, she knows she should have looked. The taxi's shunt is almost loving. It shrugs her up onto its shoulder, then off. She falls awkwardly, and stretches her hand out to catch something – a wing mirror? A handle? She watches the carton of milk spin away from her, then bounce and twist and split. Her hands don't find an anchor, and she falls from the taxi's shoulder onto her own. The milk is chugging out of the plastic carton now, making a puddle of white around her.

There is a petrolly smell to the tarmac. And then the pain seeps through the shock. Her hands have slapped hard against the road. She hasn't moved them yet, but she can feel the raw tear of pain along each palm. A word jags across her mind. Shatter.

14

Ro lets himself in to Jess's house for tea and toast. Once inside, it's hard to leave. He is ravenous for everything that Jess's kitchen has to offer. He fries some rashers, scrambles some eggs, then settles into a beanbag to rehearse his spiel. He will serve her up a slice of guilt, with a dash of enlightened self-interest. When the squat hallway clock strikes eleven, he's surprised Jess isn't back yet. He begins to pace, and then the landline rings. It keeps on ringing until the sound starts drilling through his head. It makes his heart race and his breath tight, and in the end he has to answer it.

'Yeah what?' That's all he says, but it's way too much.

'It's you,' Charlie says. 'I bloody knew you'd still be there.' This is not a friendly start. 'Jess said you'd gone.'

'Wishful thinking,' Ro shoots back, and he's pleased with that.

But Charlie isn't playing. He sounds fretful, stressed. Jess has had an accident. Knocked over by a taxi on Sisley

Road. No real danger, but kept in for observation. Ribs. Blood pressure. Concussion.

Ro says he's sorry. And he *is* sorry, but he tells Charlie he doesn't do hospitals.

'You fucking toerag. I'm not asking you to go to any hospital. I'm making sure you fuck off as far away as possible. Timbuktu? Great. Outer Mongolia? Even fucking better. I'm up to my neck here trying to extricate myself from this deal, and you are not going to be there when I get back.'

'What you don't realise—'

'I'm not interested. I'm sick to death of it all. You're a liability to the rest of us and I won't have you under my roof. That's the end of it. Now, Hana will be there in twenty minutes—'

'Hana? Jess won't like that,' Ro says. 'She's only just fired Hana.' It's a new experience for him to champion Jess's interests, and he finds it pleasing. 'If it's babysitting you're after, why don't you call in Renée?'

He articulates the name as extravagantly as possible because Renée is a ridiculous woman who deserves all the mockery he can muster. She is a booming voice beneath a wide, pink hat. Petunia Dursley made flesh.

'You can leave my mother out of this. And then you can bugger off.'

'Hang on a sec,' Ro says then. 'I've got a much better idea. *I'll* take care of Ruby.' He likes how that makes him feel. Heroic, capable.

'Are you actually kidding me? No bloody way. One word from Hana that you're still here, and I'm calling the police. And I don't think you want that.'

Ro takes a lie-down on the sofa, flicks on the TV. *Escape to the Country.* Sweet. He enjoys having the place to himself. It gives him time to think. Out on the terrace, there is an assortment of chairs including a large white ovoid with a red fabric centre he's been meaning to sample for a while now. He sits into it and it tips a little, and he imagines himself rolling down the garden like a sparrow in an egg, through the gravel and the obedient plants, and smashing into Jess's tasteful blue wall.

He has taken her iPad out there, and now he is travelling deep into the Web, where he is William Wren, journalist, a man with many questions. The efficacy of chloroform. The effects of Rohypnol. How to overpower your victim. How to disable but not to injure. Truth serums. Lie detectors. The painless winkling out of fact. He immerses himself in 4chan and Reddit, tugging on the threads he started earlier. Comments trail down the first screen and the next one and the one after that. There are jibes about lace hankies, about twiddling his moustache. But most of the comments address his fundamental question. What is the perfect drug to bend the subject to your will without rendering her inanimate?

The tranquillity only lasts another half-hour or so before the scrape of a key in the front door and the clack of heels in the hall. He jumps up to take a look, then almost collides with Hana as she enters the kitchen, hooking the strap of her bag over a chair. She slides a blue silk scarf from around her neck and shrugs off her jacket. It's like she never left.

'Well don't just stand there,' she says. 'Double espresso. Use the purple capsule. Two.'

When he doesn't move, she tilts her head to look at him. 'What's wrong? Aren't you glad to see me, Sparrow-man? Charlie told me you sneaked back in. Me too.'

She gives him a half-hearted high five, and then busies herself with the coffee machine. 'But aren't there people looking for you?' She flexes her hand and examines her nails, painted battleship grey today. 'Photographer? Journalist? Maybe even policeman? Soon, you might need to hide somewhere like your mama.'

He doesn't want to talk to Hana about his mother. 'Charlie gave you your job back then?'

'I don't need a job. This is just charity work. Telephone rings, and Charlie is begging me. Come for two, three days, just for Ruby's sake. Please, please Hana, look after Ruby so she is safe. And make sure my fuckwit brother-in-law stays away.' She shakes her head sadly. 'But it is fine with me, Sparrow, if you stay. If you play nice and be a helpful person, then so do I.'

But with Hana around, sharp little Hana with her pink cat's mouth, he can see his room for manoeuvre start to shrink in front of him. Before she offers to collect Ruby, he's on to it himself. He pulls on a hoody and a baseball cap to deflect attention, grabs the buggy and is out the door, quickening his pace across the Common, which, despite last night's rain, is like a desert shot with clumps of green.

Turning towards the bandstand, he spots Eddie's van parked in the same place as before, in between the playground and the section of Common that has been turned into a wildflower meadow. It crouches there, red and squat and covered in wild streaks of yellow paint. The notice tied to the tailgate seems like overkill, but even the spelling mistake makes him smile.

Don't buy from this man. No Peados here.

Eddie's ice-cream days are over.

There is no Mother shaking hands at the school gate today, just a dandy in a yellow tie and matching socks and a sharply cut pale grey suit. The man is an irritation – all jazz hands and banter – and Ro could happily take him by the throat for not being who he's meant to be. When Ro gets back to the house with Ruby, Hana is making herself a quinoa salad with strips of avocado and tiny moist olives. She cuts through a lime and forks its juice over the plate. Ruby doesn't seem to recognise her at first, but Hana brings her round with little pieces of chocolate crumbled onto the tray of her high chair.

Meanwhile, Hana is talking to the air. 'I have new life now, Sparrowman. They can't just expect the world to stand still for them. They can't expect to treat me like I am trash and then expect me to come back whenever they say. They shouldn't be surprised if I look after myself.'

A message pings into her phone, and she jabs at it in response. If he were Jess he would worry what this girl could do.

She turns on her heels and surveys the fridge. 'Ah,' she says. 'I forgot. Would you please be darling man and go and get some milk.'

He is not used to being given instructions, and he

stands his ground until she glances sharply up at him and shoos him along.

'You want me to have to put poor, tired Ruby in buggy? Play nice, Sparrowman.'

He gives in then, and drags a shopper off the hook on the back of the kitchen door.

The Indian woman in the shop is reading a magazine when he gets there. She gives a little start when she sees him, and is careful not to touch his hand when she passes him his change. But he doesn't let it bother him. When he gets back to the house, he notices that all the shutters at the front have been closed. He slides his key in the door but then he realises she must have put the deadlock on. He decides that it's deliberate because Hana never does things by accident. He bangs, kicks, shoulders the door. He tries to shout through the letter box, but it is bristled with something that stops him seeing through. And then he goes round the back.

At the gate, he removes the strips of Sellotape from the keypad and holds them to the light to reveal the code: 8912, 1289, 9821? The order is a matter of experimentation, but he is lucky. Charlie is predictable to the last. Year of birth, of course – 1982. The code gets Ro into the back garden, but no further. He comes right up to the bifold doors and peers inside, but there is no sign of Hana. The kitchen is empty, the door into the hallway closed. Glancing around the garden for an implement, he grasps a trowel in his fist like a dagger and begins gouging at the glass. Dig, dig, dig. But the glass is toughened, just like his mother, just like Jess, and his blows make no impact on it. He yells up at Hana's window to let her know he isn't taking this. The bitch has shut him out of his own sister's house, and he will wring her neck for it.

As he leaves, he is awash with longing for the simpler life he might have had – a place of his own and a sofa life spent drinking beer in front of an endless stream of hopeless optimists with their barn conversions and built-in barbeques, their chalets that are just off the piste.

When he reaches the café, it is still full of the after-school crowd. By the time Nefertiti has finished her shift, he has concluded that he needs more than just the one drug. He needs his mother to be compliant, of course, but that's just a means to an end. What he really requires is the truth. The shiny truth from his willing mother's mouth. There is someone on 4chan who calls himself the Go-To Guru and claims to have access to every solution you could ever need. Ro hasn't messaged Guru yet, but he will.

'What's up with you?' Nef asks as they walk back to her flat.

She is the nearest thing he's ever had to an accomplice, but he's still not sure if he can trust her. He is half thinking of trying her out for a role in all of this. He is half thinking she might know someone who could supply him. But first he needs a bed for the night.

The flat is small and smells of patchouli. It is less chintzy than he remembered, and maybe it was just the contrast between the story she told him and the airy, flowery decor that struck him then. There is a flatmate, apparently, but she isn't there today.

'Thursdays, she stays with her boyfriend. He's an electrician down in Croydon.'

Nefertiti is looking steadily at him over the rim of her glass on the opposite side of the small veneered table. She starts to jiggle her knee, as if she's wondering why the polite conversation. Because, to tell the truth, he's wondering that himself. Mostly, though, he's trying to broach the perplexing subject at the front of his brain.

'I'm looking for something,' he says. 'But I don't have a dealer.'

He has imagined a train station at dusk, a deserted shopping centre. He has thought of places like Peckham, maybe, though he's never been there. Somewhere on the East London Line. Dalston, perhaps, where he had a job once in a bar. Or New Cross.

'What kind of something?' She leans towards him, and he can smell her perfume now, like a fleshy, musky flower. 'Is it because I is black?' she says, and then she flips the side of his face with her fingers – not too hard, not too soft, and turns away laughing.

For a moment, Ro thinks he's blown it. He quenches the anger, at himself, at her. But it's not over, not yet.

She raises a finger, then shimmies herself forward and starts working her fingers into the front pocket of her jeans. She draws out a tiny plastic bag, holds it up in front of him, then drops it into the middle of her own outstretched palm. She smiles – strong white teeth, bubble-pink gums – and it's a shame she doesn't use that asset more. He reaches out and takes the baggie. And though MD isn't what he needs, not for the cottage anyway, it will do for now, for Nefertiti. It will wipe away the indignity of the school gate, the yellow tie and matching socks, the lack of progress he's been making on the cottage, the worry that he might never get his mother back. He pops open the bag and puts a pill on his tongue. She smiles that smile again and does the same.

One thing leads to another. And once they have done it up against Nefertiti's primrose-yellow wall, and collapsed panting onto the birch floor, he feels more powerful than before. Nefertiti props herself up on an elbow. She doesn't stretch for her clothes, doesn't flinch when he looks down at where he's just been. He likes that. She is bold and daring, just like him.

When she sits up, there is barely a bulge in her belly. She stretches herself into a kind of lotus position and listens, her chin in the heel of her hand, her eyes trained on him. Whatever is happening here, he likes it. He prefers being one of two. All the twos he has tried to forge have been fraught with impossible expectation, but perhaps there is an alliance to be had here.

They are coiled up on the gleaming floor, and his knees are beginning to ache, but it is warm there with her, and he's not inclined to move just yet although that is probably just the little pill talking.

'So, why do you really hate the paedo?' she asks.

'Because I think he killed my father.' He's never said such a thing out loud before. In fact, this might even be the first time that he's formed the thought. But the cat is out of the baggie now.

Her chin is still in her hand and it hops when she starts to talk.

'The paedo? Are you sure?'

'How about this, then.' He tries to concentrate on her face and nowhere else. 'She planned to run away with him, my father found out, and there was a struggle. They didn't mean to kill him.'

'Your mum and the paedo? And that all happened on the beach?'

It sounds ridiculous, of course. These things always do when you say them aloud. He should have known better. There is a slick of sweat on his forehead, and he's fighting now to recover the situation. 'OK, so he went off to get drugs – a prearranged thing – and Eddie is waiting there for him in the trees and clocks him one on the back of the head in the trees when he's out of sight.'

'But why would he do that? And your mum, how come she didn't come back to you? She isn't just going to dump you, is she?'

He needs to put the blame on Eddie.

'Well, is she?'

'Eddie stops her. He says it's them or me. And anyway, I know that you wanted him dead so you're fucked unless you come with me. And then her only option is to use her spare passport and get away from him.'

'Eddie Jacques? How come?'

'He was at the beach.'

'Really? You sure? And she's got a spare passport now?'

'You know she does.'

'Oh, OK, the thing you mentioned. I never read the papers, sorry. But why did she have another passport anyway? Did she plan all this or something?'

And she has put her finger on the very problem he doesn't want to countenance. He could curse Mags Madden for that passport. If she'd only kept it to herself. And then there's the photo taken on the beach. He's waiting for her to mention that. But Nef doesn't go there.

'What you're really saying is that you hate him because you think he stole your mum. And you know what, Ro? I can understand that.'

He supposes that *is* what he's saying.

'So, if he stole your mum. Where is she now?'

He realises right away that he can't just come out with it, pat, like that. She's here, she's round the corner, hiding in plain sight, living with Eddie Jacques. It all sounds too fortunate, too coincidental, if you put it like that. But he can't help smiling at her, like the sun has just burst inside his chest. He taps the side of his nose at her, but he doesn't think she catches on to that.

When Nefertiti puts her clothes back on she doesn't bother with her knickers, just scrunches them in her hand and shoves them into the jeans that she slides on standing up, hopping on one leg then the other. She tosses her hair forward and runs her fingers through it. Her bangles jangle and the air smells of her. She cooks him chicken and rice and pours him glass after glass of sharp white wine until he is as happy as a stupid person. They fall into Nefertiti's not-quite-double bed, and he is soon asleep.

He wakes abruptly around dawn. There is a siren, and he knows that his real world is out there, not in here. He eases himself out of bed and through the door and out into the sharpening day.

Maybe Hana has already been out of the house this morning, or perhaps she's had a visitor. Whatever the reason, she hasn't put the Chubb lock back on, just the Yale. So careless, he thinks, so very careless. If he were a different kind of man she might come to regret such an oversight. He lets himself in, and walks through the hallway towards the stairs. He climbs one storey, then another, until he is standing outside Hana's room. If it weren't for Ruby he'd have walked right in there. He'd have given her what she deserves. But he likes Ruby, who has no one better to look after her. And so he proceeds with the plan instead.

This time, he isn't limited by one small backpack, so he takes everything his mother might possibly need. Medication in case she's sick, an old pillow and a blow-up lilo from the cellar to use as a mattress. He has changed his mind about not needing to pack food, because he has the feeling that his mother will be a harder nut to crack than he first imagined. And so he includes hip flasks, a camping stove, jars of olives and roasted peppers, cans of soup. Wedged in beside the boiler, he finds a picnic rucksack with plastic plates and cutlery for two. There is even a small radio complete with earphones, in case she is afraid, in case he needs to fill her head with music.

He tops up the hip flasks with spirits from each of the

bottles he finds in Jess's walnut sideboard. Brandy, schnapps, whisky, vodka, gin. Something for everyone. He brings a hammer and some nails so he can decorate the walls of the cottage. A picture of the home place he found in Jess's upstairs loo. The Orphans on the Beach, swiped from one of Rae's old scrapbooks that he found in Jess's wardrobe, and a photo of them together, Mama and Pa.

15

Into the space between sleep and wakefulness comes a white-coated man with a clipboard. Beamed up by the side of Jess's bed, he delivers his diagnosis – cracked ribs, fever, concussion, elevated blood pressure. The bedlinen is glacial, and the doctor leaves her feeling even weaker than before – something small and weightless trapped between sheets of ice.

She feels a vague sense of unease, even in her semi-conscious state. But it is only when she wakes properly that she remembers Ro, and all the other things she should be dealing with but has left undone for however long it is that she's been here.

For the first time ever, not having a job is a relief. Then she remembers the passport, and the fact that there is a puzzle in her life now, something she has to try to decipher. The last thing she remembers is Ruby, who should have been first, not last. Her negligence alarms her. She needs to get up, right now, and find Ruby. She turns to the stainless-steel pan by the side of the bed and throws up into it.

The hospital room is small, low-lit. Wired up through a port in her hand, she waggles her fingers to make sure that she still can. She glances around for her phone to call the house, but it's nowhere to be seen. The room is comfortable, but anonymous, and there is a distant hum of air-conditioned purpose, but she has no idea how long she has been here or where they might have put her belongings. The next time she wakes, the person hovering by her bed is wearing a pale pink dress with a stark white pinny. She isn't sure whether this pink and white nurse is real or not. She stretches out her hand and, as the woman whips back and forth between this and that, she feels the starched cotton graze the back of it.

This pink and white nurse is the person to give her back her mobile phone, still partly charged, with messages from all sorts of people she never realised gave her a second thought. Not just Sarah and Martha and Max and her couple of other close friends, not just her far-flung cousins who have somehow heard about the accident, but Delia too, still in Dubai but apparently already on the warpath over what she delicately calls Jess's 'departure'. A whole three scrolls of other people have somehow heard about her accident, whether through Facebook or via the old networks of college and work, and it warms her heart. But there is nothing from Ro.

There has been a stream of texts from Charlie. To sweeten the news of his continued absence, he sends an army of emojis, an embarrassment of kisses. He says that

Martha has everything under control, and the thought of gentle Martha taking care of Ruby is a huge relief. The warm fuzz of all this kindness surrounds Jess like a cloud of candyfloss hot off the wheel until she remembers Crowe, and all the texts she hasn't answered. She watches them accumulating, green rectangle over narrowing green rectangle, on the screen of her phone.

He has been to the house twice now in search of Ro, he says, and he is losing patience. Each text is shorter, curter, less emollient than the one that preceded it. The next time the doctor appears beside her bed, he is more substantial, more of a person who could be out in the real world beyond the hum. He could be someone who knows about her, who knows about Ro. But there is no sign of that.

Charlie calls. His voice is soft, coaxing. 'How's my sweet?' he says. 'How's my lovely one?'

'Say that again,' she says, and he has the grace to laugh at himself.

'How's Ruby?' she asks.

'Oh Ruby is fine, she's great.'

'Is she going to nursery?'

'Yes. Yes, she's going. At least, I think—'

'But isn't that a complete nightmare for Martha? I mean, she's got the girls to take to Balham. How does she cope?'

He is silent for a moment, and then he tells her that there's been a change of plan.

'A what?'

'It was going to be too disruptive. And so, we, I, we thought—'

'You brought back Hana.'

'Well, it wasn't exactly like that.'

'You're a shit, Charlie. You know that? You make me sick.'

She hangs up on him, and discharges herself, which really just amounts to saying that she's leaving. She doesn't wait for the doctor. She doesn't know what she would say.

Stepping into the Uber, she feels like one of those friendless elderly women who wait forlornly for a minicab in the Sainsbury's car park, clutching at bunches of orange plastic bags. She spends the trip home examining the balding head of the cabby because it is easier to concentrate on that head than to let herself worry about Ruby.

Crossing the bridge, the tower they have spent an eternity constructing has acquired several storeys of windows since she was last over this way, while the wrapped power station has lost two of its chimneys for reconstruction. The taxi whispers along the wet streets until they are passing all the places she knows by heart – the plastic Costa, the dry-cleaner's with the smiling Cypriot couple, the Japanese restaurant, its Korean neighbour, Ruby's nursery, the Common.

Arriving at Riverton Street, she feels the first stirrings of alarm as the real world, the one she needs to do something about, reasserts itself. And then she sees them, right outside her house – the journalist from the other day, and Hana. Despite the rain, Hana is wearing a pair of tight white jeans that almost match her hair. The journalist is holding a yellow umbrella high above her so that the street light turns golden as it floods her face. She is an exclamation mark. She is trouble. Jess feels a jag of panic at the thought of coming face-to-face with both Hana and the journalist. She plays for time.

'Go round the block,' Jess tells the driver.

'This is the address,' he says, and brakes, sending a knife of pain between her ribs.

He glares at her in the rear-view mirror, and she tries to recover her composure, taking small sips of breath. 'No sweat,' she says. 'I'll pay.'

She eases herself back in the seat, and the car lurches towards the edge of the Common where thick foliage crests against the skyline like an inky wave. She directs him along the cut-through and past the derelict changing-room block with its battened roof, past the scrub where a lone man sits on the trunk of a felled tree, past the empty playground. She tells the driver to stop.

'What, here?' He looks suspicious, then wary. He winds down the window, as if he needs to assert himself by doing something she hasn't instructed.

He turns on the radio. There are tailbacks on the M4, which couldn't matter less to her right now. She scans the messages on her phone, but there's nothing new from Charlie or Ro, or anyone but Martha, who says she's stocked the fridge with breakfast things. And welcome home, by the way. She dials Martha's number, and tries to stay calm.

'Why did you let Charlie get Hana back?'

Martha seems to be having difficulty remembering who Hana is. 'Hi, Jess. You OK?'

She tries it from a different angle. 'Were you not able to have Ruby in the end?'

'Hana? You mean the old nanny? The one who left?'

'The one I sacked.'

'Oh.'

For the first time, she wonders if she is the kind of person that people feel they have to humour, if she has something in her that is like Sparrow. The thought appals her.

For a moment, Martha is silent. When she speaks, she is circumspect, evidently feeling her way.

'I did offer. I'd hate you to think I didn't offer. But Charlie said he had it covered.' She sounds like she is keen to get off the phone now. 'I'm sorry, Jess. Of course I'd have looked after Ruby. You'll have Charlie back tomorrow anyway, I hear, so things can start to get back to normal.'

Jess doesn't know what to feel about that. And she doesn't know what to say to Martha, who is kind, of course. Entirely without suspicion, and kind. She tries to soften her tone. But all she can think about is the reality of Hana taking care of Ruby, with axes to grind.

She leans forward to speak to the driver. 'Back to Riverton Street now, please.'

She gets him to stop at the other end of the street. When he cottons on that she's struggling to push the door open, he steps out to help her, so keen to get rid of her he practically lifts her out of the back seat.

As she walks towards the house, she finds herself hobbling a little, her arm pressed tight against her ribs to hold herself in place. No sooner has she reached the house two doors away from her own than she is seen. When the reporter realises who she is, his attention shifts, sudden as snow. Hana is left open-mouthed, like a cartoon-strip heroine, as the streetlit rain drizzles down on her.

Ignoring them both, Jess pushes open the gate. On the other side of the door the house feels overwarm and muggy. She pushes down the snib and leans back against the door, leaving Hana outside. She flicks the light switch, but the bulb has blown. The air is heavy with the sharp, sour tang of mouldering nappies. All she wants now is Ruby, to have her child's soft plump limbs around her, to stroke Ruby's velvet skin. But the odour of neglect makes her anxious. The dark, the silence. She stands perfectly still, and listens. From the very top of the house comes a long thin wailing, an old cry that has almost exhausted itself. Ruby.

Slowly, painfully, Jess drags herself upstairs to where Ruby is standing in her cot, her sobs hiccoughing in her chest, her face red with fisted-in tears. She cries even harder to see Jess, as if she is summoning up her last reserves of strength to keep her mother there. When she takes Ruby in her arms, the child's cries heave up from somewhere Jess recognises: the place of abandonment, somewhere no one should ever have to visit.

They gaze into one another's eyes – mother and child – and there is a moment of perfect joy. So overwhelming is that love that she is more certain than ever that Sophie would never have walked away from her children, not for all the pleasures of Goa. She is sure now that her mother is dead.

When Ruby is fed and changed, she curls up against Jess. They lie together on the huge white bed. And this is love. From downstairs, the twee game-show chime of the doorbell. Hana. *Chee chung, chee chung*, on and on and on. Finally, the doorbell stops ringing and Jess, still clinging to Ruby, closes her eyes and luxuriates in the silence. Her anger starts to melt away, until there is nothing else but the soft skin of Ruby's cheek against her own, the melding of their breath, slow and calm.

But it's as if her fury has left behind an odour. Once she notices the smell, sweet and rotten, it clogs her nostrils until she is almost unable to breathe. She untangles herself from Ruby, and switches on the bedside light. On the dressing table, there is a bouquet of dying lilies. Not a bouquet exactly, more a cluster of plastic-wrapped cones. Right away, she realises that these are the same flowers that she abandoned outside the back door. Charlie's flowers. The thick white petals are shrunken now, their edges brownish, and the stems are sappy and weak. She has always hated lilies, and inside the house they have putrefied, their pollen scattered over her dressing table like powdered spice.

She imagines Hana retrieving them from outside the back door, leaving them there for her return. Furious now, she grabs them by their necks, and whisks them from the vase. Opening the window, she flings them out into the night. Someone, in the morning probably, will see a dozen mangled flowers strewn across the gravel and wonder why. Unless that person is Hana, still loitering down there in the front garden, who has probably already seen them, and will know.

Ro catches the stink as soon as he opens the door of the cottage. He gets the air freshener he took from Jess's bathroom and sprays it round the place in great hissing arcs. White lavender is what it says on the tin, but the place still smells of shit. Someone has been smoking in here, and his mother doesn't like smoke. He's seen her flap her hand in front of her face whenever Eddie lights up.

As his eyes acclimatise, he can just about decipher a shape in the opposite corner of the room. A roll of roofing felt, perhaps. He moves closer, and sees it's softer and less evenly contoured, more like a gigantic slug. The nearer he gets, the more certain he becomes that beneath the stillness there is movement. Pump of heart and rasp of lung and surge of blood, and a brain that might be tick tick ticking its next move any moment now.

When the rain begins, it's like being inside a drum pelted with gravel. He can't blame the slug for not wanting to be outside in that. He gets it, the need for shelter. But to use his mother's sleeping bag, to steal the soft pink and green blanket. And when the creature stirs, when it lifts its head, it doesn't have an apology to offer. Oh no. It goes on the offensive instead. It starts mouthing off, though it's impossible to hear exactly what the mouth is saying, with all that gravel overhead. And though the creature on the floor is fumbling at the sleeping bag, though it is trying to find the zipper, though it is shuffling off towards the wooden hatch in the brickwork, Ro gets there first.

And even if that creature were willing to repair the wrong it's done, even if it were able to stand on its hind legs like a man, it has still ruined things by coming here at all. When Ro lifts the hammer, this could be the moment he discovers that the slug is so much stronger than it looks. But it has tangled itself up in quilted nylon, and when the first blow comes it hasn't got an answer.

Ro has already decided this can't be a token matter. With the creature almost on its feet, having slithered half-way out of the sleeping bag, he's going to have to finish it off. But when he brings the hammer down again, the creature stops, turns slightly, then falls. Nothing's certain. It might be over, but only time can tell. All he can do is wait.

Ro's heart is pulsing in his throat now. He takes pot luck with the hip flasks. Eeny, meeny, miny, gin. It tastes rank, but it blunts the edges. He keeps his eyes on the slug. In movies, he's seen them check a pulse in the neck, but the thought revolts him. He's hardly noticed that the rain has stopped when it starts again. And the slug doesn't stir. It's dark now, and the night is surprisingly cold for the time of year.

Even if it's dead, Ro knows the slug will come for him, just as Mags Madden sometimes does, with her sour breath and that papery rustling inside his ear that's just a notch too low. He waits on another half-hour or so before approaching it. He stays as still as he can, so that if there is breath to be heard, he will hear it. Then he gets to his feet and walks over there. He peers down, and can see now that it is a man, more or less. When he touches the man's brow, it is not marble yet. Not even nearly. But the fight is over and Ro is empty because there is a body now, and a body very quickly becomes an even bigger problem than a slug.

He will have to find a way to drag the dead slug out into the undergrowth. It is still tangled in the sleeping bag, and pulling the bag back up around its torso is no easy matter. And all the time, he is focused on the other slugs who must be out there somewhere and who may sense that one of their number is missing.

To cover the damage to the skull he ties on a cushion he brought to the cottage to cradle his mother's head. What if he were to leave the slug out there, in the small, enclosed patch of grass? How long would it take for feral things to come and eat it? How long till he'd be driven mad by knowing it was there? And what about the stink of it?

There is no option. If he wants to use the cottage, he will have to get rid of the slug. He tugs at it and starts to ease the body towards the door. It is hard work, and the gin is wearing off now. Outside, the dark is thinning and the birds are going wild.

There is a high gate set into the fence at the side of the garden that backs on to the wooded area where men have always gone for sex. Does anyone still go there these days, when you can grind away wherever you like? He takes a chance that they might, that the haters might still be cruising too, that there is always someone handy with a hammer lurking in a place like this.

He prises back the bolts on the high gate, and jerks it open. Birds flounce up and out of the clearing, at the centre of which a fallen tree lies like an invitation surrounded by tissues and used condoms. The birds turn up the volume somewhere out of sight, and he wonders then what else is out of sight, if there are cameras, hidden eyes, what time the dog walkers arrive.

At the far end of the clearing, there is a tangle of old cuttings, sharp criss-crossings of this and that. It's an imperfect solution, but he can't think of a better one. He can't think at all. Better to leave it in the open, uncushioned and debagged, and hope to pass it off as someone else's victim? He doesn't think so. His instinct is to conceal.

He drags the slug, still in the greenish sleeping bag, still with its pinkish-cotton head shedding feathers on the wet leaves. He drags it over to the pile of cuttings and branches and undergrowth and starts to make a nest for it. But time is thinning with the dark, and the first hints of light are in the sky. Panic assails him as he scrabbles at twigs and bracken, young green and old brown. He looks for fallen branches that might form a barricade against an inquisitive terrier, for a while at least. Because they will be here soon, the dog walkers, he is sure of that.

He arranges the heavier branches like a wooden casket around the body, then lattices the lighter vegetation on top. He takes a risk when he chooses to reinforce the structure with some planks from the cottage, but without them a large dog would have the body free in no time. Finally, he criss-crosses the entire construction with birch twigs until it looks as if it's always been there, in among the flitters of wildflowers. By now, he is exhausted and covered in burrs and brambles. He seems to be slug-free, but he feels as if he's sloshed around for hours in the black gunk of a nightclub floor. He needs coffee, carbs, sleep. He needs Nefertiti.

He can scarcely recall where exactly it was that Nefertiti lived. But he thinks he will know it by feel if he just starts off in the right direction. As far as he remembers, it was a red-brick barracks of a block with a railing extending right the way along in front. One street from the Common, he reaches the first of a series of similar estates. He turns in at the gate and stops at the corner of a building whose stained concrete staircase disappears in a dog-leg. He examines himself in a convex security mirror. He has become a fairground attraction, warped, more dirt than blood. There is surprisingly little blood.

But even so, he smells like a butcher's shop, a metal tray of meat. And he can feel Mags Madden at his back, pinching the soft skin on the inside of his arm, whispering at him. Jess. Jess. Jess.

He walks along a row of doors, all painted a peculiar green that might be Kelly or Shamrock or even Curramona. The doors have numbers, and he thinks she was a 40-something but she can't have been because the numbers run out at 33. Someone passes, a woman with a shopper and a beanie. But she doesn't even glance at him. Number 29 opens and a man sticks his head out, then pulls it right back in again. Ro is lost now. He is lost and dirty and there must be DNA and evidence spidering out all over him. He leaves the estate past the metal bins and the abandoned skeleton of a racing bike, and keeps on walking.

He walks until he's far away from the Common, until he's in the next manor, more or less, where there is a Tube station and a row of early-morning caffs and a pool. He's surprised to find a pool in operation when they've closed down all the libraries. But there it is – a brown-brick monolith – and the smell of chlorine is the smell of redemption. The girl on reception, on early shift, scarcely looks at him when he passes across his fiver and exchanges it for a fat blue rubber band to put around his wrist.

He undresses to his underpants and wades through the footbath disinfectant to a kind of ante-room by the side of the pool where there are push-button showers and plastic bottles of bright yellow multi-purpose soap. Later in the day there might be a gaggle of schoolkids in regulation blue twittering past him, a regulation teacher, but at this hour of the morning there is only the lone swimmer he hears ploughing back and forth on the other side of the divide. The water is hot and he pounds the button on the wall to keep it coming until the images in his head are only shadows of what they were. Air-drying in the tiny changing cubicle, he discards his hoody, shoving it into one of the plastic bins, but his blue shirt looks fine, respectable even. His hair could still do with a trim, but his face is clean. He looks innocent and, in this world away from slugs and pyres, perhaps he is.

In a caff on the other side of the street he drinks coffee with sweet cream, and the ordinary world settles back around him. He can't risk going back to the house because Jess will force him to speak to the police as soon as she knows he's still around. Besides, the cottage is the thing. He needs to repair the rotten hatch in the wall, and block off the door that's unsecured now. And then he remembers the efficacy of a high-vis jerkin. And the bandstand, with all the materials required to build a barricade.

16

Jess isn't aware of having slept, but there is a moment when morning arrives all at once with a sense of pressing newness – the smell of toast, the burble and grind of a faraway coffee machine, the clean Common light. Ro, Charlie, Hana. There is no one emotion tagged to each of these people. Her feelings fluctuate between rage and anxiety, inexplicable guilt and fearful apprehension, and, in the case of Ro and Charlie, love. When she remembers Ruby, alone in the dark house, she pulls the sleeping child towards her. From downstairs, a declamatory *Today* programme voice is the clue that Charlie is back. She doesn't know yet how she feels about that.

Her gaze drifts out towards the Common and the sky above, its scudding clouds reflected in the huge mirror it took three men to hang. Out there, people are doing what they always do. Stretching, jogging, being pulled along by dogs or by the magnet of a ball. The door edges open, and Charlie has brought her coffee, hot milk on the side. But the toast she smelled earlier is cold now, the butter sunk deep into it, and the paprika sprinkled on the smashed avocado reminds her of the lilies she is trying to forget. He puts the tray down next to her on the blue bedside table, then takes her in his arms, a little too tightly.

'Ouch,' he says. 'Still sore?'

Just like Charlie to think it should all be over already. No more broken bones or hearts or anything.

'Takes a while, you know.'

'Hey, I got you a present.' He has it under his arm, it seems. A small frilled box, black and white. *Fragrance by Heart*, it says.

'Looks posh.'

'Bespoke. Look, it's got your name on it.'

And so it does: *Devised for Jess Clark, who is kind and dependable and very lovely.*

'Gosh. Who sent you there?'

'I asked one of the secretaries at Rob Liston's place.'

'So, what was the brief then?'

'Something nice. Flowery. Fruity.'

She is not remotely flowery. She supposes she must be nice, then. Oh well. As for fruit, she imagines she is the English pear, Hana the small tart berry. She draws away from him, and it hurts, although the image of Charlie instructing some smart girl in Donna Karan on the flavour of his wife is funny, at least it's that. But it's not quite funny enough to divert her from all the things that aren't funny at all.

As she opens the box, she has a flash of white-hot

clarity. She glances up at Charlie but finds herself unable to meet his eye, so dazzling is the realisation that she ought never to have married him. She was so desperate not to be Sophie that she crawled in under Charlie's wing. He represented convention, security, and she thought he would keep her safe. When it came to all the things she thought she needed, Charlie had seemed perfect. His background was stolid, unexciting. There were no hippies there. Just accountants and lawyers who lived in solid houses with well-tended gardens. There was Renée, with her golf and her flower arranging. There was Ralph, with his vintage cars. There was his sensible sister who had married a GP up in Inverness. And so, she had cleaved to Charlie like he was a saviour, even though he could never have been that, she should have known. She should not blame him for marrying her, and yet sometimes she does. He is watching her, waiting for her to react to the little bottle fashioned to look like a black diamond. But she doesn't touch it.

'You brought Hana back,' she says. And it brings tears to her eyes that he could do that.

'She was the only one I could think of,' he says without even realising what it is he's said.

'You should have thought a bit harder,' she says. 'I'm just out of hospital and barely able to make the stairs, and what do I find but Ruby all alone upstairs in her cot, her nappy not changed for hours while Hana entertains the press on our own doorstep.'

Charlie walks round to the other side of the bed, where Ruby is still sleeping, perfectly still, her curls splayed across the pillow. He gathers the child into his arms and she clings to him without opening her eyes. He kisses her head, smooths down her hair.

'What was I supposed to do? I had to find someone at short notice. By the time Martha offered, it was too late. I'd already contacted Hana.'

She knows that's not true, but she hasn't got the strength to challenge it. She is just trying very hard not to cry, like a small child who has discovered that this too is just a fairy tale.

He edges on to the bed and takes her hand, and she is suddenly too exhausted to argue. She shuts her eyes and tries to make the confusion go away.

'Your brother was here, you know, when I rang. That's another reason I got in touch with Hana. I suppose I panicked a bit, really. I couldn't bear the thought of Ruby being looked after by him. The thought terrified me, to tell the truth. But it looks like he's gone now. Off on his travels again, if we're lucky. Poor old Ruby.' He puts the child down gently and pulls the duvet up over her, tucking it in around her.

Jess closes her eyes tightly, hoping fervently that this is true.

He nestles his head into her shoulder. She feels like pushing him away, but she doesn't.

'I'm only going to say this once,' she says instead, her eyes still shut. 'So listen really well. Don't ever be in touch with her again.'

'I've not the slightest inclination.'

When she dares to open them again, the expression on

his face is fervent, contrite, and then she realises he thinks it's all OK now, that she is his whatever he does.

'Let's go away, sweet,' he says. 'Just for the weekend. We could go to Renton.' He takes her hands in his and kisses them, and she can't help wondering if this newly found tenderness is because she is wounded and jobless, and therefore weaker than she was.

'Renton, Charlie? Are you kidding? I've just lost my job.'

'Well I haven't,' he says. 'I'll treat you. We'll do it all, spa treatments, massage, the lot.'

She has always collaborated in the fantasy that his job was the only one that mattered. It seemed necessary to his self-esteem that her work be characterised as a mildly admirable party trick, hardly a financial necessity.

'Don't you realise we'll run out of money by Christmas,' she says, 'unless I find another job?'

His face alters slightly, as if he has just passed an open drain.

'They gave you a package, didn't they?'

'Actually, no,' she says. 'No package. I didn't want to sign anything that would prevent me from suing the pants off them.'

'You're kidding,' he says. 'Why not? There's no way you're going to sue.'

She thinks of Miles, then of capable, implacable Delia.

'I might,' she says. 'I very well might. As for Hana—'

He looks her in the eye, and for the first time she can see a flicker of fear in there.

'Oh my darling. Don't worry about Hana. I have no desire to see her ever again,' and then he kisses her closed mouth like he hasn't done for weeks, gently, persistently, until he has opened her up.

'Where is she now, then?' she says.

'She's gone.'

'Well she was bloody here last night.'

'BA to São Paulo. She left early this morning. Must be mid-Atlantic by now. So, what do you think? Renton? It's only half an hour up the motorway.'

'Hang on a sec. Just run that by me again. How do you know all this? Did you pay for her flight?'

'Sure. Payment in lieu. For the babysitting, that is.'

She swallows hard, tries to work out what she feels about that.

'Come on, sweetheart. Let me treat you.'

She can't escape the feeling that she is being bought, and with a bad cheque, too. 'We can't afford it.'

'Sure we can.'

But his self-assurance is no longer as attractive as it once was.

'Come on, Jess,' he says. 'What harm could it do?'

She feels wrung out, exhausted, and so eventually she gives in. Yes, OK, let's go. Because, what harm in linen sheets and candlelight and all the rest of it? What harm in a change of place and some peace and quiet? But already she is weighing lies against tenderness, care against negligence, and what they have against the cold dark matter of divorce.

While Charlie goes to do a supermarket shop, Ruby and Jess sit together on the floor of the TV room. A

Teletubbies DVD sends Ruby into a flurry of excitement. She wants her scooter. She wants to play. She flings herself around on the floor. Jess has never seen her so overexcited, feverish almost. She calms the child with some milk and they spend a quiet few minutes matching pegged wooden pieces to their butterfly- and lion- and ball-shaped voids. Jess rushes to answer the landline that scarcely ever rings. But it isn't Ro.

Eddie sounds subdued, hesitant.

'What's the matter?' she asks. 'Has something happened?'

'Nothing's wrong. I just wanted to tell you that we're going away. For a while, anyway. We're going travelling again, Maya and me.'

'But won't that leave the school high and—'

'They'll have all summer to find a replacement. It won't be a problem. But we'd like to come and see you before we go. Is that OK?'

She still feels exhausted and her ribs hurt, but of course it's OK.

'We'll drop by around seven,' he says. 'I hope you're feeling a bit better, Jess. I'm sorry we didn't hear. Maya would have helped out, I hope you know that.'

'I do know. Thanks, Eddie.'

'Don't bother with food. There's no need.'

But there is need, of course, and she goes down to the cellar to take something out of the freezer for supper, very carefully negotiating the narrow wooden stairs. Down there, a shadow household is stored in cardboard boxes – duvets past their best, stained pillows, old sleeping bags that they have never had a chance to throw out. After all, who wants to spend their weekends at the dump?

Halfway along, past the rack of ordinary wine they will probably never get to before it becomes undrinkable, past the boxes of baby paraphernalia, there is an open cardboard box. A seasonal box she only discovered again last summer and whose contents she had already, annoyingly, replaced. Flask, picnic rug, an assortment of plastic cups and glasses. There was even a blow-up lilo – pink on one side, floral on the other. And it is all gone. All of it. She gazes at the open box. And, although those things mean nothing to her and have little monetary value, their disappearance gives her an excuse not to feel sorry for Hana, who is a thief now on top of everything else.

Inspector Crowe is on the doorstep soon after lunch. He has a different man with him this time, younger and not so humble. If you passed this guy in the street you would never think he was a detective, with his tight jeans, his dreads, his bluish, mirrored shades. Crowe nods as she tells them to come in, but he doesn't start to talk until they're all seated – at the breakfast bar as before, and no further on.

'You had a Princess Di moment, I hear,' he says.

She doesn't get it, and he looks irritated at having to explain.

'Chased by the paps? Anyway, you know why I'm here. You've got to let me talk to him, Jess. Because we *will* talk to him, I suppose you know that.'

She knows that.

'He upstairs then? Sleeping late?'

She shakes her head. Ruby toddles over to her and she takes the child up on her lap.

'Mind if Si takes a look?'

Perhaps she looks doubtful, because he follows the question with a statement of fact. 'We have a warrant, of course, just so you know, but I thought I'd do this the civilised way. You can go upstairs with Si, if you like.'

She doesn't need to accompany Si, with his shades and his disappointing name.

'I have no idea where my brother is,' she says.

And the pleasure of being able to speak the truth gives her strength.

'Mags Madden,' he says then. 'The woman in the caravan. We're all clear who that is, yes? Well, the pathologist over there has made her report. Mags was kicked, they say. Kicked five times in the head. Cranial BFT. Here, you might want to have a read.' He slides a printout over to her, but she doesn't want to look at it.

'Come on, Jess. Don't pretend you don't care what happened to Mags. We all care, don't we? And you must care a little more than I do, if you spent half your childhood summers in her caravan. It's not disloyal to Sparrow to care about an elderly woman who gets beaten to death.'

'How do they know she didn't fall?' And this sounds like someone else talking, making excuses.

He spreads his hands out on the counter and flutters his fingers on the surface. 'Take it from me, sweetheart.

She didn't just fall. Drunk or not, she didn't die without a lot of assistance.'

Jess turns for the coffee machine.

'No,' he says, abruptly enough to make it sound like 'Stop'. 'No coffee, thanks.' And then his voice softens. 'I'd really like if you would just listen to me. OK?'

And like the good girl she has always been, she nods and stays right where she is.

'Here's what we know. Taxi driver takes thin, pale young man to the Madden house that night. Guy hasn't been traced, but given the subsequent discovery of the passport, given that we now know that Sparrow hired a car in Holyhead – and let's face it, what other reason is there to be in Holyhead than to have come from the ferry? – given—'

Given, given, given.

Si is back downstairs again now, his shades pushed back onto his head. He has a plastic bag, and raises it in her direction. 'A couple of bits and pieces from his room. OK?'

She could object, and perhaps she should, but she doesn't. She is thinking about all the things that are missing from the cellar. She doesn't know why that disconcerts her so greatly, but it does. She can't imagine Hana having any interest in a stained pillow and a pink lilo.

'We haven't had an extradition request. Not yet, anyway, but I wouldn't rule it out.' Crowe is examining her face, and it's making her uncomfortable. She can feel herself redden under his scrutiny. What is she, after all? Just a woman without a job, in a sham marriage, with a loose cannon brother who might turn out to be a murderer.

'Would it help to talk to somebody who was there when your parents went missing? I'm not saying this woman has any answers. None she's given me anyway, but it might be good to talk to her.'

She shrugs. What is there to hear?

'She lives somewhere in Berkshire.' And he is scrolling down his phone now. 'Yeah, Datchet area. Evelyn Tuite. I can always ask her to give you a ring.'

'I'd rather not,' she says before she's really given any thought to it. She is glad when he doesn't take no for an answer, when he says that sometimes these things are better done by email, at least at first.

'I suppose,' she says.

Ruby starts to cry, and they take that as their cue to leave. Jess leads them to the door. Saying goodbye, she comes face-to-face with herself in Si's mirrored shades and is forced to look away. She knows they will be back, they say as much, but this time she is almost afraid to let them leave. She should have protected Sparrow better. She should have kept him with her from the start.

That period just after their return to England is fixed in her mind for many reasons: the relentless attention of the press, the difficulty settling in at school, the great contrast there was between the way Christmas was celebrated by Auntie Rae's family – with church, turkey, church, carols, church – and the chaotic approach of her own parents, with presents opened the moment they were received and Warninks Advocaat for everyone, served for the kids in eggcups, but served nonetheless.

It was Christmas Eve, and Jess had been sitting at the

top of the stairs on the first landing, when the man who turned out to be her paternal grandfather arrived at the door. Nestled down on the beige carpet, her nose crisp with allergens, she could see the tweed jacket, the snot-green V-neck stretched across his belly, the pate that gleamed beneath the light. She already knew that this man gave Auntie Rae money to help her to look after them, but she had barely ever met him and knew next to nothing about him other than that he thought Sparrow should be in a proper school in the countryside where they locked you in at night. As for the conversation between this man and Auntie Rae, she caught only jags and scraps before they moved into the front room and shut the door.

'The girl remembers nothing. Is that right?'

That statement triggered something in her and for the first time she was sure.

The trees, the trees, the trees. Something was moving in the trees. Sparrow told me, but I wouldn't look.

By the start of the next term Sparrow was gone. He was still too young to board, but their grandparents were keen that he live with them in the meantime and attend the school as a day boy. Jess missed him but she felt liberated from him, too. She worked hard at school, was picked for the quiz team, and soon the story of the beach was crowded out by capital cities and prime ministers, highest mountains and longest rivers. Most nights she was so exhausted by the long school day that she would fall asleep right away.

When she next saw Ro, she was shocked by how desperate he still was, how lost. He had begun to entertain the fantasy that his mother had been coerced into abandoning him, that she loved him too much, and so 'they' tore her away from him. On her own she felt powerless, but maybe that was the moment. Perhaps there was something more she could have done.

Ruby is tugging at Jess's leg now, and now there are swings to think about. Whatever else is happening, there are always swings.

Ro is lucky, there is very little blood, and by the time he has finished cleaning up, there is hardly any sign that the slug was ever there. As for securing the cottage, he has bolstered its weak spots, and made his barricade, and now he is restless, out of sorts. He curses summertime and the long wait for darkness, but when finally it descends, he stalks across the Common with his cap down, suspicious of every park-bench loiterer who might turn out to be a Crowe. He avoids the burger stall on the cut-through with its side order of cops, and picks up a kebab on the South Side instead.

The lights are on in Jess's house, but whether it's Hana in there or Jess is anyone's guess. He still has the front-door key in his pocket, but now that he is a banished orphan, a slayer of slugs, it seems politic to take the back entrance instead.

He keys in Charlie's most obvious of codes, wondering idly if this is a universal password that could unlock the essential Charlie, and slips into the dark garden. It is like entering a cinema when the film has already begun.

He stands there in front of the brightly lit screen of the kitchen window, transfixed by the high definition parade of domesticity. Jess is back, and apparently unscathed by her accident. There are no crutches or plaster casts or obviously disfiguring scars. There is warmth in there, and food, and candles. There are four of them for dinner, and Ro's eye picks out Charlie next, blue shirt open at the neck, sleeves rolled up, sitting square at the head of the table. He raises a virtual sniper rifle and blows the man away. Charlie halts, his fork halfway to his mouth, and Ro's breath catches. For a moment, it seems, the weight of his desire has been enough to make it happen. But the moment doesn't survive, and Charlie does, and, by the sound of muffled laughter from the screen, the joke is on him.

Opposite Charlie, sitting with his back to the window, is a man with a grey-gold ponytail. Eddie, of course. Jess and his mother are facing each other across the table. When Jess reaches across to touch his mother's hand, Ro's heart lurches. The gesture is casually affectionate, as if it's no big deal to be sitting in the same room as Sophie Considine, resurrected from a Goa beach.

How did he find himself shut out like this? When did he move to the other side of the glass, and become a danger to rough sleepers, a night-time peril? Seeing them all together, all fed and warm and nurtured, he could scream the whole city down with rage and indignation on behalf of all things forgotten.

'Would you mind if we left a key with you, Jess?' Maya is saying. 'If you had time to pop in now and then and just check that everything looks OK, that would be great.'

Jess finds herself examining Maya more closely than she's ever done before. Her unlined face has a kind of otherworldly benevolence about it. It's hard to guess her age, but sixtyish feels about right.

'I'll drop one over tomorrow, try and catch you before you leave for your weekend.'

Maya's silvery plait rests on her shoulder much like Sophie's might do, if this were Sophie. There is a slight accent, something flat about the vowels, but it is scarcely there at all. Swedish? She isn't sure. But yes, perhaps it could be Swedish.

For a moment, Jess is tempted to be straight with Maya, to let her know how these things run with Sparrow – a mad gush of obsession and then the slow trickle of realisation that this is one more blind alley. She could suggest they get a DNA test and just knock the whole subject on the head, but it seems unnecessary, now that Eddie and she are going away, now that Ro seems to have gone. It would sound alarmist, and Eddie has already told her how it's not good for Maya to get worked up.

Later, when they have eaten the mushroom masala she defrosted, the dhal, Jess asks Maya straight out if she met Eddie in Goa. It comes up quite naturally in the context of travel and where they might go now, on what Eddie has taken to referring to as their 'year abroad'.

Maya glances at Eddie and when he doesn't react she smiles. 'Oh no, I didn't meet Ed till I was well into my fifties. I moved here after my divorce, in fact. I'd been living in Devon, in a village in the middle of nowhere. I relied on friends for transport – never learned to drive myself – and then there was the impossibility of earning money. An income is hard to come by down in Devon.' She glances at her pearly nails. 'I'm not much of a gardener either, so I was never going to be Miss Self-Sufficiency.'

'She found her place, though,' Eddie says and squeezes Maya's hand.

'In South London. Who'd have thought?'

'By the way, Eddie,' Jess says then. 'I've been given the details of a woman who was in Goa the same time as my parents. Evelyn Tuite. I wondered if you recognised the name?'

She detects something like alarm in Eddie's face before his attention is drawn back to Charlie, and how dhal is a completely different dish if you go to Kerala.

Later, Eddie draws Jess aside. He seems agitated. 'You shouldn't do that, you know,' he says. 'You shouldn't let just anyone inside your head. You have no idea what their motive might be, who they are and where they're coming from.'

It takes Jess a moment to realise that he's referring to Evelyn Tuite. 'What harm could it do? There's nothing wrong in hearing what she has to say.'

But Eddie is shaking his head. 'I don't know what her angle is, but a woman popping up out of the blue, blast from the past, she's probably out to make mischief. God knows, she might think there's money in it, with the press interested.'

'You remember her then?'

'Yes. I bloody do. I remember her all right. She's my ex.'

Maya puts her hand on his and pats it gently. She is watching his face closely, waiting for the moment when she can catch his gaze and hold it in hers. And when the moment comes, it seems to calm him. Jess tries again. 'Well, to be fair—'

'To be fair, Jess? To some stranger? How about a bit of fairness towards those who love you.'

She has never heard him say love before, in any context. He has certainly not said he loved *her* before, and she is knocked off balance by it, she is a grown woman now, but she is still a girl without a father. Her skin, the secret one, is tender and it feels the word like a caress.

Ro doesn't launch himself towards the window and attempt to burrow through. He doesn't scream the house down. Instead, he watches the silent movie and notes it all – the murky dish that resembles porridge, the sliced mango and coconut laddu – until, after the production of a bottle – a Speyside malt, no doubt, a favourite Charlie tipple – and its rejection by the guests, the show is over.

He half considers rushing round to the other side of the house and intercepting his mother on the way out. His heart batters at the thought of Eddie's face as he reclaims her. But he has learned restraint enough to stick to the plan. He watches the bottom floor go black. Up at the top of the house, a dim light flicks on in Jess's room and then the window is swept dark again. On the first floor, however, the window of the room that was once Hana's remains stubbornly lit.

He sits down in the gravel and waits, fondling the key in his pocket, winding it through his fingers. He waits until the only sound is the occasional motorbike, the thrum of a taxi, until he comes face to face with a fox who stands and glares at him. But that first-floor light just won't go out.

17

Renton is somewhere they used to go in the good old days, all velvet sofas and long walks. Jess used to love it there, they both did. She will try not to think about the cost.

'We'll switch off our phones and leave the iPads at home. Catch a glimpse of the blood moon without all this light pollution. Stand in the middle of a field and hold hands.'

Jess can't imagine Charlie wanting to stand in the middle of a field with her and watch a moon, even a bloody one. She can't imagine either of them would ever have wanted that. She takes a side glance at him, but he seems perfectly serious.

She is in the middle of feeding Ruby when an email pings into her phone. The message is peppered with references to people called Soph and Will, though she has never heard them abbreviated like that before. Evelyn Tuite has attached two images.

The first is of Jess's mother on a beach – young,

beautiful, fey. Maybe this is *the* beach, it's hard to tell in black and white, but she thinks the throw on which her mother is sitting is the same, and her heart is scraped raw by the sight of it. She has always felt that if she only had that throw, or her mother's wicker basket perhaps, she might be able to come to terms with the reality that one moment they were there, and the next they were gone for ever. The other image is of Sophie with a man – a young-ish man, perhaps in his early thirties. This one has been taken on a beach, too, but whether it's the same beach, or even the same day, it's impossible to say.

The stranger on the other end of the email addresses her as if they already know one another. The chattiness is disconcerting.

I was in Goa, same place as your parents. Can't say it was the happiest of times, not for me anyway. You've seen this man before, but you probably don't remember him. That's Ed, my ex. He was mad keen on photography, Ed. We were going to travel the world and collect it in images. His words, not mine. In the end, we didn't get past Goa. Arrived together, went home separately. Soph was like that. She took what she wanted. Not that she wanted Ed for long, as it happened. I still have all the old pictures he took. In fact, I have shoeboxes full of people who have nothing to do with me. It seems wrong to bin photos, I always think. I'm a bit superstitious like that. I got in touch with Bill Crowe when I read about the passport in the Daily Post. *Brought it all back.*

Taking another look at the photo, she can catch a glimpse of Eddie in the smile, in the way the man holds himself, the slightly concave chest. But the hair is short and there is no beard. He looks more conventional, somehow, and she realises how instrumental Goa must have been in shaping him. Nonetheless, Eddie looks quite handsome enough to have been her mother's lover.

At the bottom of the email, there is a landline number. When Jess has put Ruby down for her nap, when she has nestled her and kissed her hair and vowed never to be the kind of woman who could walk away from her child, she punches the number into her phone.

His night in the cottage has been cold and uncomfortable. Having kept the one remaining sleeping bag for his mother, he lies curled up in a corner, well away from where he encountered the slug, with only his jacket for cover. He wakes longing for a shot of hot coffee, for something warm and comforting to eat. No one sees him elbowing his way out through the broken fencing, he is sure of that, or heading for the Costa down the road.

He dreads to think how cold the cottage would be in winter. He sits in the rear of the Costa, his back to the door, warming his hands on the supersized mug – palm, back, palm, back – while the unseasonal hot air pumped out from under the banquette scorches his calves.

He has the queasy sense that he needs to take her soon, before somebody finds the slug. But he still hasn't got the drugs. He plugs Jess's iPad in to charge and finds that the consensus on 4chan is for one unpronounceable thing, while Reddit subscribers favour another. Which, either, both? He is almost at the point of walking into the Boots next door and asking for a sudden, foolproof sleeping draught when his patience pays off. He is just approaching the final curve of his pain aux raisins when a new post appears on 4chan from someone who claims to be able to supply the perfect substance from the McDonald's on the Old Kent Road.

A delegation of mums arrives, heavy with prams and buggies slung with nappy bags, while he sets up the drop for later. He angles himself away from them, but, even so, he knows it's not wise to hang around. His belly full and his plan in place, he makes his way back to the Common. He tries hard not to look towards the place where the slug is buried, but the pull he feels towards his pyre-in-waiting is irresistible. It takes him off the path, and into a thicket of saplings and barbed scrub. Soon, he finds himself standing in the clearing, right where his head has told him not to go.

Shocked at himself for having succumbed to temptation, he shoves his hands in the pockets of his jacket and walks quickly past the spot. So far, the slug is undetectable, its resting place still latticed with twigs and tangled foliage. But there is a faint odour, he will admit; there is what Auntie Rae would have called a farmyard smell.

As he passes the side of the cottage, the barricaded door, he looks back at the Common, its great expanse filtered now through a fringe of glittering leaves. That first stretch of open field presents a problem. Even if she proves willing to come along with him, at least at first, they will be visible from all directions. He will have to take her through the chestnut trees instead. Once he's seen that the barricade is still in place, that the cottage is secure, he sets out to walk the route that he will have to take when he brings her back. Affecting a confidence he doesn't feel, mindful of the old rules of invisibility, he strides towards the school, past coaches parked in the spaces reserved for them on the red route and a long trail of cars hitched up on the pavements on the Common side, mothers and nannies and Hackett dads, jabbing at their little screens.

This will be difficult, even with his old friend the high-vis vest. But there is another worry, too. What if she doesn't conduct herself like a mother who has walked away should do, with proper contrition and regret? What then? When he gets her to the cottage, he will have a list of questions for her. And topping the lot of them, the biggie. The one he can't ignore.

Mama, oh sweet Mama.

Those nights at school when he cried so hard his pillow was salty, when he swam oceans in search of her.

Did you ever think of me?

You are not angry, he tells himself, and neither will she be. She is hoping you will come for her.

He passes the bandstand café and Nefertiti is outside, wiping down the metal tables under the huge tree. Two men are playing chess at a battered board, just like in the old days, and the Ray-Bans dads are there with their helmeted kids. So much has happened since he last saw Nef.

'Hey,' she says, waving over at him though a little less enthusiastically today.

'No sign of Eddie Jacques,' he says. 'I reckon we've got rid of him.'

'Oh yeah?' she says, scrubbing at a little scabbed stain on the corner of a table.

'Only a matter of time now till I see my mum.'

'Oh yeah?' she says again, still not looking up at him. 'We should have a party. Your mum, my mum, Lady Gaga and Donald Trump. Fucksake.'

'No need to be so aggressive, Nef.'

'Amanda. My name is Amanda, right?'

He shrugs.

'Your mum? Who are we even talking about?'

But as he opens his mouth to answer her, she gives him a go-no-further hand. 'Look, don't tell me. I really don't want to know.'

She doesn't give him a chance to tell her he thinks he's found a dealer who has what he's looking for. She just flounces off, flicking the cloth onto her shoulder and gathering glasses into a tower she carries between her hands like an offering of air. But he doesn't need her now anyway. He will stock up on supplies at Jess's house, and pick up the drugs this afternoon.

A man answers, and in a parallel domestic world from Jess's an opening door releases muffled TV voices and a clatter of plates. Evelyn Tuite lifts the phone with a rustle.

'I'm glad you called,' she says, pausing to get the name right. 'Jessica-May.'

'Jess,' she says. 'Jess is fine.'

'Bill Crowe gave me your details. He's a doll, isn't he, Bill? He told me this case had never left him, the sight of you children, all alone. And I remember you two myself, little blond sweethearts, holding hands like the babes in the wood. Some people stay in your head for all the wrong reasons, though, don't they? Bad penny always gawking up from the bottom of your bag. You know what I thought when I heard about Mags? Good riddance, that's what I thought.'

Jess is beginning to feel things spiral away from her. She moves into the bathroom and locks the door. She sits on the edge of the bath and concentrates hard.

'You knew Mags?'

'Not well. She was only there a couple of weeks.'

'Mags Madden was in Goa?'

'Sure. Didn't you know? She'd been teaching English somewhere. Delhi maybe? Job came to an end. God knows, probably fired the little tart. Came to us to have a little break, that's what she called it, not that she knew anyone there except Soph. Your mum, she really didn't want Mags coming, though they'd known each other since they were little ones. But Mags turned up anyway. And you know what? I'm no fan of Soph's, but Mags was a whole other nightmare. She was a right nasty piece of work. Little weasel of a thing with that real carroty red hair, slathered on the sun cream like you wouldn't believe. Fancied your daddy something rotten. Believe me, Soph was right to be careful.'

Jess wants it all to stop. Her first reaction is to put down the phone, but somehow she can't bring herself to do that. Because she also wants to know it all, about her mother, about Eddie.

'The day I saw the news in the paper about Mags, I had to talk to somebody about it. So I called Inspector Crowe.'

'You weren't exactly friendly with my mother, then?' Jess asks, because it seems important to establish just how much her mother might have been hated. That she expects her mother to have been hated comes as a surprise to her, but it seems she is right.

'Friendly? She was screwing my chap. What do you think? She was pretty, though, I'll give her that. Hope for your sake you got the genes. You blonde, dear? Like your mum?'

'I'm just mousy.'

'She had lovely hair, I'll say that for her. It was that silvery kind of blonde you don't find very often.'

'And she sang, didn't she,' Jess says, keen for her mother to be more than just beautiful.

'Oh she sang all right. Though there was nothing special about her singing. Nothing original, anyway. Old school, that's what she was. She had a guitar with a braided strap, for Pete's sake. In 1992.' Evelyn Tuite is taking a long drag on a cigarette, and that makes Jess long for one too. The woman exhales luxuriantly. 'She went in for that breathy style. Like one of those French singers. You know? What's her name that was married to the tiny little politician?'

'Carla Bruni.'

'Yeah. Like her, can't sing for toffee but somehow carries it off. To be honest, I thought it was a load of crap. Not that I want to speak ill of your mum, love. Really, that's not why I'm talking to you. But it wasn't singing, it was just sex.'

And the way Evelyn Tuite says the word makes it sound worse than murder. Jess can't imagine this woman on a beach in Goa. She can't imagine her young, irresponsible. And that's the thing. If Evelyn Tuite knows anything, if she can remember anything useful at all, perhaps that's because she was the only one who was sober.

'Jessica-May, you've got in touch with me because you want answers. So let me tell you what I know.'

So there *is* something. Jess wants to be able to say that she knows as much as anyone could be expected to know about a mother last seen on a Goa beach twenty-five years ago, that she doesn't need a complete stranger to tell her about her mother. But none of that is true. She is frightened, though. She isn't sure how much truth she can stand.

'Inspector Crowe,' Jess says, 'Bill, I'm sure he'll have passed on anything you told him, but thanks anyway.' And right then, she almost puts down the phone.

'Oh, I haven't told Bill any of this personal stuff,' Evelyn says. 'It's none of his business. But I'm telling you now, love. Your mum was a hard nut. She didn't need to take my Ed, but she did. Shame, really.'

And right away, Jess knows the real conversation has begun, that it has veered down a dark alley where she can't control it. And yet, she's unable to tell this woman to stop. Already she is in the middle of a fantasy where Eddie is her real pa and the reason they ended up in Goa in the first place. The thought shames her, and she misses the beginning of Evelyn's next sentence.

'Not that I blame her for straying, not per se. Just not with my bloke. Your dad – the drink and drugs and all the rest of it. That was hard. When it came to him and Mags, that must have been the last straw for her.'

Evelyn Tuite's voice has turned cold. She has something to say and Jess doesn't know if she has the strength to hear it. And then, in an instant, she loses patience. 'So what are you saying? That this was all *my pa's* fault or—'

Evelyn seems genuinely taken aback by that. 'Oh no, my love. No, no, no. That's not the way it was at all.'

Jess steels herself. 'OK. Why don't you tell me how it *was.*'

'Soph didn't need drugs. She got high as a kite on all the attention. Ed was in love with her, sure he was. Why else would he have decided to get involved with you kids? He didn't have to do that. When it came to the affair, Soph got bored with poor old Ed very, very quickly. The whole thing probably only lasted a month. Look, I know you're still in touch, so maybe I'm boiling my cabbage—'

'Yes,' Jess is feeling defensive now. 'But he's never mentioned—'

'Why would he? He was the loser, wasn't he? In the meantime, your mum had moved on to a guy called Dejan. I don't remember his surname, but he was from somewhere in the Balkans. Slovenia, Serbia, not sure which. A dealer. Eddie did some work for him for a while.'

She doesn't know why that shocks her. This was Goa, after all. But she feels crushed by disappointment.

'Eddie was a dealer?'

'I never saw the money, if he was.' And she takes another deep drag of her cigarette. 'He did a bit of running for Dejan, but that's about it. I doubt he'd tell you that, though. Don't expect he shouts about it these days. Morals were different back then. And when you're far from home, the rules don't always make much sense.'

Jess remembers Dejan, the glittering bracelet on her mother's wrist. She doesn't care to acknowledge that.

'Dejan didn't hang out at the Yellow House with the others. He was a big shot. At least, that's how we saw him. Funny bloke, with a moustache, mad keen on techno music. I think he ended up going back home, actually. Things were kicking off back there, the old country was breaking up, war starting, all that. And he seemed to think there were opportunities for him in that.'

Jess is losing patience now. 'What has this to do with my mother?'

'Like I said, you can't judge any of it by your own standards. If you don't want to engage with this, that's fine. But if you do, Dejan, he's your key. If you want to know what I think, I think she probably only really wanted your pa, except for the fact that he was out of his head most of the time. Dejan had the drugs your father needed. So, fill in the gaps.'

She doesn't care to fill in the gaps, at least not on

demand. 'I mean, thanks for telling me all this. But forgive me if I find it all a bit—'

'Sordid? I guess it was. It looks good from the outside, that lifestyle. But it was hell, specially for the women, specially if you were like me, not exactly Kate Moss. You'll find it's usually the men who do better when it comes to free love. But if you want the photos—'

'I can't imagine Eddie taking photos. I've known him most of my life, and I've never seen him with a camera.'

'What are you saying then, love? You don't believe me? You never saw him with a camera so he never had one? People change.'

'Sure.'

'You'd have to come and pick them up though.'

'How come you've got the photos if Eddie took them?'

'I took them. He wanted them back, but I held on to them. Because it would hurt, I suppose. All those photos of lovely Soph he'd never see again. You can have them, if you want. In fact, I should have given them to you children years ago.'

She needs to play for time. 'Maybe I should talk to Eddie first.'

'Up to you. As for the passport, if Mags ended up with it, my guess is Mags stole it. If she couldn't have Soph's man, she was damn well going to help herself to whatever else Soph had. As for the passport, for all we know she might have used it herself.'

'Whoever used it went to Paris.'

'All I remember is that some family had hired her, back in Europe, as a kind of in-house governess. God help them. No idea where, though. Just somewhere on the Continent.' There is another long exhalation. 'Come to think of it, she would have loved that. Taking Soph's way out.'

'Do you think my mother always intended to dis-appear?' Jess is almost afraid to hear the answer.

'Doubt it. Not without you kids. No way. She'd never have done that. Her and the little lad, they were joined at the hip. But *with* you? Yeah, maybe. Can't blame her for having an exit route.'

Jess feels a wave of relief, heartbreak, gratitude; she can't put any one tag on it.

'I'd call that sensible, really, if you're married to a smack addict. Wouldn't you? Look, I don't know what happened, I really don't. But it was a tiny village, with nothing much in the way of public transport. The only bus came once a week. There'd have been taxis, of course. Tuk-tuks. But apart from that you'd be pretty much stuck there until someone was willing to come and get you out. She must have had transport. If you ask me, Dejan drove her out in that big jeep of his.'

Jess is about to put an end to the call, but she can tell that Evelyn doesn't want to let her go.

'And just one other thing. The newspaper said you kids were playing at the water's edge while your mother read. Well, Sophie never read. She might have picked out a few chords on the guitar, or plaited her hair. But she never read.'

Jess can hear steps on the stairs outside the bedroom. Charlie wants to beat the traffic, so they'll have time to accustom Ruby to the hotel babysitter. She hasn't figured out what this woman's agenda is. For all she knows, she could be a reporter, a fantasist, a fraud. No reason to think the *Daily Post* is finished with her yet. The thought of that makes her decisive. And so she tells Evelyn Tuite, quite suddenly, that she has to go, that someone is looking for her.

'Before you go. That photo? The one the papers keep on printing? Ed took that. She got him to take photos of her, of you and the boy.'

It's a banal end to a lifelong conundrum, but it will have to do.

'He sent it to the papers. I think he thought if she saw you kids it would make her come back. I think he thought she would come back to him, you see. Even then.'

'Eddie was on the beach that day? I didn't realise.' She is feeling sick, and now she just wants to get away. She wants to try to work this out in her head.

'Oh no, dear. I never suggested that. Don't get me wrong. It wasn't taken on the day she disappeared anyway. It was taken, I dunno, a couple of weeks before? Before she dumped him and took up with Dejan. He took it one day they spent together on the beach with you kids.'

But she remembers no such day, and she is sure she would remember. What if Eddie had been there, in the trees, perhaps, photographing them from a distance while their parents were being attacked, or abducted? What if he did it after the event? Without even realising it, she has cut the call. If Evelyn rings back, she will pretend the call failed. But she doesn't ring back, and this is all that Jess is left with. A little more, but not much, and not better.

'Jess? You OK?' Charlie is in the bedroom now. She can hear him sliding open drawers and pulling his weekend bag down from the top of the wardrobe.

'Yes, I'm fine. I'll be out in a sec.' She flushes the loo and runs the water, soaping Evelyn Tuite away, for now at least.

By the time she leaves the bathroom, Charlie is downstairs. She has already packed, but then she remembers the walk, the moon in the field, and goes in search of a warm jacket. Her Barbour seems to have disappeared and so she goes to borrow one of Charlie's instead. It's while she is retrieving it from his wardrobe that she finds the package. At first, she's confused as to how her gift from Charlie can have repackaged itself when she left the naked bottle on the bathroom shelf. Not that she will ever use the scent – too cloying, too much violet in the blend. Yet here it is again. *Fragrance by Heart*. Even as she opens it, she knows. And it is as bad as it could be. *Devised for Hana Schweitzer de Abreu, my everything.*

Charlie has already clipped Ruby into her car seat in the back of the big black 4X4 that Jess never has any inclination to drive. As he gets behind the wheel, there is a determination about him, a set to his chin. If they were celebrities, and the two pressmen from earlier in the week were a swarm of paparazzi, this scene would be captioned, 'Fighting to save their marriage'.

She will not fight for him. Meanwhile, Ruby is giving her newest toy – a black and white goblin – a contented chew. By the time they reach the M4, she has fallen asleep, her head drooping forward like a tender-stalked flower.

Charlie puts his foot down. Once they're past Heathrow, the traffic thins and the light thickens. She refuses to think about Hana. Instead, she flicks back through her emails and finds the message from Evelyn. She reads and rereads it, but when they reach the hotel, she still hasn't decided what to do. Charlie carries Ruby into the hotel in her car seat as if she is a gift.

The hotel at Renton has been updated since they were last there. There is still the cantilever staircase spiralling out of one corner, the baronial fireplace in another, but these days the elks are lit in pink neon, and sombre paintings with a Rothko heft to them are paired with Corinne Days. The reception area smells as fragrant as something dreamed up by *Fragrance by Heart*. And yes, it is all as lovely as she remembers it. But everywhere, she imagines Hana. In the lobby, in the lift, even in the big plush bedroom they have been allocated overlooking the lawns. She can't think why she agreed to come here.

At lunch, she is so exhausted she doesn't really notice the food, but it is tastefully arranged and drizzled on. There is starched white linen and off-pink orchids, beeswax candles and petits fours. How could she not be happy when so much trouble has been taken? She places her hand on the table next to the gleaming array of cutlery, and examines it closely. The nails are painted dark grey, but she can't think when they were painted or why she chose the colour. Her tiny engagement solitaire has been trumped by a brash marquise-cut stone, a present from

Charlie when Ruby was born. This is not her hand. It is not her life. Charlie covers that stranger's hand with his own, and his touch feels nauseating, warm and moist. She pulls away, then reaches for her napkin to cover the moment. Her face burns, and she lets the stiff, cool linen soothe it.

'I have a package to pick up,' she says. 'For Martha.'

'Do you want me—'

'No, no. It's fine. I need a breather anyway. It all feels, I don't know, a bit overwhelming I guess.'

'It's a nice place.'

'Sure. I know. It's just—'

He frowns slightly, but he doesn't press for more.

Once she's made the decision to pay a visit to Evelyn Tuite, the rest is easy. It takes a matter of minutes to arrange a golf lesson for Charlie followed by a massage, to book Ruby in with the resident babysitter. Driving out of Renton, over the cattle grid and through the stone columns, she begins to breathe again.

It takes less than half an hour to get to Evelyn's house, in a cul-de-sac off a suburban road off Junction 5. It's hard to find a parking spot because most of the kerb has been swallowed up by driveways onto paved-over front gardens, so she reverses out again and leaves the jeep in the car park of the Harvester instead. The path up to Evelyn's house is edged on either side in white-painted concrete shells; the house itself is a grey semi, braced with blinds. It suddenly strikes Jess that perhaps she should have rung ahead, but it's too late now.

On the phone, it had been hard to imagine a woman

in her mid-sixties, but of course that's what Evelyn is. Her hair has an inch of growth, more white than grey, and she is wearing a kind of batik shift over a pair of black leggings. She looks tired, heavy, disappointed.

'Evelyn, I'm sorry to rock up like this. It's Jess. We spoke on the phone?'

'I didn't think you'd come,' she says, standing back to let Jess in. It's hard to gauge what she's thinking.

As soon as she enters the house, Jess feels like she has upset some unseen apple cart. She is led into a room that is evidently not used very often. A pair of sofas covered in Indian cotton throws face one another across a glass coffee table on which there are two shoeboxes, one Clarks, the other Nike. Within seconds of sitting down, Jess realises she has chosen the wrong seat, even though she was careful to select what seemed to her to be the place of least status, a low Victorian nursing chair. And then it strikes her that the very fact that she selected that chair was probably enough to raise it in the pecking order, that any chair she chose would have been the wrong one.

Something about the house, hugged as it is into the damp corner of a cul-de-sac, and the fact that Jess is not entirely sure whether she is welcome, flattens the atmosphere and makes it hang heavily around them. Evelyn must be one of the last people on earth to smoke indoors. She makes a performance of it, flinging her butts onto the dead coals in the tiled fireplace. Jess can hardly resist touching the shoeboxes, but Evelyn hasn't offered them again. She seems different face-to-face. Quieter. Surly and tight-lipped.

Jess has the thought that perhaps she reminds Evelyn of one or other of her parents, maybe that accounts for the change. Her whole life has been an attempt not to be like Sophie. But maybe that's the problem.

'You must be hungry,' Evelyn says. 'Can I make you something to eat?'

'Oh no,' she says, her mind flicking back to lunch at the hotel. 'I'm fine.'

But Evelyn persists. 'Surely I could make you a sandwich at least. Come on now, what would you like?'

She is not hungry, and besides she does not want to eat anything in this house. But she is keen not to be rude either. Cheese, maybe? There is no cheese. Ham? No ham either, and definitely no tuna. She is embarrassed then to have taken the bait at all. Evelyn disappears into the kitchen and re-emerges a couple of minutes later with a red toast rack filled with triangles of toast, some spread with Marmite, others with honey.

Evelyn slides a press cutting out from behind a painted vase on the mantelpiece. Jess wonders if it is kept there, or if it's been placed there on the offchance that she'll visit.

' "Tragic Sophie and those Orphans on the Beach". All that palaver. Don't tell me she wouldn't have loved all that. Typical Soph. In some ways, she got exactly what she wanted.'

Her malevolence is astonishing, but Jess is on her turf and for a moment she is shocked into silence.

'She was an attention-seeker, Jessica-May. I hate to say it, but it's true. I'm sorry you were dragged halfway round the world for the sake of that woman's vanity.'

Inside her own head, Jess is protesting that it's too harsh to say that kind of thing about her mother and expect her just to take it. But Jess is desperate to find out what's inside the shoeboxes, and so she just nods and forces down the over-milky tea until she has the opportunity to get away.

18

It was easy to get into the house while Charlie was pack-
ing up the car. Ruby, strapped into her car seat like a con-
vict, was the only one to notice him. She raised her hand
and gave him a little royal wave. Ro Ro Ro your boat.
Inside the house, Ro stepped behind the cellar door and
waited for Jess to come downstairs. Once he heard her
setting the alarm, and the front door was slammed shut,
he counted to a hundred before stepping back out again.
He steeled himself against the scream of the alarm, then
calmly keyed in Charlie's birth date to switch it off.

In the kitchen, he stocks up on provisions: canned
fruit and rice pudding and baked beans, more jars of
olives and sun-dried tomatoes and two packets of salty
crackers. The thought of a mission successfully under way
has given him an appetite, and he helps himself to cheese
and ham, a large bowl of lentil salad, a banana. To kill
time before the meeting on the Old Kent Road, he flops
onto the sofa and watches a documentary about Roswell

until he realises he knows it all anyway. When the doorbell rings, his first thought is of a large black bird in a police hat.

He scoots into Jess's empty drawing room and peeks through the shutters. But this is not the disaster he was expecting, this is joy. Because his mother has come for him. She is standing looking back out at the street, and then she turns and tries the bell again. As she raises her hand, he spots her ghostly tattoo. If it were anyone else, he would melt back into the dark hallway. There is a calculation to be made here, gift horse or not. She rings again, then checks her watch and glances back at the street. But he is terrified of losing her, and so he rushes for the door and cracks it open just a sliver, for fear of prying eyes.

She looks surprised to see him, startled even. 'Oh, hello,' she manages. 'William. I didn't know you were still here. I thought . . . but never mind. Is Jess there? Or have I missed them?'

It's Jess she's come to see. Of course it is.

He thinks quickly. No, no, not at all. Jess has just popped out, Charlie too, and won't she come in? And he can't help thinking spider and fly, though he pushes the thought away.

'I didn't see the car outside so I wondered . . .' She hesitates a moment on the doorstep and he realises then that she won't cross the threshold unless he invites her to. He is not good at reacting to things he hasn't initiated.

'You don't mind, do you, if I just wait a few minutes? I'd love to see them to say goodbye. It's been so sudden, but that's Eddie for you. We're going away, you see. Big trip.'

Big trip?

Fate has gifted her to him, and already it is threatening to swipe her away. The irony of it – when he is only half a day from the perfect subduing, truth-revealing drug – to have her here without the means to capture her. The thought floors him, and he is struck dumb. Syllables bubble on his tongue, but they don't form into words.

As they walk into the kitchen – or rather, as his mother walks into the kitchen and he follows her – it is obvious that this is going to be a superficial encounter, a useless one. She stands there awkwardly by Jess's big American fridge until he stretches out his arm and gestures to a chair. No breakfast bar for her. She lowers herself into place and spreads her fingers out across the slightly sticky tablecloth that Jess uses to protect her precious walnut table from Ruby. And he is embarrassed by it, on Jess's behalf. He tugs at it until she lifts her hands and he is able to slide it away.

'That's better,' he says.

She looks slightly taken aback, but then she smiles. He spots her inching up the cuff of her jacket. And it breaks his heart to see that his mother is looking at her watch. What's ten minutes of her life, after all she owes him? But all she can do, after depriving him of twenty-odd years of love, is check the time. And his heart drains into his eyes, his ears. It floods into his capillaries, into the tiny alveoli in his lungs, until he is drenched in all its pent-up sorrows.

'How come I haven't met you here long ago, with Jess and Ruby?'

His throat has closed itself off, and he stretches his neck to free it. 'I've been travelling,' he says.

'Nice.'

Not nice, not nice, not nice. He needs to break through that kind of blandness if there's to be any progress here.

'Actually, it wears you down after a while.'

'I'm sorry to hear that.'

How could she be sorry, when she has no idea whatsoever?

'I haven't been *travel* travelling, you see. Not *your* kind of travelling, off to ashrams and things.'

'No, well, I didn't—'

'I've been in Ireland, most recently.'

And he looks at her again to see if that remark has found its place. If she's putting two and two together and making Mags. If she's giving him some respect for that, at least. But no, she doesn't seem to have any particular interest in Ireland.

'Oh,' she says. 'A little colder than where we're going.'

Well, no, as it happens, he thinks, visualising the cottage and all its draughts. No colder than that.

'I've never really had the time to travel much,' she says.

He's astonished. Is she kidding herself, or trying to put him off the track?

'It's a regret of mine. But something has to give. That's why it was so lovely when Eddie suggested this trip out of the blue—'

He thinks about the van, the yellow cock and balls, and he can't help but smile. Not exactly out of the blue.

'Bit last-minute, though,' he says.

She makes a gesture, as if it's all been beyond her control. 'It's not just the job, either. There are grandchildren up in Liverpool and . . .'

Grandchildren? What grandchildren? You have a grandchild here. Your *children* are here, for God's sake. And he is sure that all of this is written on his face, but yet again she doesn't take him up on it. She just nods and smiles. And stretches her hand out to the tablecloth that he has now folded up at one end of the table, as if to say he should have left it where it was.

'I don't want to disturb you any longer,' she says. 'Your sister is worried about you, you know. All she wants is for you to talk to the policeman so that they can clear up all the confusion. You know what they're like once they get an idea in their heads.'

She laughs, and he wonders why, and then he realises that she isn't laughing at him, but at the very idea that anyone could think he could have done such a thing. Oh, the faith there is in mothers.

'She'll be so glad that you're here, William. Make sure you wait for her.'

Her pronunciation makes that name sound more elegant than it's ever done before. Will-i-am. He might even start to use it again, now that he's heard it from the horse's mouth. But she is on her feet now and slinging the bag up onto her shoulder. A lock of greyish-blondish hair has escaped from the clasp at the back of her head. In a gesture that is almost girlish, she tucks it behind her ear.

It's only now, when she's on the point of leaving, that he wonders if he has frightened her away. The thought horrifies him. He does not want to frighten his mother, or to shame her either. He does not want to chase her away. There is nothing he wants less.

She is moving ahead of him into the hall that is flooded by deep-dyed sunshine cast onto the tiles in slices of ruby and indigo and lemon. She is moving purposefully in her Birkenstocks, though not that quickly really. He wonders if she has trouble with her knees and hips, if he can keep her comfortable in the cottage he has made for her, if she will be cold. She stands on the sisal mat at the front door, as if waiting for him to open it for her. As he stretches over her, he imagines a faint scent of mango.

She turns towards him. 'I don't know what to say about your news, William, about your mother and the passport. I am very sorry if it's painful for you.' She smiles sadly, and he jerks at the door to let her out. 'Are you staying long?' she asks.

'I haven't decided yet,' he says. His stomach is churning now, tight with panic and disappointment and frustration. He should have said something when he had the chance.

He conjures up that secret cord between them, and, when he tugs hard on it and she doesn't move away, it seems to have worked. Until she does move, and he can feel himself begin to lose her. He touches the back of her hand, runs his finger lightly across the pinched and puckered skin. But she flinches and pulls her hand away. And he can't be sure if that's just a reflex or if she is detaching herself from him again.

Her head drops as she hurries through the door. He watches her make her way down the gravel path between Jess's large pots of lavender and box. She doesn't look back, even though she might never see him again. That's when he decides to follow her. He waits until she has turned the corner at the end of the street before walking through the gate. It doesn't take long to catch up with her. On the Common, she chooses the path of least resistance, the one through the copse where they can't be seen from the road, from the playing fields, from the great prairie itself. It is her gift to him.

He takes her from behind, one hand around her waist, the other on her mouth. She is very light, more sparrow than he is himself. When he lets her see him, so she knows not to be afraid, she looks him in the eye as if she can see right into him, as if she can see all his pain. And for an instant he thinks that this will go all right. But as soon as he releases his hand, she opens her mouth. He perceives the unborn scream in the split second before it breaks all over him. Immediately, he quenches it in the sleeve of his parka.

He manoeuvres her across the uneven ground of the copse, all exposed tree roots and tangles of bracken and thorn. A sandal drops from her foot and, when he stops to retrieve it, he almost loses her. As she twists away, he grabs her wrist and manages to hold her there, but he knows he has to find that sandal – a dung-coloured

Birkenstock, so easy to lose among the camouflage. And while she stands there at arm's length from him, taking sharp little in breaths and long, laboured exhalations, he can tell she is less nervous than before. And that's good, because he doesn't want her to be nervous. But it's bad, too, because he needs her to be malleable.

The sandal is just out of reach, sole upwards, just next to a fallen tree. He has to pull her along in order to get to it. Perhaps he's not holding her quite tight enough for fear of snapping those sparrow bones, but while he's bending down to grasp the sandal, she breaks for it. Plunging into the undergrowth like it's a knee-high sea, she is faster than he'd ever thought possible. He is proud of her spirit, but he can't let her make the beach of freedom just beyond the copse.

When he catches her she is sobbing, his poor lost mother. She is crying the oceans he once cried himself, but he strokes her head and says, 'There, there,' like he's seen a mother do on-screen, and for a moment she is still. The skin around her eyes is bluish, and her mouth is slack. As he takes her towards the cottage, she starts to murmur, 'Please, please, please.'

But she is not even looking at him. She is pleading with someone, but not with him. And although he has found her and is bringing her home, he doesn't feel the happiness he'd hoped for. He steps through the man-sized hole in the fence and bends her head under, the way he's seen them do on TV cop shows. He knows now to keep a hold on her, so he removes the elements of his barricade one-handed, pulls back the door, and shifts the planks and bricks into the cottage to build it up again on the inside.

She moves as far away from him as possible, choosing the most distant wall. She seems to be shutting herself off from him, muttering something to herself in a foreign language while her fingers tug at her clothing. He realises then that it's God she's been pleading with, or maybe Buddha. No way is she begging him.

Once he has them barricaded in, he moves towards her.

'What's wrong?' he asks, and when he hears his own voice, still harsh and urgent from what he's had to do, he softens it. 'What are you saying?'

She shakes her head like she's trying to shake it off, her eyes closed tight, their lids almost translucent. He had hoped admissions would flow out of her, but he can't see what he is gaining here. It alarms him to think how long it might take for her to crack. Because he hasn't got so long. Not with a body in the woods.

She opens her eyes very slowly, squinting against the light. And now that she seems to have rejoined him, he starts to point to all the things he's gathered for her. He shows her the photo he put up on the wall, the one of Jess and him on the beach, but she doesn't appreciate any of it, and that makes him sick.

'Sparrow,' she says.

And he hasn't heard her call him that since that day on the beach.

Stay away from the water, Sparrow. Don't go in too deep.

She clears her throat and wipes her eyes so that there's a black streak of mascara across her cheekbone.

'Why have you brought me here?'

Her voice is steadier now. She seems to have come through the worst of the panic, and he's not sure if that's because she is learning to trust him or because she thinks she's found a way out. He wants to call her Mama, but there is a sternness about her now that doesn't invite it.

'Eddie told me what you think, Sparrow,' she says, 'but it isn't true. I am not Sophie. I am not even Mary. I am Maya Hallström and I am sorry for what happened to you.'

He invites her to sit on the lilo he has blown up for her, but she shakes her head, a furious little shake.

'Are you going to stand here all night?' he asks.

She seems to crumple at the prospect. Her head droops onto her chest, and she starts to slide down the wall and onto the bare floor. He draws Jess's pink and green blanket over her, but she pushes it away.

'You let me go now, Sparrow, and I won't even tell Eddie, I promise you this for life.' She is speaking with a shallow voice, as if she doesn't have the energy for more.

But his attention is jolted away from her by what he hears outside. There are people out there, much closer than anyone ought to be. He is not sure whether they have made their way to this side of the wooden fence until he hears their voices close by and decides they probably have.

The only sound from her is a squeak, as if she's afraid to risk a scream. But he can't take any chances, so he ties her gauzy scarf around her mouth. Outside, someone is rattling at the bolt, the oversized one on the main door. And maybe any moment now they will be through that door and there will be a decision to take. Make a hostage of his mother? Or give himself in? He can see the hope in her eyes as they flicker towards the opaque window, and it breaks his heart to think she might want to be rescued from her own long-lost son.

But the men leave as quickly as they came. Their voices recede as they move off, and he and his mother sit facing one another across the floor. Without asking, she unties her own scarf and flings it away. It makes an arc, then floats slowly to the ground. She says nothing, just sits there looking at him, and he feels that he has ceded ground to her. She refuses everything he offers her until he takes out a bottle of water. Her eyes follow it, and when he hands it to her she gulps it down.

It is too quiet in the room, and so he starts to tell her about all the places he has roamed in search of her.

'Manchester, Darlington, Kerry, Cork, Lille, Paris, Freiburg, all over India, but mainly Goa and Rajasthan, Durham, Newcastle, Dublin . . .'

Perhaps he should have brought a map with him. He might have stuck it up on the wall and she'd have seen then the lengths he's gone to. Because she's looking blankly back at him now, and he isn't sure if that's because she doesn't know where those places are, which is surely unlikely. Perhaps she can't believe the distances he's gone for her. Maybe she's feeling guilty for leaving him on that beach.

When the coughing starts, it is more like a succession of caught breaths than a proper cough. In out, in out, in out. And then he notices the whistling sound that accompanies each exhalation.

'Have another drink of water,' he says. 'That will help.'

It feels oddly satisfying to be mothering his own mother.

But soon she is getting agitated, and her chest is bellowing in and out with the effort it takes to breathe. She starts to try to tell him something. And she isn't begging God or Buddha, not this time. This time, she is begging him. He gets right up close to her, and listens hard. She isn't asking him to let her go, not any more. She is asking for her inhaler.

After leaving Evelyn, Jess is desperate to look inside the shoeboxes, Clarks and Nike, marked *Goa 1* and *Goa 2* in black felt tip. Away from the cul-de-sac, she finds somewhere to stop and has a quick rifle through the top few layers of photos. But it's getting late now. The babysitter was only booked for a couple of hours, and Charlie will be wondering where she is.

Back at the hotel, Charlie is red-faced from his sauna, and already changed for dinner. Jess sees no need to endure another formal meal. She would rather skip dinner altogether and spend the evening with Evelyn Tuite's shoeboxes. Although, so far, she has recognised no one in those first few layers, she can think of nothing else. She is just about to plead a headache when the babysitter arrives at the door for the dinner shift. Jess hasn't got the heart to turn her away.

Dinner is eaten in near silence, as if uttering anything at all risks straying into the swamp. Besides, Jess's mind is whirring away from Charlie, from Hana too. She is sharp with anticipation. For the first time, there is the real prospect of finding answers, hope even.

They relieve the babysitter early, and Ruby is still awake and ready to play. Charlie flicks on the TV, ostensibly to catch the end of the main evening news, but more likely to offer a distraction. Jess is just wiping off the last traces of makeup when the local bulletin from BBC London comes on. A familiar street name causes her to glance towards the screen.

A reporter is standing on the edge of the Common, *her* Common, with a tsunami of greenery surging up behind him. But this is no longer a place where people play, it is no longer the prairie at the bottom of her garden. Braced with police tape, it has become a location, the scene of a crime. She finds herself scrolling through the mental lists of all her friends and neighbours, then the database of people she has half glimpsed at a shop counter, in a café, at the swings. The reporter is talking about extraordinary events, about violent incidents. Two in one day, in the same small area.

'Here, in leafy South London,' he is saying, 'in a small area between two commons that is known as Nappy Valley, it's hard to believe how suddenly someone can vanish. The missing woman is Maya Hallström, a local nursery-school teacher, Swedish national and long-time resident of the UK. Mrs Hallström, aged sixty-three and a divorced mother of two, lived near the Common with her partner. She was last seen this morning while on her way to drop off keys with friends on Riverton Street, which borders the west end of the Common. In an extraordinary turn of events, police with sniffer dogs searching for Mrs Hallström later uncovered a body concealed in undergrowth not far from where she is believed to have disappeared. The deceased, an unidentified male, had suffered a blunt force trauma to the head. The incidents are not thought to be connected.'

All her life, Jess has been expecting disaster. And now that it has occurred she is light-headed with the horror of it. Out of nowhere, she remembers a group of women in Auntie Rae's kitchen discussing the men in 'that family' and how they were. Weak, defective. Some faulty wiring, some gene gone wrong.

'I shouldn't be surprised if he ends up like the father,' one of the women had said, 'shoving poison into himself.'

She glances over at Charlie, who doesn't seem to have noticed the TV news. He is holding Ruby, whose nappy needs changing, at arm's length, while still managing to play a game of backgammon on his phone.

'Oh my God, did you see that, Charlie? Did you hear about Maya?'

Charlie places Ruby next to her goblin, and he and Jess sit down on the bottom of the bed and watch the screen. She takes his hand and grips it tightly, because all she can think of now is Ro, and what he might have done to Maya.

The reporter is talking about the Common, and how it is an amenity for all kinds of groups from Sunday footballers to the local bowls club. The camera pans to a scene outside the café, where people are sitting at metal tables under the dappled light. Meanwhile, the reporter is saying, life proceeds as normal.

Jess looks, then looks again. She pulls her hand away from Charlie's.

'It's Hana. Outside the café. See?'

'Oh, I don't think—'

'You can't miss her, Charlie. There. She's looking straight at the camera.'

'I guess it must be archive footage.'

'What the fuck? Why can't you just tell the truth for once?'

Charlie reaches for the remote, Ruby dangling from his hip, and switches Hana off. Ruby's eyes dart from one parent to the other and then she starts to cry, tipping her head right back and screaming into the ceiling. She senses that her little world has fractured, and she is right. Charlie jiggles her, changes hip, but she is inconsolable.

Desperate for news of Maya, Jess turns on the phone she'd agreed to keep switched off and the messages come flooding through. Eddie, Eddie, Eddie, Crowe, Crowe, Crowe. Sixteen missed calls, a dozen WhatsApp messages, so many emails. She tries Eddie first, even though she is ashamed, so ashamed. But his number is constantly engaged.

She gets through to Crowe on the first attempt, and he comes straight to the point.

'You need to give me your brother,' he says. 'If you persist in shielding him, you'll be obstructing us. Understand? And Jess, you help me, I'll help you.'

She doesn't need to ask him what he means. He is only too happy to tell her.

'I want Sparrow. Understand? You give me Sparrow, and I'll give you everything I've been able to find out about your mother.'

She is so exasperated that he could still think she has any idea where Ro is that the words tumble out of her. 'I've no idea where he is. But I'm on my way. We're heading straight back now.'

'You don't know where he is?'

'I sent him away,' she says, and then the thought she can't afford. Perhaps she should have kept him close, perhaps she could have stopped this.

'I've spoken to Eddie Jacques, of course, and he's beside himself. He's told me the history, about your mother – the affair, and all the rest of it. No time for secrets now.'

Eddie. The thought of what he must be going through brings tears to her eyes. She dreads speaking to Eddie.

'We'll find her,' Crowe says. 'I'm convinced of that. But first we need to find Sparrow.'

'You never found my mother,' she says. She blurts it out and is ashamed because he needs to concentrate on Maya now.

He pauses a moment. 'No, and I don't think we will,' he says.

She is shocked just how much she wants him to be wrong.

'After all this time, it's a jigsaw. There's no open book I can give you.'

And even though she is aware that he might be feeding her snippets to be passed on should she be in touch with Ro, she doesn't care. She can almost hear him calculating what it's in his interest to tell her, and whether that might improve his chances of getting Sparrow in return.

'We've been focusing our enquiries on a man called Dejan Gorivic. Gorivic came from Slovenia originally, had a bit of a racket going in Goa. Drugs mainly, a bit of protection too. There was a file on him, way back, but nobody made the connection with your parents. They were looking for a missing couple, of course, not a woman on her own, so perhaps that skewed things. They can't have known that your mother and Gorivic were having an affair either. She seems to have been quite successful in keeping it quiet. Anyway, Gorivic had a serious road accident a few days after your parents disappeared and a European woman, who was assumed at the time to be a girlfriend, was fatally injured. That was on the road between Candolim, where Dejan Gorivic had various business interests, for which read rackets, and the place where you were living. Given that we now know that Sophie went off with Gorivic, that Gorivic was your father's dealer, my best guess is that the dead woman was your mother.'

Her ears feel as if they are stuffed with cotton wool.

'We can't be sure, of course. There was no description, nothing to identify her other than that she was thought to be in her thirties. This being India, she was cremated within a matter of days. My guess is, your mother was held against her will. Maybe it made sense to get her out of the way while they got rid of Will. Maybe she did go along with something, then changed her mind. To be fair to the authorities, things were much more difficult back then. No Internet, of course, poor communications. Took a while to link bits of information. Were proper procedures followed? I doubt that. They didn't exactly break their arses trying to find out who she was. Why not? A woman in a car with a drug dealer? He'd have had the means to bribe his way out of trouble, for a while at least. Gorivic left India soon after the accident. He went back to Slovenia, and ended up working in the casino business in Portorož. Came a cropper himself a few years later. Knifed on the seafront late one night.'

There is no comfort in any of this. If anything, it is simply the cue for a whole new set of nightmares. It would break Ro's heart.

'I don't want my brother to be told.'

'I'll be the judge of that, Jess, when I track him down. I don't think he'll have gone far. But he's not in Riverton Street anyway. We've been in there already.'

She visualises a boot in her beautiful grey door, though she knows that's venal of her. But apparently the neighbours were obliging with the keys, and while her marriage has been shattered, her hopes too, the grey door is still intact.

19

They drive back to London straight away. Ruby is asleep before they've even joined the motorway, and the dread that is always there, lurking at the pit of Jess's stomach, cranks ever tighter as they approach the city. They sweep through Hammersmith and down the Fulham Palace Road, then through the zig and zag of side streets towards the bridge. From the back seat, she can hear her phone, thrumming mutely in the depths of her bag. She strains to reach it, but it's too far away. It's hard to find anywhere to park on Riverton Street, which is crammed with the chunky seven-seaters that are the vehicles of choice around here. There are no journalists on the doorstep – she is grateful to Inspector Crowe for that at least – but as they walk into the hall, she realises with a shock that the police have taken up residence in her house. She starts to say something to Charlie, but he has already passed ahead of her, and is climbing the stairs with Ruby slumped in his arms.

Two plain-clothes men are slouching in the drawing room, peering at a screen. Two more are in the kitchen, making coffee from her machine. They look up briefly, nod at her, then return to what they were doing before she walked into her own home.

She should have heeded the warning signs, the desperate infatuation that seldom turns out well. She longs for Ro to be stretched out on a sofa, watching one of those programmes he likes – unsolved mysteries, the renovation of perfect family homes. She imagines him restored to shining innocence and planning his next trip.

But there is no Ro.

And it is all making sense now – the missing items from the cellar, the obsession, the feeling she had that he was still somehow close. She can hear Auntie Rae in her ear – reaping and sowing. Rae was a great one for telling you what you should have done.

The policemen don't seem to want to interact with her, and that makes her wonder if they suspect her too. She takes what she needs upstairs – the shoeboxes of photos, a bottle of Chianti Classico with a single glass – while Charlie tucks Ruby into the bed that Jess will never share with him again.

The story of Maya is ripping its way through her, its various implications and dark possibilities coming at her in squalls of realisation. By comparison, the end of her marriage is just a small black cloud, hovering overhead and fat with rain. She locks herself in the spare room with her phone and these new comforts. Even the past is less frightening than the future.

She reopens the Clarks box, the one with the earliest photos. There is still no one she recognises in there, except for a plump, sour-looking girl in shorts who could, just possibly, be Evelyn. She wonders if it is possible to chart Eddie's love life, the transfer of affections from one girl to the next by his subjects, some of whom he has concentrated on to a forensic degree. Visual essays on knees and shoulders. If there was anything more obviously erotic in there, it has been removed.

The Nike box, *Goa 2*, is where her parents are. In the handful of pictures she can find of him, her father is reclining – on a brightly coloured rug, surrounded by cushions that are equally bright, on a patch of scuffed grass under a tree. His features are out of sync with one another, as if his eyes have forgotten that his mouth is happy. His interaction with the camera is uncertain, the mood he projects impossible to decode. There are pictures she finds hard to look at. The one she has to turn face down has her father kissing someone who could only be Mags Madden. Twenty-five years ago, Mags must have been in her mid-thirties, probably only a year or two older than Jess is now. She is tiny and very, very white with a great shock of bright red hair. In another image, Mags is clinging on to Pa and gazing straight at the camera, as if daring it to look away. Her determination is arresting, even now.

At first, Jess is astonished that there don't seem to be any photos of Sophie at all. And then she finds, in a brown envelope near the bottom of the box, an entire bundle of Sophies. The shock of it is overwhelming, but while Jess cries harsh, raw tears, Sophie is unperturbed. She gazes back – smiling, pensive, coquettish – fiddling with her plait or strumming on her guitar. Now and then, she is even playing with her children. But none of those pictures has been taken on a beach.

Whatever the setting or her expression, the message Jess receives from these images is always the same. I am dead, gone. Nothing more to see here. Move on.

In one of the last photos in the bundle, Sophie is sitting at a bar beside a thickset man with a comic-opera moustache. She doesn't even need to ask Evelyn. She is sure that this is Dejan. He is glaring into the camera, as if challenging the photographer, who has responded by slicing his face in two. She feels a rush of hatred for him.

Jess opens the bottle of wine and works her way steadily through it, quarter-glass by quarter-glass. As she reaches the halfway point, she starts forcing it down like medicine. Around three in the morning, she goes upstairs, all the way up to their room, where Charlie is asleep, still fully dressed, as if he might have to make a swift getaway, with Ruby pulled tightly in to him.

She picks up the phone to try Eddie again, and sees there are three voice messages. One is from the woman at the *Daily Post*, one from another journalist and the third from someone who is also probably a reporter. She calls herself Amanda Rowley and says she works at the café on the Common. She got Jess's number from a neighbour and could she call back urgently please. Jess doesn't know anyone who works in the café, and besides it's the middle of the night now anyway.

Dialling Eddie's number, it breaks her heart to hear the dart of hope in his voice when he picks up.

'It's only me,' she says. 'I guess there's still no news.'

'If he so much as—'

'I know,' she says. 'But he won't.'

'You heard they think he killed Mags. Kicked her in the head. Jesus Christ.'

'That's only a rumour, Eddie. There's no basis for that at all.'

'It's time to face realities,' he says.

And he's right, of course. It feels absurd now to think that Charlie and she might have been standing in the middle of a field tonight, glass of champagne in hand, looking at the moon, while her own brother was holding Maya hostage. Now, her marriage is over and her brother is a kidnapper, perhaps worse. But because this is a night of realities, terrible and frightening and unforeseen, it seems just possible to ask Eddie about an old love while the new one is in such danger. She approaches it as gently as she can.

'I've been to see Evelyn,' she says. 'You never told me.'

'How do you tell a child that you've been sleeping with her mother?'

'Haven't been a child for a while now, Eddie.'

'I decided it was better to say nothing. Besides, it was over by then. She had left. What was the point of upsetting you?'

'She told you something, though, didn't she? I really need to know what it was. Will you tell me?'

He is quiet. She can hear his breath rise and fall.

'She told me she was going away with Dejan. Just for a few days. She said she had to find a way to keep him off Will's back, that she didn't love Dejan but that Will owed him so much money they could never have paid him back. She told me she was leaving Will, but she had to get him back to England first, get him into rehab, all that. Look, Jess. It's hard to say this now. But I thought she loved me. I didn't realise there was such a queue.' And he laughs so bitterly to himself that she finds herself compelled to apologise on behalf of a mother she never really knew.

'And I began to question everything. She had a cold streak, Sophie. I worried about what she asked me to do. I began to worry that I'd been used.'

She forces down another mouthful of wine. It tastes thick now, sour. She hardly dares ask the obvious question.

'What did she ask you to do?'

'She told me you were all going to the beach that day, that she would slip away so as not to upset you kids by saying goodbye. Although she left you with Will, she didn't really trust him not to fall asleep, to remember to feed you, all that, so she asked me to nip down and make sure everything was OK.'

'And did you?'

'When I got there, Will was gone, she was gone. You kids were at the water's edge.'

'And you were in the trees. But you didn't come over, you didn't do anything.'

'It's my greatest regret. But I wasn't meant to be there. I panicked.'

'Weren't you afraid for us?'

'I knew Will was in danger from Dejan and that lot. But then again he might just as easily have wandered off. I didn't put two and two together like I should have done.'

'But you didn't even try to comfort us.'

'I wasn't, like, some kind of scout leader, Jess. Times were different then. You knew where the Yellow House was, after all, and you were a self-possessed little girl. I knew you would look after Sparrow. It was only when Will didn't turn up, and people were saying that Dejan had killed him, or had him killed, that I got worried. When you didn't arrive back at the Yellow House, I went to the police station and claimed you. They let me take you back there until Rae was able to come and get you.'

He hasn't mentioned working for Dejan himself. She doesn't mention that either for fear of closing off his flow.

'And the photo?'

'It was mine, yeah. I sent it to the papers. I thought it would drive her to her senses, bring her back. But I never heard from her again. I don't think she left India, Jess. My guess is she thought she could play Dejan, and found she couldn't. My guess is she tried to get away from him, but . . .'

He doesn't finish, and she is glad of that, because she doesn't want to hear the end of that sentence. Her throat feels constricted, as if someone she has never met has got his hands around it and is pressing hard. The silence between them holds the weight of their shared loss, and yet there are questions too.

'One more thing, Eddie. I just don't understand why you didn't mention that Mags was in Goa, too.'

He seems to choke up then. 'Do we have to talk about this now, Jess? All I can think about right now is Maya.'

And Jess has no option but to accept that this is not the time.

Ro has talked and talked, but his mother has said very little. She has been shivering, sobbing quietly to herself. When she catches a coughing fit, it seems to turn her inside out, and he feels every gasp and splutter. She has accepted more water, but nothing else – no food, and nothing from the hip flasks. He tries to drape the pink and green blanket, so soft and light, around her shoulders but she shrinks away.

'My inhaler,' is all she will say.

'Hold out your hand,' he says, and she begins to whimper.

He is shocked by her reaction. 'Oh no,' he says. 'No, no. I'm not going to hurt you. I just want to look, that's all.'

He has seen that expression before; it's one the supposedly sane give people they think are mad. But gradually she moves her hand towards him. She turns away, as if she can't bear to look, and her fingers curl. Gently, he flattens them out and scrutinises the deep lines that cross her palm, the scrape of fate, the finer cuts of life and sun and heart and head.

'You see?' he says, though she isn't even trying to,

sitting there with her eyes shut. 'We are the same. Your life is just like mine. Your fate—'

But she seems unable to keep her hand still, and her palm becomes a blur. Her reply is almost swallowed by another coughing fit, but he catches it. 'Not the same,' she is saying.

Guilt, he thinks. Denial.

The cottage gets darker with the day, and there is nothing to be done about that. He has come prepared with a small blue camping cylinder from the back of Jess's cellar, a contraption he dare not use that produces stark white light. If he could have a candle or two he would, but he is afraid to chance it.

To soften her heart, he starts to tell the story of the beach. He concentrates hard on her face, but she is refusing to look at him. He understands how it must be shaming to hear him talk about that day. But she is barely even listening. Most women do him the honour of that, at least.

He searches for the moment in the story that hits home. He can see she is awake but the light has grown too dim to work out whether the expression on her face has changed, whether he has moved her yet. When he gets to the bit about the cut foot, the tears, the blood and salt, she seems to lift her head. And there is hope now.

'Mama,' he says. 'Where did you go?'

'If I said I was your mother, Sparrow,' she blurts out, 'what good would it do? It isn't true. It will never be true.' Her voice sounds husky, and he can't help thinking that she's been crying, which is good.

'Acceptance starts with denial,' he says. He came across that somewhere, perhaps that therapist at school, perhaps online.

But the words hover there unanswered.

She is asleep now, more or less, on the lilo she finally agreed to use, under the pink and green blanket she was glad of in the end. The story came to nothing, and he rues the lack of tranquillisers and truth serums, things to erase the will and salve the conscience. He comes in close and puts his ear to her chest. Her breath is coming fast and shallow. Jess has an inhaler. He's sure he's seen one somewhere. But whether one inhaler is the same as another, he has no idea. It is dark now and even with his headphones off it is completely quiet. At this hour there are none of the normal sounds of the Common – the punt of a ball, the dry sirocco of traffic in the distance. For a while earlier, there was a helicopter overhead – a burglary, an escapee, a missing woman? But everything is quiet now. He has peeled back a corner of tarp, and there is a strange light around.

When he leaves the cottage and barricades the door behind him, the moon is shining, its ghost reflection hovering. It has shrunk and reddened now, more nut than disc, a red marble skelped by a scrape of white along its left curve. As he stalks through the black field of the Common, he hears the helicopter return. Its hollow drone drills into the back of his head, its stuttering searchlight seeks him out, but he ducks and weaves as it passes beyond him and over towards the bandstand where it hovers as if pulled there by a magnet. The stars are still out, hordes of them, jostling for position with the unblinking satellites. A bird, or perhaps a bat, crosses his line of vision. It is gone in an instant, flickering into the trees. Just as he's about to step into the road, he glances back. The far trees seem to have advanced, their outlines clearer than before. It's as if the whole Common is shrinking in on itself. When he sees the arc lights in the copse, he realises that they were the source of the strange light he noticed earlier. He knows then that they have found the slug. He quickens his step because a sick, unwilling mother in the cottage doesn't seem so smart now that they are almost on to him. He is glad he thought of the gag. It's only when he reaches the road that he realises there are police cars parked up all the way as far as the school. Riverton Street itself appears to be blocked off, and for a moment he panics until he remembers that it is always better to stride boldly than to mince or cower or creep.

He accesses Jess's house from an adjacent road. The blinds are still down, the plantation shutters closed. He moves as if his trainers barely touch the ground, and the silence clogs his ears. Time and the sky are on the move. Tick tock, tick tock. He slides in his key, slips quietly into the house, and makes for the medicine cabinet Jess keeps below the vegetable racks. It's an impeccable archive of pillboxes and blister packs, but there is nothing that could possibly be inhaled. He swipes it all, shovelling it into his pockets because, as Auntie Rae would say, you never know the hour or the day.

It's only as he turns to go that he sees the men sitting smoking in Jess's garden, their backs to the bifold doors, surrounded by water bottles and cans of Red Bull. Remembering the undesirability of sudden movements, he edges his way very slowly along the breakfast bar that is littered with half-drunk cups from Costa and Caffè Nero. He slips silently past a man who is snoring faintly, his crossed legs ending in scuffed white trainers, and out the door.

As he moves back on to the Common, he knows it's over.

The blue light of an ambulance circles in front of the cottage, and three cop cars are parked up on the grass around it like white rays from a blue sun. The thought that maybe she has died should break his heart, but it doesn't. Because he is sure now that this is not his mother. No mother could abandon him twice.

With his pockets full of options, he turns his back on Maya Hallström, on the blue light and the cottage and the body laid out on its funeral pyre in Jess's sleeping bag. And as he walks away, he soars up, high above the Common, until it's all so much smaller than a sparrow's wing.

Around dawn, Jess feels certain that Ro is near. She straightens herself and gallops down the stairs. The front door is open, which puzzles and irritates her in equal measure. As for the police, there are more of them than there were before, and they seem to have commandeered the kitchen as an incident room.

'Where is he?'

The man she addresses looks up at her as if she's being hysterical.

'Where's who?'

'My brother, of course. Where is he?'

'Well, you're hardly likely to find him in the lions' den, are you?'

He doesn't look like a lion to her.

Crowe arrives with a bounce in his step, like a man who has been given a last-minute reprieve. 'She's in the ambulance now, being treated for an asthma attack.'

Jess's eyes cloud over with relief, her heart thudding for love of Ro.

'And my brother?'

'She hasn't identified him.'

'Sorry?'

'She said it was just some poor devil, that she didn't see the man's face. But that's not to say—'

'Sparrow isn't even there?'

'She's still quite poorly, Jess. We haven't had a chance to talk to her properly yet. The medics have priority right now.'

The lawyer in her sees the opportunity and takes over. 'So you have created an entire scenario based around my brother, who, it now appears, had absolutely nothing to do with this.'

'You can hold it right there, Jess. Just so you know, that place is full of stuff that Sparrow must have picked up somewhere or other. If he's been in there, we'll find his DNA all over it. We'll get him whether you want us to or not.'

She knows for sure now – the stained pillows, the pink lilo – and her eyes water.

'Talking of DNA, he can ditch the notion that Maya is any relative. There's no match whatsoever. She really is a Swede, from Uppsala actually. Nice, unremarkable background. Father a pastor, mother a teacher. Married once, divorced once, two children, six grandchildren. Nothing out of the ordinary at all.'

Part of her still wants to take Ro by his hand, to lead him towards normality and convention and teach him his seven times table. A tiny bit of her still believes some of this is possible, even now.

'I think he did it, Jess. And what's more, I think he killed Mags Madden. You think that too, Jess. I know you do. Surely you realise your brother's sick.'

'Sick?' The word offends her.

'Unwell. You need to think very hard about where he might have gone.'

As he walks away she knows. She runs upstairs and pauses at her bedroom door to watch her husband sleep. And in that moment she can feel her fear of life after this marriage and this house begin to fall away. It is simply a matter of lowering a shield, and she doesn't know why it has taken her this long to realise that. She kisses the small orange bundle that is Ruby, curled on the other side of the bed, and slips back down the stairs.

The press have returned. It is not just a single journalist now. Outside, there are photographers, five or six at least. If they spot her, her chances of finding Ro are zero.

The police have congregated in the drawing room. The door is closed, but she can hear Crowe's voice addressing them.

She hurries into the garden, out through the gate and onto the Common. The first dog walkers are out already as she passes the scaffolded bandstand and the shuttered café. Although she hasn't looked for it since they were children, she finds the place without difficulty. Behind the café, a row of black bins conceals the entrance to a narrow, roofless corridor where the back wall of the café is tracked by another wall, perhaps the beginnings of an outbuilding that was never constructed. She isn't even sure the place is still accessible, but when she notices that a bin has been shunted aside, she slips in behind. The space is narrow, no more than a metre wide. No sunlight reaches here; it smells of damp and rot. It feels like the past, and she has to force herself to enter it.

When she finds him, he looks as if he's sleeping. With his knees pulled right up to his chin, he occupies all the available space, wedged between the walls, trapped in his own secret place. His head is resting on the crook of his arm and there is a feather clutched in one hand. She calls out to him, but the sound is dampened, swallowed by the narrow walls. She calls until her voice escapes from her and becomes a kind of wail. She moves sideways along the narrow passage, her feet crunching over plastic pill bottles and countless empty blister packs, then sinking into mulch. She can hardly see for the blur in her eyes. When she gets right up close, she doesn't try to rouse him. There will be no happy-ever-after now. It is better to let him sleep. And though he looks as if he might wake at any moment, she knows that Sparrow has already gone.

In the narrow, lightening strip of sky above her head, there are whirling shapes that could be birds or ghosts or discarded theories spiralling away and out of reach. But as her eyes clear, those shapes begin to thin and fade until they are nothing more than scudding clouds.

The yelp of a nearby siren catches her attention. They will have followed her, she is sure. She will stay with Sparrow until they take him. She will hold his hand, and keep it warm. And as she waits for them to claim him, she squints against the breaking sky and all the wisps of possibility beyond her gravelled garden, its high walls and locked gate.

ACKNOWLEDGEMENTS

Thank you to my agent, Zoe Waldie, for her keen insights and unfailing support, to my editor, Emma Mitchell, for making a round of edits such an enlightening and positive experience, and to all the other people at Hutchinson and Windmill who have helped *The Orphans* along, especially Jocasta Hamilton, Laura Brooke, Laurie Ip Fung Chun, and Laura Deacon.

As ever, I appreciate the friendship and support of many writer friends. Special thanks go to Elise, Anne, Roger, Jude, Gavin, Oana, Vicky, Clare, and Sue. It would be a lonely road if we couldn't share the joys, the woes, the travellers' tales.

Thanks to Café la Baita on Clapham Common for inspiration and sustenance, to the wonderful Tyrone Guthrie Centre at Annaghmakerrig, where a section of this book was written, and to Sara Cohen for her expert advice.

Finally, heartfelt thanks to my family — to my sons, Patrick, Conor and Rory, and to Mike, my love and my greatest friend.

SIREN

THERE'S ALWAYS
SOMEONE WATCHING...

Ireland, 2004

Róisín Burns has spent over twenty-five years living a lie.

Brian Lonergan, a rising politician, has used the time
to reinvent himself.

But scandal is brewing around him, and Róisín
knows the truth.

Lonergan stole her life as a young girl. And now
she wants it back.

But he is still one step ahead . . .

'A nail-bitingly tense tale, with writing
as sharp and pointed as arrows'
Independent

'Gripping . . . A masterful crime debut'
Stuart Neville, author of
Those We Left Behind

Turn over to read an extract

Róisín sensed the danger long before she'd had a chance to think it, when it was just a quivering of something in the air outside the room. Not quite a sound, not quite. Then from the other side of the wall, a thud, a gasp, a dull thump like a fist in a pillow. They broke off from kissing, and she felt his sharp intake of breath as if it were her own. He scrambled off the bed towards the window.

'No, no,' he was murmuring. 'Fucking no.'

He found his shoe, began battering at the glass. But the men were in the room now and the window wouldn't break.

It didn't sound like much, just a dart puncturing a board. But it got him. As his body slumped backwards from the window, Róisín lurched across to try to reach him, but one of the gunmen had her by the hair. She kicked and scrabbed and punched at him, but he flung her out on to the landing like she was nothing.